The Ins & Outs

OF A WOMAN'S

DREAM

JENNA LEE SERIES BOOK 2

ALSO AVAILABLE BY SONNY
The Ups and Downs of a Woman's Heart, Book 1

COMING SOON
The Back and Forth of a Woman's Love, Book 3

SONNY D. STONE

Publishing Coordinator – Sharon Kizziah-Holmes
Cover Design – Jaycee DeLorenzo

INDIE
PUB
PRESS
an imprint of A & S Publishing
A & S Holmes, Inc.

ISBN -13: 978-1-951772-80-2

Dedication

Sharon Stone, thank you for being my daily encourager, proofer, entertainment and bestie. Jackie and Greg you two are a great example of true love. Kayla and Kourtney you are sunshine and laughter rolled up with a pinch of orneriness. Missy, thanks for your ideas and encouragement. Kristi thanks for your enthusiasm and support. Stan and Steve you two are beyond words, love you all. Special thanks to all who purchased my books.

Acknowledgments

To my publishing coordinator who is professional and supportive, thank you Sharon.

Chapter 1

Memory Lane

On my flight headed back home, my mind flooded with childhood memories of summer visits at Granny's house. To the childhood experiences I held dear of my friend and now my recent ex-fiancé, Jacob. The first time I snuck out of my Granny's house (or any house for that matter), was because of him.

It was a hot summer Kentucky night and Granny didn't like to waste money. She thought air conditioning wasn't something to use on a daily basis and certainly not when it "cooled off" at night. Consequently, I had my upstairs bedroom window open to get a breeze so I could attempt to sleep.

I was probably eight or nine years old at the time and Jacob would have been eleven or twelve, since he's three years older than me. He climbed Granny's huge old oak tree in the backyard, jumped from the tree over onto the roof, and climbed over to my window to wake me up (not that I could sleep in that heat anyway).

I had no clue he even knew which room I was staying in, or that he would even think of me and try to come over in the middle of the night, but he had a plan. Since the window was open, he just whispered my name. "Jenna, Jenna, wake up." I rolled over and there was Jacob, standing in front of my window. "How can you sleep when it's so hot in here? It's like an oven; it's cooler outside."

"I'm not asleep. As you can see, I'm talking to you. What are you doing in my bedroom? If Granny hears you, she will skin you alive, and she has good hearing. What do you want?"

"Jenna, get dressed quickly. One of our horses is having a baby and I thought you would want to see it because it's pretty cool, especially to see for the first time. Do you want to come with me?"

"Yes, quick, turn-around so I can get dressed." I threw on my jean shorts, a tee-shirt, and tennis shoes and followed him out the window, onto the roof, down the tree, and across the field. I tend to live on the klutzy side of life, so Jacob was helpful to get me to the ground safely.

Oh, yeah, I almost forgot, he even had chigger and mosquito spray for me to use so my Granny wouldn't know I was out in the weeds at night. Even at a young age he was thinking about all the details, or maybe he had lots of experience doing this. I'll never know.

Anyway, we ran through the field to one of Jacob's Grandpa's livestock barns, and we made it in time to see the miraculous birth. It was so sweet to experience this event.

This baby horse, a colt, had long legs, much longer than I expected. And, it was a stud, a boy colt. He lay wet and exhausted in the hay for a while. After a few minutes, his mom smelled him, licked him, and then the colt tried to stand up. He got his footing, wobbled a few steps and stopped, regained his balance again, and found his mommy, the mare, and had no trouble walking over to her for a drink of milk.

I was so glad that Jacob thought of me and came to get me that night. It was a great moment, and a special memory I share with him. The colt was so cute, but the mare was very protective of her new stud, so I didn't get into the stall to pet him.

We named the colt Gingerbread because of his ginger coloring. It was a registered thoroughbred colt, so they had paperwork that called him something much longer, and one that reflected his expensive bloodline, but we called him Gingerbread that night.

I don't think I ever thanked Jacob for thinking of me and coming to get me, to share that amazing experience. He was thoughtful and I was an excited kid who didn't even say thank you. Jacob was cute back then, but he was just one of the boys to me. He was older, and I never thought of him as boyfriend material. He was just a great guy that lived down the road from my Granny's farm.

Oh, I remember another summer visit that we'd played together, me, Jeff, my brother, Jacob, and his brothers. I'm pretty sure it was flag football, but after a day of fun, we'd all gone to our own Grandma's houses to clean up for supper.

Granny had a dinner bell outside that was on a large, wooden stand, about ten feet tall. The bell was the size of a boom box back in the day. It had a long rope on it so you could swing the bell. It was a heavy-duty bell that had a great sound when it was rung. When it was time for lunch or dinner, Granny would ring that bell one time, and we would come running from wherever we were on the farm.

That was before cell phones and no matter where we were playing, we could hear the bell, and head toward Granny's. I always wanted to ring the bell, but Granny said it was only for meals and emergencies. This was especially beneficial where our grandparents, who were neighbors, lived in the miles and miles of the beautiful green grassy hills of Kentucky.

My Granny and Partner went to bed early at night. Granny would say "early to bed, early to rise, makes a man healthy, wealthy, and wise." Oh, and she didn't think there was anything decent on television. So, after they went to bed, we weren't allowed to watch TV. They only had one television and it was in the living room on the main floor.

It wasn't until many years later, when the younger grandkids came along, that the rules changed, and they got to watch TV and videos. Things were much stricter for Jeff and me because we were the first two grandkids. Then along came all the other cousins and I think Granny was just thrilled there was Walt Disney, DVD players, and videos for those rainy days of summer breaks.

I recall another time, I was probably 14 years old, therefore, Jeff would have been 16, and we were trying to go to sleep at Granny's. I once again heard Jacob's voice outside my window. "Hey, Jenna, get Jeff, and let's go to town. My brothers are down in the truck. Put your swimsuit on under your clothes and come with us, and hurry."

So, I tiptoed down the hall to wake Jeff. Jeff made a lot of noise getting his bathing suit and shorts on, but Granny and Partner luckily were sound sleepers. Then Jeff came to my room where I was dressed and waiting for him.

We climbed out on the roof, down the tree, and ran over to Jacob's truck. Jacob told me "Get behind the steering wheel and steer my truck. The rest of us will push the truck down the gravel road." There was no power steering when the truck wasn't turned on, so steering this truck was no easy task for me. I'm sure pushing that truck on gravel wasn't easy for them.

They said their Grandma Ruth had very good hearing, and if she thought they were gone, she would take their car keys and they would be grounded. So, they all pushed the truck to the end of the dirt road, about a mile, to make sure that didn't happen. I thought it was kind of funny, but they knew their Grandma, and knew she meant what she said. No one messed with Ms. Ruth.

We finally made it out to the end of the road to the highway, and then I got bumped over to the middle of the front seat. Four of us were in the front seat, and four were in the back bed of the truck. The truck was started and purring down the highway. We didn't have the seatbelt laws back then like we do now, or rules like you can't sit on the tail gate of a truck going down the highway, but somehow, we all managed to survive our childhood innocence.

Jacob may have had his drivers permit at that time. I'm not sure he was even old enough to drive without an adult, but out on large farms, they let boys drive a lot younger. Nevertheless, he drove us in to a nice little town, Eudora, that had a public tennis court and a pool. Of course, everything was closed because it was late at night, or it could have been early morning hours, I don't remember.

Anyway, Jacob knew where the lights were for the courts and pool area. There was a large, black handle next to a metal box, hammered onto a power pole. He just pushed it up and the lights to the tennis courts and the pool all came on, so we could see the ball to play tennis.

The Jamison boys had tennis rackets and balls for all eight of us and we played tennis on the same court, at the same time. We had four of us on each half side of the court. It was great coverage, two people up near the net and two at the back of the court for each side. We kept the ball going back and forth for long periods of time and had a total blast.

I'd played tennis before, but this was the most fun ever. I think they should rethink the game as a team sport, because it was a highlight in my memories of sporting events. (Well, that and mud volleyball game I played in college, but that's an entirely different story). The game was fast paced, and we hardly ever missed the ball. It was very competitive each person had to guard their section and go for it!

It never occurred to me at the time, that this was public property, and we were breaking the law by trespassing. I just thought we were having fun, and I was a lucky girl surrounded by great looking, fun guys and didn't think we were hurting anyone. After we were hot and sweaty from the summer night and from playing an hour or so of tennis, we decided to climb the fence around the pool area and go swimming to cool off.

I told Jeff I couldn't climb the metal chain linked fence, so Andrew and Jacob moved a heavy wooden picnic table over to the fence. I climbed on the table and only had a couple steps on the fence to be inside the pool area. We shimmied off our shorts, shirts, and shoes and with suits underneath, cooled off in the pool and had the best time ever!

A huge public pool all to ourselves, diving boards, a blast! It was so much fun, we were laughing and relaxing in the pool for about twenty minutes or so. The boys were taking turns showing off on the high dive until all of a sudden, out of nowhere, we saw a police car pulling into the parking lot.

No siren, just his flashing lights, and coming into the park at a slow speed. Then a bright search light from this police car scanned over the swimming pool. I was next to Jacob at that moment, and he shoved me to the edge of the pool wall. Then, without warning, he pushed my head under water. We all sank down under the water, each of us trying to stay out of the spotlights of the police officers.

We were like cockroaches when you turn on the lights. We were immediately flat against the walls of the pool, underwater, and watching to stay in the shadows. The water was still full of motion from all our jumping, swimming, moving, and wet footprints were all over the sidewalks around the pool. Jacob's truck was the only car in the parking lot and our clothes were in piles by the fence.

Suddenly, it occurred to me that we could all go to jail for our actions. Granny would never let us hear the end of it. The guilt trip would last a lifetime. In that split second. I could see her face and hear the disappointment in her voice in my mind. *How could you two leave my house without permission? I live in a small rural community my reputation is tarnished.*

I guess the police just wanted us to get our butts home and knew we weren't tearing up things, we were just cooling off and having fun. The officers went over to the light pole, turned off the lights, and then they left.

I think if Jacob's Grandma didn't own half the countryside, we'd have been in jail for sure that night. But they had mercy on us and left without saying a word, like they didn't know we were there.

As soon as that police car drove off, we were out of the pool, grabbed our clothes, and I moved over that fence with a new ease I didn't have getting into the pool area. Jacob drove us home immediately. I was hitting Jacob in the arm yelling at him, "We could have been arrested!" Jacob just laughed and said to be sure and be quiet when we were getting back into Grandmas' house.

Our clothes were wet, so it was very hard getting back up that tree and on the roof into my room at Granny's. But somehow, with Jeff's help, I made it back into the house unharmed and undetected. We hung our wet bathing suits, shorts, and shirts in the windows of our bedrooms, and they were completely dry by the next morning, if that tells you how hot it was upstairs.

Granny never knew and we loved that we were able to sneak out without getting in trouble. We didn't make a habit of sneaking out, at least I didn't, but had great memories of our almost arrested sneak out experience with Jacob and the other Jamison brothers.

Granny never locked her doors. Most people back then knew everyone in the area and felt safe not to lock their doors at night, or day for that matter. They even left keys in the cars or under the driver's car mat. But when we stayed at Granny and Partner's house, their wooden stairs creaked loudly when you walked up or down them, so if you didn't want to be heard, you didn't use the stairs.

Jacob always had a way of making me leave my common sense and follow him blindly. But I didn't regret doing it. I always had a good time with him. I don't know how he could talk me into things. He didn't even really have to try, he'd just mention it, and I'd want to be there with him. I wonder if he had that power over all women, or if it was just me? I don't think I want to know the answer to that question.

A stewardess came down the aisle and asked, "Would you care for a drink and a snack?"

"Yes, please. I need a Diet Dr. Pepper and pretzels if you have them."

"Sorry ma'am, we don't carry Dr. Pepper. The only diet soda is Diet Pepsi."

"I'll take the diet drink and pretzels, please. Thanks."

As I was eating the smallest bag of pretzels I'd ever seen, I continued to reminisce about my summer visits to Granny's and my interactions with the man I fell in love with, and the neighbor boy I spent my summers with, Jacob.

I remember another time when my Mom and Dad were still married, and we went to Granny and Partner's for a visit. I think it must have been summer, but I'm not sure. Jacob came over to Granny's to see Jeff and me. We were playing cards, so he joined in on the fun. I think we were playing a game called spoons.

My dad and grandparents went to sleep around ten p.m. that evening and my mom was going to bed too, about thirty minutes later after visiting with us a little longer. We told her we were thirsty and wanted to run to town to get a Dr. Pepper. Mom said okay, so we took Jacob's truck, a black pickup with a stick shift on the column and headed to town.

Jacob thought this was a good opportunity to teach me how to drive a stick shift, even though I told him, "No, I don't want to drive a stick shift. I don't know how." So, as he was driving down the highway, he literally climbed out the truck window while going about sixty miles an hour and left me closest to the wheel.

Jeff quickly pushed me over behind the wheel. Jacob walked back around in the bed of his pickup truck, told Jeff to scoot over, and he slid into the passenger seat of his truck through the window. I told him I wasn't going to slow the truck down, so I wouldn't have to worry about a clutch or gears. It made Jacob nervous, so he traded places with Jeff, then with me, and we were back to our original positions in the truck.

Then we stopped at a local gas station and bought our Dr. Peppers. And we needed chocolate if we were going to have soda pops. We were talking and thought it would be fun to drive out by the lake and see if we recognized any of the boats out on the water, fishing.

Then Jacob thought it would be cool to show us a place called Wells Overlook on the other side of the lake. It was a tall wooden tower that you could climb and see out over the hills and water.

We decided we could sit up there and talk and watch the sunrise. We had a great time, it was beautiful, and then Jeff insisted we get home before everyone woke up and realized we weren't home yet. We watched a beautiful sunrise, joked around, the boys had a spitting contest from the tall tower, and then we headed back home.

Jeff told Jacob to turn off the truck at the end of the road and we'd push his truck into the driveway, so we didn't wake the house. Well, before we even rolled into the driveway, mom came running out of the house crying. Jacob started the truck and drove straight for her. She told us she couldn't sleep worrying about us being gone so long. So, she woke up my dad and he and Partner were out looking for us, checking the hospitals, and she told Jacob he should go home too.

I could not believe that an innocent night could get us into so much trouble. It was the only time my dad ever grounded me. I was the only one who got in trouble, how unfair was that, just because I was the girl? Dad took Jeff and Jacob out in the boat the next day and I didn't get to go.

Not fair, but I didn't protest, because my dad was really mad, and I just wanted things to cool down. My dad had never been mad at me before and I didn't want him to be mad or not trust me.

Granny was spouting off things like, "A girl should guard her reputation, being out that time of night. Only bad girls are out at all hours of the night." She just fed fuel to the fire instead of letting it blow over. But the story of going out for a Dr. Pepper never did lose its enjoyment for my brother and cousins to tease me, even years later.

The flight attendant brought me back from memory lane when she announced that I needed to set my chair in the upright position and put my seatbelt back on for our pending landing. My thoughts went back to Jacob and me as children, so free, so much fun together.

Now I'm in love with him. No longer Jacob the fun-loving boy, but Jacob the handsome, smart man. And he just threw me away, like the trash. How could he do that to an old friend, much less a new lover? How am I going to ever get over him? I really don't think I ever will. He just ejected me from his life, no warning, just delete button, and I'm erased and out of his life.

Chapter 2

Bumpy Ride

I thought the fasten seatbelts lights and dings meant that we were landing, but no such luck. We were entering turbulent air. There was a storm in Missouri and my plane was hitting air pockets that felt like driving in a car and hitting deep potholes straight on. I was bouncing completely out of my seat with some of the hits. Little kids were screaming and crying, and I just sat there thinking, this flight is almost symbolic of me and Jacob.

I thought everything was going along great, smooth sailing if you will, and then when it's time for a landing, we hit a rough patch. I'm here, strapped in, riding it out, and Jacob bailed, not by my side. Life throws bumps in the road. You have to be strong enough to stand on your own, no matter what you've been through or are going through. Eventually the plane will land. I have to get my luggage and just walk away. Walk away from the love of my life.

I thought I'd never know love in that way, with someone

I treasured more than my own life. I have to walk away from my dream of pure love and happiness, because the only other choice I have is to fall apart, and I won't do that. I'm stronger than that, somewhere, deep down, I have to be.

The only thing I have left is a broken heart that stays with me aching, ripping, and tearing from the inside out. With every thought of Jacob, whether in my past or my recent past, my heart breaks. With all the I could haves and I should haves that are running through my mind, how do I stop thinking about him? How could I hurt so much?

Finally, the plane landed and I'm back home. This trip is over, time to move on Jenna. It's time for me to pick up my broken mind, will, emotions, and walk on. Just put one foot in front of the other, move forward. If all I can do is stand, then I'll stand, but I will not be a pathetic, needy, whiney woman. I despise that picture and won't be that person, no matter what happens. That is not who I am or ever will be.

I am a survivor, and I will get through this. I just need to take baby steps at first. I can begin again I know I can do it. Jenna, trust God not to give you more than you can handle. Keep up the positive self-talk. That's a good first step to recovery.

Some nice man at the luggage carousel was trying to talk to me, and all I wanted, was to be left alone. I see young lovers meeting each other off the plane, hugging, kissing, embracing with tenderness and joy, and it just makes my heart hurt that much more. How is that even possible? How selfish am I that I can't be happy for these total strangers that are around me happy in love?

So self-consumed, absorbed, don't be so inward, Jenna. Be positive you will get through this temporary rough patch. Now is not forever, it just feels like it. Mind over matter, my positive nature has to kick in or I would just crumble and die right here and now. I have to be strong. I can do this because I have no other choice. Jacob took my choices, stole my heart, and kicked me out of his home, his state, his life. I'm gone in more ways than one.

I'm back at home, sweet home, and I'm heartbroken! My life feels like a heart shaped piñata that's been beaten so hard that all my sweetness for life is just gone. I'm beyond empty. The man of my dreams told me, in so many words, that he didn't trust me and thrust me out of his life.

For the first time in my life, I really was happy, and I felt like a piece of my personal sized puzzle that had been missing, incomplete, was finally in place. I was a whole person and completely happy with him. I let myself be vulnerable and took down my guard, and now I'm an empty shell of a person without him.

Everything just happened so fast at the end. I was leaving and here I am, thousands of miles apart from him. How could our love that burned so hot, so fast, be over so soon? How could I let this happen? All these questions and I'm not going to get the answers.

I have to let all the questions, pain, hurt, and rejection go. That's the only way I can be healthy and free to move on with my life. The past is behind me, and he doesn't want to be my future. I have to make my own new future without him. I know in my head this is smart thinking, but to get my heart there will take hard work and time. It's so hard.

Jacob bought me a new car and we named her "baby". Now I'm a single parent raising her on my own. He paid for it in full, but now that we're apart, I can't let him give me such a loving gift. I accepted the gift when I thought he loved me, and we were engaged. But, since he's decided he doesn't love me or want me, I'm going to have to pay him back, every penny. Problem is, I don't have the financial security that Jacob has with his business.

I'm a single teacher, and pretty much live from paycheck to paycheck, like millions of hard-working Americans, so I'm going to be financially stretched to pay him back. I guess I could start with a couple of hundred a month for the rest of my life or until it's paid off. Why did I get such a nice car? Oh, I remember why. "Nothing but the best for my Jenna."

I miss him every day, in some big and some very small ways, but I have to move on for my sanity. I need to realize I will never be that happy again, but I need to believe that there is happiness out there for me. I just have to heal and move on. I need to be brave and put myself out there again. In time I might be able to feel again, to care again, and to love. It could happen. I could find someone to care about me. Be positive and expect the best. That's my self-talk these days, expect a miracle. Lightning can strike twice. I know this to be true because Jeff, my brother, has actually been struck by lightning twice.

Jeff was on the golf course and it started to rain. He and his buddies wanted to finish their round of golf, so they kept playing in the rain. Jeff, in metal cleats, swung his club. Lightning struck him, lifted him up off the ground threw him about fifty feet away. Flat on his back, the force of the lightening blew his club out of his hands, and the shoes off his feet. His buddies were over to him quickly and helped him to the clubhouse.

Once they knew Jeff was going to be okay, the stories they told of Jeff's near-death golf game became a humorous favorite for all to hear. But to hear Jeff retell it from his perspective was hysterical, and the story gets funnier every year as Jeff adds his flare. I know this is a serious subject and not funny, but Jeff is so animated you can't help but laugh hearing him retell his story.

The second time Jeff was stuck by lightning, he was hauling horses for his boys to a horse show and his truck stalled. It was raining and he climbed up into the engine area of the truck to see what was happening.

The boys were getting rain gear on inside the truck when the lightning hit Jeff. He went flying across the parking lot. The bolt was so strong, it knocked out all the electricity at the Taco Bell across the street from where he was stalled. Jeff's wife and sons jumped out of the truck and ran to him. They had paramedics called and ran tests after that. My mom and I were waiting to meet them at the horse show just a few miles further east.

When he finally arrived at the horse show, both his hands were still hot to touch. He was a weird color, sort of yellow green, pale looking and was understandably shaken up. I would be too, but now he just adds this lightning experience to his "I just about died" stories that seem to grow like his fishing stories. My "smoking hot" brother, got to love him!

A couple days after I'd been home and unpacked, and tried to get my life back to normal, I decided to contact Jacob. I wrote my first check to Mr. Jacob Jamison, in the amount of $200.00 and in the memo section I wrote Baby's first re-payment. I didn't know how he'd respond. I decided I would just mail the check to him. No note, no letter, no begging him to come back to me, nothing. Just cold hard cash.

With all his expenses lately, some because of me, I think he'll just keep the check. Oh my gosh, I completely forgot about our engagement rings we ordered when he came to Missouri to see me.

I quickly called the jewelers in Branson to cancel our wedding ring order, only to find out that Jacob had already cancelled our rings. I should have known he would be ten steps ahead of me and I'm sort of glad I didn't have to deal with any more problems right then. I'll just assume that he had deleted all memories of me that linked us together.

I needed to find something new to do, something with no Jacob connections. Something for fun, pure enjoyment, to keep my mind busy and entertained, maybe take a dance class. No, I'd need a partner. I know, possibly a photography class. I want something or someone to keep my interest and challenge me. Find anything to keep me from missing him. I knew the aching, hurting, and crying in the shower each morning would end in time. But part of me was afraid to let go of the pain, because then he really will be out of my life and honestly, I didn't want to let go of him completely.

Reality is, I'd have to face the fact that I'm alone again. I have to face the cold, hard certainty that I'd blown yet another relationship. That I'd loved and lost, and experienced the mind-numbing happiness, and the heart wrenching pain of losing something that meant everything to me. I had no idea what I did or why it ended, but it was over. I was alone and empty and need something new.

A week later was a huge day for me. After I got home from work, I went out to the mailbox to get my mail, and there it was a letter from Jacob. I stopped breathing. I had to tell myself to breath, so I could get air to think.

My first letter ever from him and here it was in my hands. He has beautiful handwriting. He wrote neater than me with all his letters written in upper case, and they are all the same size, so precise and exact, beautiful just like Jacob. He wrote my name, he sent me a letter. I was so excited to receive a letter from him that I literally screamed when it finally registered in my brain that it was from him.

My neighbor was outside at the same time and asked me if I was okay. I just nodded, waved, and ran inside the house with my letter that was more precious to me than gold. I gently opened it, making sure I didn't tear anything. I unfolded the handwritten treasure, and this is what it said:

Dear Jenna,

I hope you are doing well.

Enclosed you will find your check for $200.00.

I don't need your money so keep it, all of it.

The car is yours free and clear like we discussed before purchase.

Best Wishes Always,
Jacob

It wasn't exactly what I wanted to hear, but it's proof that he had been thinking of me, at least for a few minutes. He could have just sent me an e-mail, or just tore up the check without a word, but he took the time to wish me well and let me know he wouldn't be taking my money.

That was sweet of him. Now, what was my next move? Oh, dear Lord, I've got it, this will be perfect, no, genius! I am so happy with me right now. I'm jumping up and down and doing my happy dance. My dogs are trying to figure out what I'm doing. They are barking and chasing around me, and this was me, being totally giddy!

After I stopped dancing around my living room, I grabbed my purse, found my car keys, then drove directly to the mall. I went up the escalator to the bedding department. Jacob loved my Egyptian sheets. They are off the charts, the softest things, highest thread count you can buy, that I've ever slept on. He wanted a set of these sheets when we were together, so I will send him a set.

Color, what color should I buy? Blue, I want his set to be blue, to match how I feel without him, and blue to match his beautiful crystal blue eyes. Wow, I'd forgotten how much I'd paid for those fine sheets. There goes that $200 and then some. But he will love them and he's worth it. If he is sleeping with other women, then at least I will be there with him too, in some very small way. How desperate did I sound? Buy sheets and get out of here.

Now for the letter, what do you say back to him? Keep it short, sweet, and to the point. No pouring out your heart, no begging, no needy woman, just be strong Jenna, you can do this. I smiled. I just wish I could see his face when he gets his package and reads my handwritten note.

I had to write and re-write the note over and over to get

it to look just the way I wanted. His handwriting is so much better than mine. Seriously a computer e-mail or a text would have been so much easier. But I'm going for the dramatic effect. I did great with this purchase, no it was better than great, it was perfect!

Dear Jacob,
I'm fine. Hope you and your family are well too.
Enclosed you will find your earlier request.
Fondly,
Jenna

Now I think I can finally move on. I got to say goodbye to him, sort of, with my letter, my humor, and on my terms. Okay, I was going to be okay. I could begin again. I knew I could, for real now. I felt a spark of happy today, and it felt good from my head to my toes. It didn't last long, this feeling, but it was a start. I'm headed in the right direction of life without Jacob. I was past the desperateness of hoping and on my way to healing. Goodbye dear, beautiful Jacob, goodbye!

Chapter 3

Picture That

I was teaching my kindergarteners today, and I had recess duty. I'd just gotten through talking with a student who was yelling, "On your mark, get sex, go" to his friends, and I suggested he just say "1-2-3 go" to start the race with his friends. I turned my head, cracking up thinking that kids say the dandiest things, when another kindergartener from a different classroom came up to me.

"Ms. Jenna?"

"Yes sir?"

"My sister is in fourth grade, and she thinks you are fat."

I just looked at him and said, "Well, Johnny, what do you think about that?" He gave me a full head to toe, to head look.

"No, I don't think so."

I said, "Thanks Johnny, and you should be careful when you talk to girls about their weight because it could hurt their feelings. Now go play. You've got five more minutes before I blow the whistle to go inside."

Great, have I gained weight? It's possible, with stress from the breakup, and food as my new best friend. I probably have packed on some pounds. I've been living in sort of a fog since the breakup. I seem to be hungry all the time. I guess this is my wakeup call to see things clearly and get my priorities in order. It starts tonight. It's Friday night and now I had something to do.

I decided to throw out junk food and chocolate supplies and take a good look at myself in the full-length mirror.

The Saturday business flyer had a local community college's courses listed. Hey, photography classes in the evenings. That would be fun. Tuesdays and Thursdays. I could do that if I rearranged my afterschool tutoring jobs. It sounded like just the ticket for a fun and interesting change.

It was to start in a couple of weeks, I thought I'd call and see what kind of a camera they recommend I should use for the class. I would need to buy one. I'll look online and see what I can learn about cameras and options too. There was no one to talk to in person on a Friday evening, so I had to leave a message. I hope to hear back from the community college on Monday, so I can get a camera and use it a bit before class starts.

Monday came and the college had forwarded my call to the photography instructor. He returned my call and was very friendly. He said he lived near two great stores that sell quality cameras, the Lawrence Photo Shop or Best Buy. He indicated he would be glad to meet with me and help me find a good camera, without the pressure of a camera salesclerk, possibly on commission.

So, I would have a camera for class, and I would have some time to get familiar with it before classes began. I told him I really appreciated his willingness to help me and that I could meet him after four-thirty, if that would work for his schedule. He asked to make it five o'clock and actually that would be easier for me to travel across town anyway.

I told him I drive a new red Chevy SUV, and my name is Jenna. I'll stand outside the front door of the photo shop until you get there, and we can go inside together. He said his name is Brandon and that he would meet me at five at the front door of the camera shop.

I was using Google on my phone at the stop lights all the way across town, lots of lights, to find out something about cameras, so I didn't look and sound like a complete idiot in front of my new professor.

I'd forgotten everything I'd found out on-line earlier and didn't have the notes I'd written down from the internet. If I didn't write things down, I'd forget them, and now I'm forgetting where I put my notes. It was getting bad. Anyway, I drove into the parking lot a couple minutes before five, so I was really glad we changed the time for later.

I jumped out of my car with phone and purse in hand and stood at the door reading camera reviews on-line while waiting for my future professor, Brandon. I was absorbed in my phone when I heard his deep, friendly voice.

"Jenna?"

"Yes, Brandon?"

I was turning off my phone as I looked up. I was happy to see a very nice-looking man. No, he was better than nice, he was fine looking. No, he was handsome, very handsome.

What did I do in front of this man? For a first impression that you only have once to get right, I fumble my phone. And as I'm reaching forward to catch it before it scratches my screen by landing on the ground, it somehow ends up sliding down the front of my future professors' stomach, and he stopped it as it slid to his belt. My hands are trying to catch my phone and I'm trying not to touch my professors' body. I just looked at him. Shaking my head, no, and apologizing.

"Here you go Jenna, here's your phone."

It was important at this point for me to focus. "Thank

you, so much, for coming to help me select a good camera… I'm really excited to take your class. My photography experiences have pretty much been with my cell phone and a digital camera that has auto everything, just point, shoot, and hope for a good shot experience.

I wanted a camera that would allow me to use the information you teach in class to become a really accomplished photographer, with time and practice. Sort of something I can grow into with experience and time."

"What kind of pictures do you enjoy taking?"

"I love outdoor pictures, still life, animals, and people too. So much beauty and humor there to capture and enjoy. I just want to capture the essence of those special things, to share that joy with others. Does that help you know where we should start shopping?"

"Yes, we have a starting point. Let's go inside and see what they have available and what would be a good fit for you. Do you have a price range you want to target?"

"I am more concerned with getting a quality camera that will last for several years of great pictures. But would love to get a deal, so I don't spend too much money, if that helps you at all."

We headed inside and his manly cologne hit me. Wow, he smelled good too! Ring, is he wearing a wedding ring? I nonchalantly looked down at his hand, and no ring. Hmm, he looks close to my age. What am I doing?

This man is a stranger and helping me find a high-priced item. Pay attention to the cameras, not the man holding the cameras. Brandon was very careful to explain things to me in an easy-to-understand way, without treating me like a child. I appreciated his skill. He will be a great teacher to help me learn the tools of the trade.

I spent way more time and money than I had intended, and bought an additional very expensive lens, that actually cost more than the camera itself. How was that possible, I didn't know, but I charged it on my credit card. I was very excited and couldn't wait to go take some pictures with my new camera.

While paying my bill, I thanked Brandon one more time, and told him I was really looking forward to taking his class. He just smiled and said he was looking forward to getting to know me better too. I looked in his eyes and I thought I saw a twinkle when he said that. Was he flirting with me? I didn't even know what to say. I was shocked, I just smiled.

"Thanks again for your help. I feel confident and excited about my high dollar purchase!"

Brandon walked me to my car. "I was wondering if you don't have plans already, would you like to go somewhere and grab a bite for dinner?"

I had no plans and this kind, good looking man, just asked me out. Why not be brave, fight for happiness. "I didn't have plans and just happened to be hungry. Do you have any place in particular in mind?"

"Well, that depends. Do you have any food allergies or dislikes?"

"Not really, I like everything except green peppers."

"How does pizza sound for a Friday night?"

"I love pizza, one of my favorite foods."

So, I followed him to the mom-and-pop pizza parlor called Artis Pizza, not too far down the road from where we were located. As I followed him, I was thinking about Brandon. He was tall, well taller than me, I guess he's 6'3ish. And I like a man with meat on him, not just skin and bones, and he's very fit and in shape. He had brown eyes and I was so thankful they weren't blue. No one could ever compete with Jacob's blue eyes. Brandon's hair was thick, sandy blonde hair.

Once we were at the pizza shop, Brandon was a gentleman, opening the door for me, and pulling out my chair. I've never had a man treat me so respectfully with good manners. I appreciated and enjoyed the experience.

"Brandon, I keep saying thank you. Why don't you tell me about yourself?

"I teach Art History at Missouri State University. I am also an adjunct professor at the community college for photography. I'm single and enjoy long walks along the beach, but living in Missouri, I don't get many of those." Then he winked at me and something inside me fluttered.

"Well, you've always got spring break and summers."

"Yes, people often think instructors have all this time off, but I actually work every other summer, so I can travel and take groups of students to different sites, to experience photography in other geological areas. We tour famous art exhibits on those occasions too. How about yourself, what do you do?"

"Well, I'm at the opposite end of the spectrum of the teaching scale. I teach kindergarten. I love their questions, energy, humor, and honesty. I love that each day is a challenge and fun. I have the best job ever and I know it. I too work summers but being single and not on the professor pay scale, I have to work every summer to keep up with rising gas prices and expenses. I totally splurged on this camera, and the lens, but I really wanted to. Actually, I needed something new to focus my energy and attention."

"I don't mean to pry, but from your comment, I'm wondering are you divorced or had a recent break up?"

"Yes, sadly on both counts."

"Sorry. Do you have kids?"

"No."

"Do you?"

"Yes, I have a beautiful daughter in high school. She lives part time with me, part time with her mom. But since her mom's recently remarried, she spends more time with her mom and their new big house, with stepbrothers and stepsisters. She's always been an only child, so she is enjoying having brothers and sisters right now."

"Brandon, a teenage daughter needs a good relationship

with her dad. No one can ever take the place of a dad in a girl's heart, ever. It's a great responsibility to love her and listen to her through all her talking, non-stop talking. A teenage girl's stress processing mechanism is talk and talk, and then talk some more.

Then there are those emotional hormones that young girls are trying to figure out. That's a tough job for you, to know when to say something and when to let things just blow over. I'm so glad you two are in the same town so you can be involved in her everyday life. That gives a girl security to know her dad is there for her. I'm sorry, I sort of ramble when I feel strongly about something."

"No, I think your thoughts and comments were really sweet things to say. I've dated a lot since my divorce, even joined one of those on-line dating sites. But the women they've connected me with are more impressed with my career title and could care less about my child, the love of my life.

In all my dating experiences, not one of those matches was as thoughtful and honest as you just were about my love for my daughter. You are a refreshing woman, Jenna. I'm so glad you called for help and I'm so glad I'm the one who took your call."

"Well get used to it." I felt my face blush. "Oh, I mean get used to me needing assistance in the field of photography, not that I would be calling you all the time. I probably crossed over some sort of invisible line between professor and student already, and I wouldn't want to cause you any negative consequences for being with me. I didn't mean "being with me". I meant student dating a professor, not that this is a date. I think I'm just going to shut up now."

Laughing he said, "Jenna, we are fine. The dating police are off duty on weekends. I am not crossing any lines. You aren't even my student yet. You don't need to worry about me. I take full responsibility for my actions, always have and always will."

"Brandon, are you saying this is a date?"

"Well let's recap things, shall we? We've been together for the last three and a half almost four hours, enjoying one another's company, and talking non-stop. There have been no awkward pauses or lack of interesting conversation. If this isn't a date, then how about you go out with me and we will have our second first date?"

I couldn't believe he just said those exact words to me. Jacob and I had something of a hard time nailing down our first date too. How could I let history repeat itself? I must have looked like a deer in the headlights because Brandon quickly said my name.

"Jenna, I'm not pressuring you, please don't feel that way. If you don't want to date me, I can still be your instructor and it won't be weird, I promise. There is no pressure. I just enjoy your company."

"No, I'm sorry Brandon, it's not that. It's just your choice of words, "our second first date". That just happened to me in my last relationship, and it broke off as fast as it started. I was just caught off guard when you said those exact words. I'm sorry for the look of apparent horror on my face. I just wasn't prepared for your "second-first date" reference."

"You said I caught you off guard. Do you feel like you need to be on guard around me?"

"I'm a woman, and I think it's my self-preservation mode to be on guard to some extent, especially around good-looking men. Brandon, if you still want to, I would be honored to go out with you on a formal date. But I need to take it slow and set some ground rules. When I'm in your class, you will have to treat me the same as everyone else. If that can happen, then we can date. If not, I'll see you in class, professor."

"I think I can live with those ground rules. What are you doing tomorrow night?"

"Ha, ha. I said I need to take things slow."

"Okay then, how about next Friday or Saturday night? Can I call and talk with you tomorrow or is that too soon?"

"Yes, that would be fine, but only because you said, "talk with" and not "talk to" me."

"Wow, you are going to be a challenge for me aren't you, Ms. Jenna?"

"Honestly, that's probably true, but not intentional on my part, so I should apologize before we even go out. Brandon, you should run, seriously, if you know what's good for you. Run and don't look back."

"And Jenna has a sense of humor too, good to know. Thanks for having dinner with me and I will call you tomorrow."

"Thanks for dinner and the camera shopping. Talk to you tomorrow, if you call."

"Oh, I'll call you, Jenna. You will learn I'm a man of my word."

Chapter 4

First Date

Finally, I had someone to spend my time with that enjoyed spending time with me. I enjoyed meeting Brandon and getting to know and appreciate him. He's was a really good instructor. I had my first class with him, and I kept feeling like I had some special secret from the rest of the class.

I felt giddy and just wanted to laugh but pulled myself back to reality and focus my attention on the instructor and class. I should listen, so if he asks me something about what he said in class, I can ask intelligent questions when it's just him and me alone, together.

After our second class together, Brandon and I were going out for our first official date. We had planned an afternoon of picture taking and an evening including dinner. It was a perfect day for being outside together and taking pictures. We had been talking on the phone every day since we met two weeks prior.

Now, here we were together on our first date, having a blast laughing, appreciating each other's humor, and getting up close and personal tips on how to improve my photos. We had great times together. Our interactions were natural and comfortable. Brandon was a good man. He was attentive yet gave me space. He was balanced and trustworthy. And best of all was his amazing sense of humor. He made me laugh a lot. I loved that he was local.

I care about Brandon and enjoy every moment we are together. It's just, he wasn't Jacob. No one will ever be Jacob and I needed to forget my every memory of him if I was ever going to really allow myself to be happy again. Goodbye Jacob. My mind has let you go, but my heart needs to let you go too. Heart, say hello to Brandon.

On our date, Brandon brought a picnic basket and blanket. We sat in the sun under a weeping willow tree by a bubbling brook and talked. We walked around, took pictures, and laughed for hours. We got some great pictures from our day together.

My two favorite picture moments were the ones I took laying under the tree and looking up through the weeping willow branches, to the rays of sun, and the clouds above. My other favorite pictures were of Brandon being swarmed by geese when he was throwing bread chunks to them on the water.

Most of my pictures were blurry of the geese incident because I was laughing so hard. I couldn't see to focus or hold the camera still. I'm going to have to work on that skill and buy a tripod.

Brandon is fun and secure enough about himself to be a good sport. Like when he was being swarmed by geese, so I could get pictures, and laugh my sides off. I'm laughing again just thinking about our time together, and it's real, not forced.

Brandon is bringing me back to life and I adore him for that. My heart is feeling happy again and I didn't think that would ever be possible.

The sun was going down and as always, I was hungry. I just wanted to stay at Dogwood Canyon first date, picture perfect location, with the romantic waterfalls, caves, animals, and flowers. It was so pretty and peaceful, but I wanted a shower and have a good dinner too. We headed back to town to get ready for dinner. He was going to pick me up in two hours.

I wasn't crying in the shower anymore. I jumped in the shower and actually caught myself humming. After shaving my legs and washing my hair, I was really looking forward to kissing Brandon tonight for the first time. But, of course, only after eating a good dinner.

Brandon was on time and at the door with flowers in hand. How sweet could he possibly be? I don't know how he found the time to get them and be on time, but he's stunning. He may get his kiss before dinner! I hugged him at the door, took the flowers, and walked to the kitchen to find a vase to display his expression of thoughtfulness. I turned around in the kitchen and he was right behind me.

It was there in my kitchen where we had our first embrace. He walked to me all handsome and smelling heavenly, and without hesitation, gave me a sweet, tender kiss on the lips. He stepped back and asked, "Are you ready to go eat?" I was starving, but are we done kissing so soon? He was being respectful of me, taking it slow like I told him. After all, it was our first date.

"Yes, I'm starved. Are you hungry?"

"Fresh air always makes me hungry. How does Houlihan's sound?"

"Great, let's go."

We sat by a fire pit outside while we were waiting to be seated and enjoyed the best fried mushroom appetizers I'd ever eaten. Each mushroom was about the size of a man's large fist, and I'm pretty sure I ate two of the five before the main course arrived.

This night was great, the company, ambience, a handsome, kind man, and comfortable conversation. We had an enjoyable day and evening for our first date. During our table conversation, he reached across the table and took my hand. He just talked and slid his hand across the top of mine, and it sent goose bumps down both my arms and back.

"There's a bar down the road that's up scale and classy. Would you like to stop by the club for a drink or two, or call it a night?"

It was already 9:30 after we ate, and I was tired. It didn't really hit me until my tummy was full. "Brandon, it's been a wonderful first date, but if you don't mind taking me home, I am a little tired."

"Will we call it a good night?"

"Oh, most definitely. It has been a great day and a wonderful night. Thank you so much for a remarkable first date. Did our date meet all your expectations?"

"Yes and no. But only because I haven't gotten to kiss you goodnight yet."

He smiled at me and I thought I'd melt, was terrific! He had a beautiful smile. Large white teeth, and full luscious lips. I was really the lucky one here. He was a catch. Smiling, I felt warm and happy. Yes, happy. How could this happen for me after Jacob? I didn't think it was possible for me to breathe after Jacob, and here I was with a handsome man, and for the first time in months and months, I feel happy, content, and glad to be alive.

Brandon walked me to my door, and we stepped one step inside the entry way and he was all man and all over me. We bumped into my kitchen table, then onto my couch.

Brandon and I came up for air and unwrapped ourselves from one another. We sat up on the couch and just stared at each other. It was like electricity between us. This was intense and I needed to ask him to leave, or my first date rule of no sex would be a past tense standard. I scooted away from Brandon.

"Slow, I told you I have to do this slow."

"Jenna, I feel like you are sending mixed messages. One message loud and clear with your words, but a totally different message with your body. I'm sorry if I crossed your comfort zone."

"No, it's not that I'm uncomfortable with you at all. I just don't want to have any regrets."

"I have no regrets with you. Just a few more kisses and I'll say goodnight."

"More kissing? Ever heard of leave them wanting more?"

"Oh, I will leave wanting more."

I blushed and he laughed. I love his laugh. It makes me happy inside just to see him smile, but his laugh, thrills me deeply.

"Now, get back over here and kiss me."

Kissing resumed and it was hard, very hard to stop our intimate interactions. I had standards and morals, but we are friends, and we liked one another. I wanted to be with him, and he obviously wanted to be with me. We are adults, why do I feel like a sinner when I find a man that's amazing? Then it happened, but not what you think. It was about 10:45 and my phone rang.

Who would be calling me at this time of night? "Brandon, I need to take this. I usually don't get calls this late."

"Sure. Do you want to me to go or wait?"

"Just give me a minute, then I will walk you to the door."

I looked at my caller I.D. and the name and number said, "A Boyfriend Jacob". OMG, not one word in six months, half a year, and now I finally go out on my first date and he calls when I'm making out? Is this possible? How can this happen to me? What was I thinking? This could only happen to me! I had to answer the phone.

"Hello?"

"Jenna?"

"Yes, who is this?"

"It's Andrew, Jacob's brother. Jacob's been in a serious accident."

"Oh no, is he okay?"

"No Jenna, they are air lifting him to the medical center in Louisville. The only thing we know is there was a car accident, and he handed his phone to the medic and said your name, just your name, for a contact. The EMT is a friend of mine, so he called me and that's why I'm calling you."

"Andrew, should I come? I want to be there, but if anything happens to him, I wouldn't survive it, I know I wouldn't."

"Come if you want to see him, but if you plan on coming, you should come right now. Things don't look good for his survival."

"Andrew, I will be there as soon as it is humanly possible. I'm leaving as soon as I can make arrangements." I hung up the phone and looked at Brandon.

"I have to fly out of state because a close friend has been in a serious car wreck. Would you be willing to feed and care for my dogs Molly and Moose, while I'm gone? It might be several days, maybe a week, if there's a funeral. I'm sorry to ask you to do this, but at this late hour, I don't have a lot of options."

"Sure, whatever you need me to do, I'll be here for you." He hugged me and I felt his warmth and strength.

"I'm sorry to ask you to do this, but it's late and I need you to go, so I can think to pack. Wait, don't go, I need your help. Would you call the airport and get me a ticket? My credit card is in my purse. Just charge whatever it costs to fly to Louisville, Kentucky's closest airport. And if you wouldn't mind, will you drive me to the airport, so my car is here at home in my garage?"

"Okay, you pack, and I'll make your arrangements for the flight. But only if you promise me, you will not drive to the hospital from the airport. Just take a taxi. You don't need the pressure and stress of standing in lines filling out papers to rent a car. And then trying to get directions and fighting traffic in a new city, when you are upset about your friend and you're tired. Just get a taxi because you shouldn't drive when you are upset. And I can see you are in a daze right now. I'll help anyway I can. Do you need some cash?"

"Thanks for the offer and help. I don't need money. I can't even think right now, okay. Please make the call and I'll be out with you in a couple of minutes. I just need to pack quickly."

I was already in my bedroom throwing in underwear, bras, jeans, shirts, jackets, because hospitals are so cold, and my camera. I'm not sure why I packed my camera, but I did. My makeup bag and hair dryer, more clothes, one pair of tennis shoes, and socks. I was dressed up for my date, so I just left my clothes on and Brandon drove me to the airport.

"Please phone me when you know something. I'll be here and you can call me anytime day or night. I'm here for you."

"Thanks. I left my girlfriend's phone number in the doggie supplies, so if you want relief from dog duty, she knows my dogs and would gladly take care of them. Feel free to call her."

I kissed him for being there for me. I kissed him for taking care of my dogs, and I kissed him for not asking me a bunch of questions. I kissed him to end our date. Part of me just wanted to stay with Brandon and leave the past behind me, where I had just put it. But it's Jacob. He called my name, only my name, and he may not be alive when I get there. I have no choice. I have to go see him.

I thanked Brandon and said goodbye while he lifted my

suitcase out of the trunk. I just ran through the airport doors in my high heels. I heard the final boarding call for my departing flight. I was so relieved I'd made it in time. I needed to get to Jacob. I couldn't breathe just thinking about him hurt and it was tearing me to pieces inside all over again. I don't know if I could heal from saying goodbye to him twice.

Here I was in the air, all cell phones need to be turned off, and I haven't told my mom or my brother that I'm not home, but on my way to be at Jacobs side. Jacob said my name, just my name. But why? Was he afraid of dying with regrets? Will I get there in time to tell him how sorry I am and that I still love him. I just got over him and here I am running back into his arms?

What will I do when I see him? Will they let me see him? I'm not family? Jacob, please be okay. God help Jacob! Finally, the take off your seatbelts sign came on, so I could turn on my phone. I'll text mom and Jeff and let them know where I am, and what I'm doing, and why. That was a long text, but it helped me process things. I felt bad for how I left Brandon, so I texted him too.

"Brandon, thanks again for being there for me. If you want to take the dogs to my vet, they will keep them for the week. I would just pay them for taking them while I was gone. They have my credit card on file, and they can call me tomorrow to approve the charges. It would be fine if my girlfriend Jackie can't watch them. I know it would be easier for you. I have all their vet information under a magnet on my fridge."

I felt bad for asking him to take on such a big responsibility. I put him on the spot, and he had no choice but to say yes, he'd help, or he'd look like a jerk. This way, he had a way out of dealing with my dogs twice daily. I texted to inform him I was going to try to close my eyes before I landed in Kentucky, to get some rest.

Brandon texted me back, "Don't worry about your dogs.

I'll be glad to take care of them for you. I look forward to hearing from you tomorrow. Do you want me to contact your school, or have you already called them?"

I told him, "No, I'd do that, but thanked him for reminding me." Great, work, I'd forgotten all about work. So, I got on my phone, called the substitute service, and reserved a substitute for my classroom for the week.

Then I called Ms. Becky, my school secretary, to leave her a message on the school phone, so she would know what is going on with me. She is a friend and would tell the principal and not blab all my business to others that work with me, except to keep them in the loop.

Now my mind was racing. I left Brandon my house keys and my car keys if he needed them. I had a first date, and basically gave him access to my home and all my personal items. He could snoop, whatever.

I shouldn't have asked him to be responsible for my dogs and house while I am gone. I was just in shock, and he was there. I don't want to use Brandon. I hope he will understand when I get back and tell him everything, I owe him that. He's a good man.

Sleep, I needed to rest before I got off the plane and had to face Jacob and his family. Please God, let him be okay! Please help me when I see Jacob, help me help Jacob. I feel like I already suffered a death with Jacob when he killed our relationship. And now, how am I going to be able to see him, not care about him, and have all those feelings for him again.

I've worked so hard to heal, how can I do this alone? I have no choice. I have to go for Jacob, for what we were to each other, and because he gave them my name to contact, just mine. Why?

Chapter 5

My Jacob

I landed at the airport and quickly asked how far it was to the hospital. I decided to just get a taxi like Brandon recommended. I had the taxi driver drop me off at the door of the hospital. I grabbed my bag on wheels, headed to the emergency room, and there was the whole male Jamison family in the waiting room.

I was not welcomed with hugs and smiles, just stares and glares. Thankfully, Andrew walked up to me and gave me a hug, a sincere bear hug. He leaned down to whisper in my ear, "Let's walk out in the hallway so we can talk privately. Leave your luggage in here with the family, Jenna. It will be fine."

"Andrew, how's Jacob? Please tell me he's alive."

"Jenna, Jacob was in a car accident. He was hit head on. The other driver didn't make it."

My mind was racing. I know that it's usually the drunk driver that's the one who lives. If the other driver is already gone, my hopes were fading for Jacob's survival.

"Was it a drunk driver? That's what this is all about? He lost his fiancé to a drunk driver and now he's hit by a drunk driver too? Is that all you do out here is drink? Sorry, I shouldn't have said that. I'm just worried about Jacob. Andrew, hold me, I think I'm going to…."

And I did, I fainted, and when I came to, I woke up in Andrews arms. He looked so concerned, I felt so bad. I'd never fainted before, but I had no strength to stand. He carried me to the family waiting room. They got me some orange juice, and someone was getting me food from a vending machine.

I didn't want anything, I didn't want all this attention, and I was so embarrassed. I hated being weak and didn't really want an audience. I'm not some needy girl, and all I wanted was to see Jacob. I just finished my juice when a surgeon walked into the waiting room. He asked if he could speak frankly to all in the room or did, we need a private room? He then received a nod from Jacob's father, so he told us about Jacob's condition.

"Doctor, how is Jacob?"

"He came through the surgeries and now it's a waiting game. He had a lot of internal bleeding that's a major concern. There are broken bones where his seatbelt held him, and his nose was broken from the air bag. He has head injuries, and we won't know how serious the brain injuries are until we bring him out of the medically-induced coma. We are working to reduce the swelling on the brain, keep his vitals monitored, and pain killers flowing."

Then the questions came from several directions. "Is he going to be okay? Will he have a full recovery?" "How long will he be in the hospital?"

"It's too soon to tell, the next 48 hours are crucial."

"Can he hear us? If we talk to him, will he know it's us?"

"Sometimes they can hear you, but he won't be able to

respond because he has a breathing tube down his throat. We will take the tube out after he is ready to speak, if all goes well."

I forgot anyone else was even in the room and I just blurted out, "Can I go see him? Andrew, please go in with me to see him."

Jacob's dad was there and all his uncles, brothers, and apparently a few girlfriends too. So, Jacob's dad, brother Andrew, and I went into his ICU room first. My heart couldn't take it. I tried to make myself strong for Jacob. Do not faint and don't throw up. Just be here for Jacob. All I could do was pray silent prayers. When I saw tears in his dad's and brother's eyes, I had to sit down before I crashed again.

I didn't leave that hospital chair. I lost all track of time and days. I forgot about my luggage, everything. I stayed in that chair all night, through all the nurse visits, and family coming in and out crying, and staring at me. I didn't care. Jacob called out for me and I'm sending him all my love and prayers. I'm not leaving this room until they make me. He once told me to pound on his chest to bring him back to life, and I'm here ready to do that if I need to.

I must have dozed off because I heard Jacob groaning and I was suddenly fully awake and aware of everything. He was trying to reach for the breathing tube, but they had his arms restrained. The doctor was immediately notified and was in the room rather quickly to join the nurses.

He instructed Jacob to squeeze his hand if he wanted the tube removed. He squeezed. I was so happy he could think, understand, and respond quickly. I stood at the foot of his bed smiling at him, hoping he would see me, and recognize me. But he was in pain and dealing with all his physical limitations.

The doctor unrestrained his hands and asked him to use a board or his fingers to communicate. Using numbers from one to ten, ten being the highest, indicate your pain level.

And my strong, brave, Jacob held up ten fingers.

His dad, who had just rushed back into his room, immediately commanded the doctor and nurses to give him more pain meds. But Jacob gave the doctor thumbs down to his dad's emotional plea. Then our eyes met, and I knew that he knew who I was.

He tried to say my name, but still couldn't talk without great pain. I quickly moved from the end of his bed to the side of his bed and held his hand. He just faded out of consciousness. The Dr. said this was a good sign and that we should know more tomorrow. He took the tube out of his throat while he was out so he could talk the next time he tried to speak.

I stepped out into the hall to use the restroom and to see the family. The news had spread about Jacobs's accident and half the town was in the waiting room. I noticed three women, very pretty women, pacing in the waiting room.

I wondered if these women were acquainted with the new blue sheets, I'd sent him. This is not the time to play the jealous ex-girlfriend. I feel all alone and selfish for thinking about myself at a time like this. Just the stares from this family, like I'm the enemy, I hate it. But he went through a lot with my family in the past, so this is nothing in the big scheme of things. I can deal with the looks for Jacob's sake.

I called to talk to my principal to let her know what was happening. I was really worried that I would be fired for missing so much work this year because of Partner's death, then Granny's death so soon afterwards.

But I couldn't leave until I knew Jacob was going to be okay. I can give him up and I can stay away from him only when I know he's happy and healthy. But if he needs me, I'm staying, I have no choice.

Andrew took me around my waist and walked me down to the lunchroom at the hospital. He's a great guy and I know he's worried about his brother. But still, he is kind enough to make sure I am eating. Guess he doesn't want to have to pick me up off the floor again.

"Thank you for helping me get through this terrible time. I love Jacob and always will. Why did he call my name? Why did you call me? I was finally moving on, and here I am back to loving the man of my dreams, and he's got machines hooked up all over him."

"Jenna, he's going to be okay. I wanted you to be here for him so he would fight to live. Jenna, I know my brother and he hasn't been the same since you left him."

"What do you mean, I left him, Andrew? He kicked me out, he sent me packing. It was him wanting me gone, not me leaving him." Why would he tell his family I left him? It's not the truth. "Andrew we've been gone a while. We should get back to Jacob's room and make sure he's okay."

I don't know where the time went, but I was back in the chair, sleeping next to Jacob's bed, and then I felt his hand in mine. He squeezed my hand and I quickly sat up. He was sitting up in his bed and looking at me.

"Oh Jacob, thank God, thank you Jesus! I was so afraid I was going to lose you. Sorry, I shouldn't have said that last part, I'm just so happy you are okay."

"Jenna."

"Yes?"

"I love you."

"What did you say?"

"I love you Jenna, always have, and always will. I'm sorry for how this all has played out, I just wanted to protect you from my family."

"If you loved me, how could you kick me out of your life, push me away?" Honestly, doesn't he remember the deal breaker for me? Not control all our options in some macho, manly, self-sacrificing crap. "Jacob, life is too short. We can't be apart ever again. If you weren't in so much pain right now, I'd climb in there and show you what I think about you."

"Babe, don't let these tubes and bruises stop you."

"You asked for it, scoot over." Just then it occurred to me. I've been in this room four days, five nights, and I didn't change my clothes, only underwear, because I didn't want to be away from Jacob that long. I couldn't get in bed with him, all gross and dirty. He needs clean and sterile.

"Wait, I need a shower first. I can't get in bed with you. I haven't left this room for four days and I feel gross. I need to go somewhere and take a shower so you can stay germ free and get out of here sooner. I'm going to go get your dad. Do you need anything?"

"Just you. I'm so glad you are here. I love you."

"Jacob, look at me, and know this as an eternal fact. I love you forever. Together, apart, wherever you are, you have my heart always. I'm so glad you are going to be okay."

"My head really hurts. Would you turn off the lights?"

"Sure babe. I'll get a cold cloth for your head too and get your dad. Are you okay if I run, get a hotel room so I can take a shower?"

"First go and get Andrew for me."

I motioned for Andrew and he came running from the hallway into Jacob's room. "Andrew, Jacob wants to talk to you and I'm going to talk to his nurse. Leave the lights out, they hurt his eyes."

"Andrew, you take Jenna and get her a hotel room next to the hospital so she can take a damn shower. Four days and it never occurred to you that the woman I love would want a shower, or somewhere to change her clothes.

What were you thinking? You step up and make sure she is taken care of for me. Car rides to hospital, airport, whatever she wants. And she won't ask for anything, that's why she's sat in a damn chair for four days with no shower, nothing. You have to do this for me Andrew, you have to. Tell me you are on this."

"Bro, we have all been here 24/7 worried sick about

you, not your ex-girl. Sorry if I missed some clues, but I was here to pick her up when she fainted."

"She fainted? You let her hit the ground? Damn it, Andrew! Don't tell me anything else except that you are going to take care of Jenna for me. You've got to do it for me, you're my go to man. Can I count on you to take care of Jenna?

Say yes, before I have to get out of this bed and take care of things myself. Oh, and one more thing. If something goes bad for me in here, she gets everything I have or ever would have. I love you bro, and the family, but she is my life. You take care of her."

"Okay, okay, got the sermon loud and clear. I didn't think about her being all gross because she looked so good, I thought she was fine. I tried to be there for her as a buffer with the rest of the family, so I've been busy on your behalf this entire time.

She's not the only one who loves you and was worried about you. I'm relieved that you are going to be okay. I'll go make room arrangements for Jenna now. Hey, I don't want to add any stress to your condition, but a couple of your women have been here on and off in the family waiting room. What do you want me to tell them?"

"Tell everyone thanks for coming, but I've requested that they go home and not worry about me. Tell them I'm going to be fine. Tell them I will give them a call when I'm home and had time to recuperate. I don't want Jenna around my substitutes. I would never want to hurt her that way."

"Well, you've been out for four days, so I think she's sort of figured out who the girls are and the role they play in your life. What's it she calls them? Oh yeah "the evil eyers." I'll go get things organized and on track for you bro, don't worry; I've got your back. Glad you're here to get your back."

"Wait, how's my truck?"

"They did CPR on it and it's at the shop getting repaired. It's going to live."

The nurse came in and Andrew came outside his room so the nurse could do her private stuff for Jacob. Andrew told me he got a scolding for not making sure I was cared for in a proper way.

"Andrew, I'm sorry. You and I have a special bond and you have been nothing but good to me. I never said anything about you not being there for me, I don't know where he got that. I'm sorry he gave you a hard time on my account, Andrew. I'm so glad he's going to be okay."

"I see why Jacob loves you so much. You really are a caring, remarkable person. Most women around here are so critical and negative. You are like a light wherever you are."

"Thank you, I don't feel like sunshine right now, but a shower will work wonders." After the nurse said Jacob needed to rest, I told him if he didn't mind, I was going to the hotel to shower and sleep for a couple of hours and that I'd be back later.

"I don't want to see you back here today. You stay at the hotel, get in the hot tub, relax, and sleep. I will look forward to seeing you in your comfy jeans tomorrow. You look so dressed up. Did I interrupt something back home?"

"Jacob, I am really tired. I'll see you tomorrow." I couldn't tell him about Brandon, not when he's on his near-death bed. And besides, that is none of his business. He left me I didn't do anything wrong. He's got three hot women all pacing the floor next to me for days. No, he gets nothing on the dating front from me. Not now, maybe not ever.

Chapter 6

Recovery

After the doctor told the family Jacob should have a full recovery, Andrew communicated with his family that he was walking me down the street to the hotel. I invited him to crash at the hotel with me since everyone was out of town and sleeping in chairs for a week at the hospital too.

He said if I wouldn't tell, he wouldn't either. I felt safe with Andrew and knew I could trust him. I jumped in the shower and when I got out, Andrew was already in the king-sized bed, snoring. I just laughed, he sounded like Jacob when he was sleeping. That made me smile.

I had pajamas on and slipped into bed. I don't know how long it had been since I slept in a bed without nurses coming in, machines going off. I slept. I didn't wake up until I heard Andrew in the shower. I sat up disoriented, trying to think. We'd slept all afternoon Friday and most of Saturday.

It's three o'clock. How could two strangers sleep in the same bed together for so long and not wake? We were physically and emotionally exhausted. Andrew came out in a towel wrapped around his waist, and he looked sexy. I quickly looked away and told him if he'd let me in the bathroom to get ready, he could have the room to get dressed. He just smiled and asked me if I needed a towel.

"Very funny, you keep that towel on. You don't want me to tell Jacob we slept together last night, do you?"

"Oh, you don't play fair, little Ms. Jenna."

"You forget I grew up with a brother and all boy cousins, I learned from the best. Now, let me in the bathroom so I can grab a shower and change for breakfast, or lunch, or dinner, whatever. Are you hungry? Cause I'm starving."

"Yes, I'm always hungry. Don't be a girl and take hours and hours in there. Let's go eat."

"Give me thirty minutes and I'll be showered, dressed, and ready to go eat!"

"Yeah right. I've dated a lot of girls and there is no humanly way possible that you can be ready to leave this room in thirty minutes. No girl has ever been that quick. They need hours. Girls say thirty minutes, but in man time, that means an hour or two."

I told him to look at the clock. As he did, I locked the bathroom door, and jumped into the shower. Twenty-eight minutes later, I headed out of the room to the hotel lobby for food. They had a restaurant, and we were really sick of hospital food.

We had a good meal together. We both ate like a couple of pigs and I didn't care. It tasted so good. I couldn't remember the last time I had eaten. I'd lived on coffee for days and wasn't sure I'd ever sleep again. But I guess I did.

"Andrew, thanks for taking good care of me this past week. I've been sort of worried out of my mind, so if I did or said anything unkind, please forgive me."

"Just shut up. You have been a picture of grace under fire, and I couldn't like you any more than I do. So, finish your last couple of bites and your soda, and we are off to the hospital."

"Do you think they would let me get a Diet Dr. Pepper to go? They don't serve Diet Dr. Pepper in the hospital vending machines and I don't know if I can drink another cup of coffee from the hospital. It's just terrible."

"I'll go buy you some Diet Dr. Pepper at the store. You just tell me when you're thirsty and your wish is my command. Okay, let's go, off to the exciting world of the hospital. They are moving Jacob out of ICU today to a regular room. This is a good thing. He's going to recover and be fine. Jenna, I'm glad you were here for him. He needed your positive energy."

"Andrew, it wasn't positive energy, it was pure prayers. All the happy light bulb thoughts in the world couldn't make the healing power that we needed for Jacob. Only God has the power to heal. And I am one thankful woman that God spared his life, for me, for us. God is a good God."

"Why did God allow Jacob to almost die and be in so much pain if God is so good?"

"Andrew, are we going to have this conversation again? I believe the Bible is the inspired word of God. That it is the truth. That God's son Jesus lived a sinless life and died to save a very flawed human race. God is merciful, patient, and loving. He truly is my strength.

Can you imagine what a mess I would be without Him? He is a living spirit that I invited to come into my heart and save me from my sinful nature, and to love and worship a God that created this universe. I serve a big God, and I know He's healing Jacob, as much as I know He is real today. I don't know why bad things happen to people, but I do know that God will be with us, through anything. I read a great book by Corrie Ten Boom and she quotes, "There is never a pit so deep, that God isn't deeper still."

Andrew, I've had my share of pits and found that God is faithful and has given me strength beyond anything I could have produced on my own. I will always believe and trust in God, even when I don't have all the answers."

"Well preacher Jenna, thanks for the sermon. Maybe I won't have to go to church on Sunday."

"Great, then give me your tithes."

"What are you serious?"

"Yeah, Andrew, cause I'm all about getting your money. Do you really not know me at all yet?" With that, I got out of the car so he could park and walked quickly into the hospital. I've been around Andrew too long we needed a break from each other.

Jacob had already been moved to his new room and was sitting up in bed. He looked terrible, but wonderful at the same time. I walked straight into the room, right up to his bedside, and in front of all who were there, kissed him as gently as I could.

Jacob wouldn't have a namby pamby kiss. He grabbed my arm in his, pulled me down to his bed, and there we gave each other affectionate, passionate kisses. I heard him groan, and I thought it was from pain, but he pulled me in tighter. I just wanted to jump in that bed with him and never leave his side. I bumped his broken nose and I felt him flinch. I knew that pain when I broke my foot and Jacob bumped it before I had my cast on. It's mind-numbing pain. So, I pulled away. He just smiled.

"My Jenna."

"My Jacob."

"Babe…" then he stopped and looked at his family in the room. "Guys could I have a few minutes with Jenna?" So, everyone cleared out.

"Jenna, you haven't been eating. You are skinny. What happened to you?"

"You, you big idiot, you happened to me. I detest

hospitals. When are they going to release you to my care?"

"Your care?"

"Yes, my care. We are not spending any more time apart. Not anymore. I probably don't have a job left to go back to anyway. So, what does the doctor say?"

"If things progress as expected, I can go home tomorrow."

I squealed in delight. "So soon, are you okay for that?"

He just laughed at me. "I love all your sights and sounds."

"How's your head?"

"Throbbing," he said with a sexy smile.

"Not there Jacob. I mean, do you have a headache? How are you feeling?"

Once again he chuckles and says "My girl knows me well. I'm fine. I'm going to be fine. I may look like hell, but really I feel much better."

"How many pain pills are you taking?"

"Why, do I sound like I'm talking out of my head?"

"Not really, I just want to know what we're dealing with. Someone close to me was addicted to prescription pain killers and it was the catalyst that tore their marriage apart. So, I just don't want to go down that road with you. I don't want you in pain, but I won't stand by a man who wants to disappear in a drugged-out state of mind, which slowly eats away at everything. I just want to know what we are dealing with here. I'm not going into this with blinders on. I can't afford to do that with my heart, not again."

"Don't get yourself all worked up. I haven't been on pain meds for the last eight hours, just extra strength Tylenol. I'm fine and going to have a full recovery. We need to make plans. Are you serious about moving out here and being with me?"

"I am, if you are. But we shouldn't make any life changing decisions during a high stress time like now. We should wait until you are healthy, rested, and can think things out clearly. I usually make a pros and cons list and jot down all my thoughts into those categories so I can see it, and reflect, before I jump into a major decision."

"I'm marrying you, and frankly my dear, it can't be soon enough. Now get your boney ass in my bed."

I didn't even hesitate. I moved to his other side, where there were no tubes connected to machines, and shimmied next to him in that single bed. These sheets leave something to be desired.

"Oh yes, I intended to thank you personally for the thoughtful gift you sent me. Every night in bed with the sheets, making me think of you, making me want you more... The government should hire you for the intelligence warfare division. You could teach them a thing or two."

"Oh, so you got them and liked them? I'm so glad. I just wanted you to be happy."

"Yes, I know exactly what you wanted, and your mission was accomplished. The first night I actually cried when I got in bed and there was no Jenna next to me. See what you've done to me?"

"Just tell me why did you kick me out of your life? No warning? No conversation, pretty much just cold shut the door, goodbye. It was so out of the blue for me, I was blindsided. I thought you were happy. I was happy, then BANG get out, and don't come back! You broke my heart."

"I thought I was protecting you from my family, their power, and money. By getting you out of the picture, I thought I was protecting you and your family, the best way I knew how."

"See, Jacob, that was your big mistake. You tried to control the situation by controlling me. But baby, you can't control love. You can't control every situation and people. We weren't a business deal, we had a relationship, we were a team. You needed to trust me and include me in the decision-making process for our futures.

I know, in your mind, you must have thought you were protecting me. But all I could see was the man I love, throwing me away like trash to the curb. I saw when things got tough, you didn't stand with me, you left me alone. When I needed you most, you abandoned me, drew a line in the sand, and stood against me with your family, and their legal actions behind it."

"I'm so sorry I put you through that. I've been miserable without you. I've wanted to call you every day. The legal stuff between our families is finally settled through the courts, and now I am free to love again, and give you the time and attention a new wife deserves."

"Oh, I love you, Jacob, and always will, but I am no foregone conclusion. You made decisions that tore my world apart. It takes time to rebuild trust. We are not getting married anytime soon and that, my dear Jacob, is my final word on the matter. As far as our future together, we are on hiatus for the next six months."

"Six months? Why six months?"

"Because that's how long your actions have broken my heart and kept us apart. Actually, it's been longer than that, but I'm giving you the benefit of those months. Not another word of marriage until we are six months out. And now that I think about it, if I still have a job to go back to, I want to finish the year teaching with my kids. Then if we are still a couple, we can talk about us dating, and see what happens."

"All these dates and stipulations, what has happened to you?"

"I told you what happened to me Mr. Jamison, and I warned you about my honesty policy on day one. So, you are just reaping what you've sowed. I'm not trying to play God here. I'm just trying to protect myself from you, until I can feel safe enough to trust you with my heart again. You have no idea what I've gone through."

"When you were here in the hospital with me, you were

dressed up, short black dress and high heels, not your average attire. Are you dating someone? Is that why you don't want to get back together with me? Is it someone else?"

"Jacob, it's been over six months. So yes, there is someone else in my life now, and when I go back home, I'm going to tell him everything I've been through with you."

"So, you can tell him your every thought and dream and he can make them come true for you?"

I could see the hurt and pain I was causing him, so I just said in a quiet voice, "He's not you."

"What do you mean by that?"

"I mean, you changed my path in life when you kicked me out and pushed me away. And, now out of the blue, you've suddenly changed your mind again and want me back? I'm not just going to jump when you say jump. I have a life and feelings, and people in my life I care about, and they care about me.

This isn't an easy situation, and we are going to have to take the time necessary to see if we will ever be who we once were together. I'm so sorry you were hurt, and my heart can truly beat again knowing that you will be okay. You need time to heal physically, and we need time to heal emotionally too.

Please don't think that I am trying to punish you. I'm just doing what couples do. They talk things out before they make decisions that affect one another. I love you, and I'm the kind of girl that can't turn love on and off like a light switch, thus all the pain I've suffered because of your actions.

I don't know what we are going to do, but I do know we have each other and plenty of time to figure this all out."

"If you are so happy with Mr. Wonderful, don't let me get in your way."

"Fine, if you want to kick me out the door again, then

just keep it up. Quit on us again. You are so quick to kick me out. How secure do you think that makes me feel with our relationship, when your first go to response is to leave, or for you to want me to go? You are just supporting my very real concerns.

If you don't want me, then that's that. I will never beg any man to love me. You talk of loving me in one breath and leaving me in the next? How can you expect me to give up my life when I don't know if I can trust you anymore? Don't you understand how this looks and feels to me?

You have to tell me what you want, not just internalize things and leave me out of the thinking and decision-making processes that you go through in your mind. If you want me to go, I will leave and never come back, if that's what you want. I've done it before, and I didn't die. But if you want to work on us having a future together, then we can take it day by day, and see if and what develops. What are you thinking now?"

"So, would we be monogamous during this time apart?"

"I should have known you'd go straight to a sex question. Do you want to be?"

"Don't answer a question with a question with me. I've negotiated million-dollar deals, I know this song and dance."

"Oh, is this a song and dance? I will ask whatever I want to ask you. Answer me. What do you want? Your family will be coming back into the room and I need to know what you want?"

"You are so…. infuriating! But I've never loved anyone more than I love you. You are worth fighting for and I do see things a little differently now that you've told me how you feel. I'm sorry for all the pain I've caused you, I really am. I want to work on us, even if it's long distance for a while, if that's my only choice. I'm fine and you should go back and see if you can save your career. I think we should be monogamous. Six months won't be that long.

And, in case I haven't told you already, thank you for coming when you heard I was hurt. You will never know how my heart started truly beating again when I opened my eyes and saw you at the foot of my bed. I thought I was hallucinating at first, but your eyes pierced through to my soul, and I knew you were here for me. Thank you for bringing me back to life. I was dead without you."

"I'm so glad you are okay, and my heart is beating again too. Come to think of it, my breathing is much better now that I know you are going to be fine. But you know I am dating someone else now, so I am not making any promises to you on the no sex agreement. Six months apart, no strings attached. You are free to date and be happy too.

I'm not putting my life on hold ever again. If I don't value my life and my time, no one else will. I will always love you, but if our paths don't cross again, I will always care about you and wish you nothing but the best. Before I leave, can I have a goodbye kiss? It's going to have to last us six months or maybe forever."

I looked in his eyes and they were watery, and I thought if I see one tear, I will never leave this room, never leave his side. I can't be such a weakling. He turned on his side facing me, and we kissed like we'd never see each other again. I almost cried, it was so familiar, so what I'd longed for, for such a long time. I love this man.

Why didn't I just tell him I had only been on one date? I could ease his pain. I don't want to play games with the man I love, but he hurt me. He ripped my heart into pieces and stood on his porch without as much as a tear. I cried my eyes out for months. He has to know he can't play that way with me ever again. I'm a game changer kind of woman. If he wants me, he's going to have to play by my rules now.

What else could I say? I was able to say goodbye on my terms. I hope it's not forever goodbye, but I need time, and he needs to know what it feels like when a girl tells him no.

I'm sure he hasn't heard that before. I'm sure I'm the first to do that.

Chapter 7

Brandon

I had been texting Brandon every day from the hospital when Jacob slept, just letting him know I was fine and that I missed him. I did miss him. We just started dating and I'm sure Brandon is going to give me my house keys back, show me my dogs are still alive, and I'll never hear from him again. I'm going to be in the category of one of those high maintenance girls and I'll never see or hear from him again, unless it's in class. Brandon is a great guy, and deserves someone special, for him and his daughter.

I wanted to tell him my Jacob story, but with only one date under our belt, I thought I'd give him time to know me before I truly scared him off forever. Brandon wanted to pick me up at the airport and take me to dinner and then to my place. I couldn't think of anyone I'd rather have hugging me at the airport, so I told him I would love that, and couldn't wait to see a friendly face.

I hit the very small airplane bathroom, to freshen up

before we landed. I did the best I could, fresh layer of makeup, perfume, even tried to fix my hair. I had a nice pair of jeans, boots, and a really cute top with a jacket. The take your seats dinger went off in the plane so I knew we were soon to land, and I needed to take my seat. The next thing I knew, I was at the luggage return area hoping that my luggage made this flight, since I had to de-plane and re-plane another time. But as luck would have it, my luggage was here.

Then I saw Brandon. He walked across the terminal wearing black jeans, black shirt and a rust colored, brushed suede blazer. He came up to me and smelled so good; he had to hold me up because my knees went weak at the sight of him.

"Are you okay?"

How embarrassing. I didn't want to tell him that one sight of him made me limp in the knees. But you know what, I've been with a man that doesn't tell me the truth about how he feels, so I can't make the same mistakes with Brandon. So, I had no choice, I told him what just happened in a whisper in his ear. He just squeezed me tighter and turned the embarrassing moment into feeling loved and accepted.

He looked me in my eyes and said, "I've missed you more than I could have imagined." He picked up my luggage and we headed out to his car. As we walked to the car we talked.

"Did you eat while you were gone? You look so thin. What can I get you to eat?"

"I was stressed and didn't want to leave my friend until I knew he was going to live. So, I really didn't eat my usual huge amounts of food. Thank goodness you fed me well before I left!"

"What do you want to eat?"

"Actually, I'm hungry for fried shrimp. I have no idea why, but how does Lambert's sound to you? The place of the hand tossed rolls. It's on 65 Highway and on the way to my place, if that sounds good to you."

"Sure. I'm familiar with that landmark establishment. I'll take you wherever you want to go eat. I've only had a salad today, so Lambert's fried okra, fried potatoes, fried chicken, fried shrimp, it all sounds like great comfort food. We will celebrate the comfort that I have knowing you are back safe and sound at home.

While you were gone and I was in your house, I looked at the framed art on your walls. You have a really good eye for perspective, line of sight, lots of great things you are doing already very well in your photographic work. Where did you get all the different frames?"

I knew he had purposefully changed the subject off of my stressful hospital stay. He is attentive, caring, and we have interests that are the same. I look forward to talking to him about my visits to flea markets and antique shops.

"I enjoy going to antique and flea markets in this area. They have lots of them to explore. That's where I purchased my frames. Are you fond of going to those kinds of places?"

"Yes, I don't go every weekend or anything like that, but maybe once a year, it's kind of fun. How about you, do you go to those kinds of places often?"

"I've gone on an occasion maybe two or three times a year, if I'm looking for a specific item. Like looking for picture frames. The next time I go, I'll call you to be my antiquing partner. But, if you need a certain size frame, I've bought some that were good deals. I'll have to show you my frame collection before you go and spend money on new ones. I stored several extra frames under the bed in my guest bedroom if you ever want to check them out." It felt so good to be home, and not dealing with Jacob, his family, or Jacob's revolving door he loves me, he loves me not merry-go-round.

Lamberts served us so much food, I made up for not

eating for a week. I ate way too much, but they kept coming by our table with bowls of food from the kitchen. How can you say no to hot sourdough rolls with butter and honey, and hot fried potatoes with onions? Again, with the full tummy I'm starting to feel really drowsy. Brandon could see I was fading fast.

"You've had a long trip, and now that you are full, are you ready to go home?"

"If you don't mind. I'm really tired now that all the blood in my body is rushing to my stomach to sort out the massive amounts of food I just ate."

He just laughed, walked me to the car, and opened my door, again with the manners. He's thoughtful. He makes me feel like a princess on his arm. Then he waited for my seatbelt to be fastened and he said, "Good, you are finally here and trapped so you can't get away from me. I'm going to kiss that sweet face of yours."

He started on my forehead, down my nose, on my lips, then both my cheeks. When he started down my neck, and I couldn't take it anymore. I grabbed his face in my hands and began kissing him with emotion and feeling I didn't even know I had for him. "I wondered how far you'd let me go before you kissed me back. I see you are a woman of discriminating taste, just far enough, but not too far. A woman who knows what she wants. Good to know."

"Do you always fasten down your women before you attack them?"

"Only if they like it. Do you like it?"

"Kissing you, who wouldn't like it? But just so you know, I read all those Fifty Shades of Gray books and it was more like fifty shades of red for embarrassing. I'm probably the only reader who skipped over most of the sex bondage sections to get on with the love story they were developing with the main characters. So, are you into the kinkier side of sex, Brandon?"

"I'm not into bondage, domination, or being dominated.

I just keep it real. That's what I want, that's how I roll. A loving, honest, and real relationship. Sound like anything you are interested in?"

"With you, I think I could be persuaded. My life is just so complicated, but I want to share it with you, if you still want to date me."

"Why wouldn't I want to date you? You flew off to be there for a man you care about. You make sacrifices with your work and money to be there for a friend. Why wouldn't I want a person like that in my life? Jenna, is there something you want to tell me about your trip, and this friend Jacob?"

"Yes, there's a lot I want to tell you, but not tonight. I'm so tired, I really just want to soak in a bubble bath and go to bed."

"Hmm, want some company with those bubbles?"

"Brandon, as tempting as that sounds, I said slow, remember?"

"Yes, I remember the kiss in your kitchen, dining room, living room, my car. Yes, Jenna, I remember our every touch. We are almost to your house. I'll help you in with the luggage, and then I'll leave you to your bubbles and sleep. Are you a night owl or morning person? I'm a morning person."

"Good, someone has to be an early bird because I'm a night owl, not tonight, but usually a night owl. They say opposites attract, so we should be good to go, don't you think?"

"Yes, we are good to go."

"Brandon, I'm so sorry. I don't even think I asked you about your week. Sorry I was so self-absorbed."

"That's fine. My week was busy with my everyday obligations, then driving out of town every morning and every night to take care of two affectionate puggles.

Molly had to be sitting, touching me on the couch. She likes to lick my hand and Moose, he had to be on the other side of me, and he snores really loud. It was hard to have my laptop on my lap and dogs on each side of me, but I managed to get my work done. They sort of grew on me and we are old buds now. Moose went running with me one time, and I thought I was going to have to administer CPR to help him breath by the time we got back to your house. I didn't run with him again after that."

"I also took you up on your offer that if it was easier for me, I could stay at your place, and I did one night. I must say your sheets are the softest sheets I've ever slept on. The only thing that could have been better would have been if…well never mind." He smiled a sexy smile, and I just melted inside, and smiled back knowing what he was going to say but didn't.

We reached my house, and he brought my luggage inside. I for some strange reason was getting my second wind. I told him if he wanted, he could stay.

"You mean all night?"

I wanted to know Brandon. Do we have magic together like Jacob and I had? Could I have that with another man?

"As much as I appreciate your offer, I have daughter duties in the morning, so I need to get back to my place early to meet Kourtney. We will have our time, there's no rush. I'm here for you, you should know by now that you can count on me. We are friends and I enjoy your company. We will have another time when you are emotionally rested and ready for more. I want to be your more, Jenna."

I couldn't take it any longer, I held his face in my hands and the kissing began. He was an excellent kisser. His lips were large, firm, and soft. I couldn't get enough. He seems to be the whole package, looks, brains, consideration, and he communicates. My heart was beating so hard I was sure he could hear it.

"We've had this discussion. You say one thing with your lips and another with your body. What do you want?"

"I want you, but shouldn't we wait until you know the

whole Jacob story."

"If you need to tell me that before we are together, then... Jenna, what do you want? Am I leaving or staying?"

"What if we compromise and you just stay, and we cuddle?"

"I think you know that's not what will happen if I stay."

"Okay then, I'm sorry I'm so indecisive. That's probably a good clue that we should wait until there are no doubts."

"I'll just be going then. Good-bye Molly and Moose. If you can't tell, I'm really glad you are home. Walk me to the door and I'll talk to you tomorrow." Much kissing occurred, then he was out the door to his car, and leaving for the night.

There is no way I could take a bath without drowning from lack of strength in my legs again. I'm not sure how or why he has that effect on me, but it's like my body wants me to surrender to him. I want that too, but I need to think with my heart and my head. I'm not twenty years old anymore. I have to act responsible. I have to be mature.

I was brushing my teeth and my phone rang, it was Jacob. OMG, I forgot to call him and tell him I made it home safe and sound. I answered the phone. "Jacob, so sorry I didn't call yet. I was just brushing my teeth for bed."

"You made it and you are home and had a good flight?"

"Yes, I'm home. I stopped and ate a huge meal. You would be proud at the amount of food I consumed tonight. Now with a very full belly, I'm off to bed. How are you feeling tonight?"

"Angry that once I'm out of your sight, I'm out of your mind. You said you'd call when you landed, and you didn't. Do you know how worried I've been?"

"I said I'm sorry. You are a smart man with travel experience. You know how hectic it is at the airport getting luggage, a ride to pick you up, getting food to eat, and drive home. I'm sorry, sorry, sorry. I said I'd call when I got home.

I haven't been home long. I was just brushing my teeth then going to bed with my phone in hand to call you and wish you pleasant dreams goodnight. I don't want you to stress over where I am or what I'm doing. You need to concentrate on getting better and get your life back to normal."

"What if I don't want normal anymore, it's not enough."

"What do you want?"

"You know what I want."

"No, I don't. That's why we are on a six-month hiatus. Again, I am sorry, I hope you are feeling better. Why don't you call me when they let you go home? Jacob, can I tell you something without you getting mad or blowing it up out of proportion?"

"Anything, what is it?"

"Well, Andrew loves you very much, and, , ,"

"Andrew, is this discussion going to be about Andrew?"

"Yes."

"Then no, I don't want to hear it. I'm tired. I've been stressed about getting a phone call from the woman I love, so I'll call you another time to talk about my brother."

"Don't pout, Jacob, it's not handsome on you. Pleasant dreams and I'm sorry. I'm not perfect, I just spent a week of hell wishing and hoping and praying for you, and you can't give me one late phone call? See why we need a break? No trust, no relationship."

"Yes, I get it Jenna, you're always right, I'm always wrong. Good night." Click.

I should have called him at the airport. That was all on me. I cannot believe I didn't call him like I said I would. Apparently, I seem to cause Jacob stress. I screw up and he has no trust for me or tolerance for my mistakes.

No trust, plus no patience, equals no relationship. Why do I let him break my heart over and over? Why? Love is messy, and I continually get myself into messes, however unintentional they might be. Jacob needs neat and tidy. I'm sort of a, well I don't even know how to finish that sentence. But I don't fit in a neat and tidy box by any stretch of the imagination.

I would have to work on that, but for now, bed I have to be at work tomorrow. Dear God help me have energy to inspire my kindergarteners tomorrow. They deserve my best. I can't wait to get back to my kids.

Before I recharged my phone, I texted Brandon and said "Before you go to sleep, I just wanted to wish you pleasant dreams. Have a great day tomorrow, Brandon. I'm so glad you are in my life. You are an unexpected joy."

Chapter 8

The Truth

Driving home from work, on my way to my next three hours of tutoring, I had a light bulb Ah Ha moment. Or it could have been just a common sense idea, but the thought was this. Before I had a heart to heart with Brandon, I needed to have a heart to heart with myself.

Jenna, get your paper and pencil and write down the pros and cons of Jacob, and the pros and cons of Brandon. In case either of them would ever find this list, I should not put their names on it. I'll use number one for Jacob because I knew him first, and number two for Brandon because he brought me back "two" life. I need to make the list, study it, pray about it, and then talk to Brandon, because that's the kind of relationship we have. A truthful relationship.

I texted Jeff and my mom and caught them up on my cast free status and Jacob's health update.

Jeff texted back "I'm so proud of you for laying down

the law to Jacob. For once, your precious Jacob will have to work to earn and keep your love."

I quickly corrected him. "He already has my love, and I will always carry part of him with me. I knew more love from him in our short time together, than I did my fourteen years of marriage all rolled into one. I loved Tom, and in a small part, will always love my ex-husband, but Jacob was and is a large part of my heart forever."

"I can't believe you are so defensive of Jacob. Stay strong Sis and make him earn your trust. Don't give in to his womanizing ways."

"Jeff, I love him. I just don't know if that's enough to make our relationship work, and it takes more than love. It takes commitment and trust to make a lasting relationship. I have to have the trust and honesty, it's a must for me. I just don't know where my future will take me. I'm dating a great guy, Brandon, and I'm not sure what our future is, if we have a future. But I'm going to tell him about Jacob and see where we go from there."

I compiled my list of number one, and number two, and the data did not lead me to a clear, conclusive, landslide choice. That was not what I expected. But I was totally honest with myself and tried to be fair with both men.

I tore the comparison list into shreds, so this could never come back to haunt me, or hurt them. I had no men in my life for years, just going through life in neutral, then all of a sudden two men, amazing, off the charts, hot men, want me. It's like I hit my head and I'm living in an alternate universe or something.

I've decided that I'm going to share my life experiences with Brandon and tell him the whole story of Jacob and me. I don't need his whole story of his ex-wife, but I hope he wants to share that part of his life with me too. I would love to know his past. I guess I'll see after pouring out my heart, if he is still interested in me. Then I'm going all in with my professor, my friend, and maybe soon to be, my lover.

Brandon had called me every day since I'd been home. He sounded so glad to have me back and then I got a wake-up call, per se. I went to my photography class early and there was an extremely attractive, well-endowed woman in my class. I remembered her from earlier classes because she is stunning. She came up to talk to me before class started and was really nice. Her name is Kayla.

"Jenna, we missed you last Tuesday and Thursday in class. If you need to copy my notes you are welcome to. I hope everything was okay for you."

"Thanks. I had to be unexpectedly out of state due to a car accident where a drunk driver hit a close friend of mine, head-on. They had to life flight him, but he's going to heal and have a full recovery."

"I'm so glad your friend is going to be okay. Something kind of exciting happened for me last week too. I'll tell you a secret. Last week Brandon, our instructor, asked me out to dinner after class. I didn't know if I should go out with him, but he's such a great guy.

We just talked about photography and had the best time. But he hasn't called me at all this week. I don't know what I did. I thought we had a connection, but I guess it was just wishful thinking. He is so good looking don't you think so?"

"Yes, he's easy on the eyes, Kayla. I'm sure the reason he hasn't called you isn't from anything you said or did. You should just talk to him, give him a chance to be honest with you."

"I thought about calling him, but I didn't want things to be weird in class. We have such great dynamics in here, I don't want to do or say anything that would make me not want to come to class."

"Well, if he's a jerk about it, you don't have to date him. But that's up to you. I think class is about to start, so I'm going to move back to my seat. Good luck, Kayla."

"Thanks. Hey maybe we can go out sometime for a

coffee or drink?"

"Sure."

I could not believe my ears. I'm gone one week and he's dating someone else? Wait, back up Jenna, do Brandon and I have an exclusive relationship? No, we don't. I was with another man all last week, he was with another woman, and I have no rights on him. But good to know I'm not his only hugging, squeezing, and kissing deliverer. I looked up from the back of the room, and noticed that Brandon saw us talking together and looking up at him.

He just smiled. I bet he was a bit uncomfortable right then. Why would he pick a woman he knew I would talk with and find out about his activities? Maybe it wasn't all about me. Maybe it was just a good-looking man having dinner with a good-looking woman. Do not be a needy girlfriend, if that's what I am. Note to self, maybe the pouring out my heart to him about Jacob should be postponed, until I find out what I have with Brandon, what I am to him, if anything.

The class was helpful and informative, and we had positive interaction throughout the entire class time, just like always. After class, I saw Kayla pack up her stuff and head up to the front of the class to Brandon. I just slipped out the back door to go for a walk. It was too early to go home, so I went to the mall and just walked inside to be alone, but not alone. I stopped to get a coffee. It was so good, a big difference from hospital coffee. I wondered how Jacob was doing. I sat in a big cushy chair at the mall and texted him. I sipped my coffee drink of choice, Venti Caramel Macchiato, and started my text.

"Jacob, I haven't heard from you and I was just thinking about you. I hope you are recovering at home and doing well."

I stayed in the chair until I finished my coffee, but no response from Jacob. That's okay. He could be in his shower or doing something besides sitting by the phone waiting for me to call. Well, I made the attempt to keep in contact, the ball is now in his court. Just as I was putting away my phone, I get a text from Brandon.

"Where are you?"

"I'm at the mall."

"Are you interested in having dinner together tonight?"

Don't pout Jenna. Don't be immature, give the man a chance to be honest with you. "Sure, what did you have in mind?"

"How about Famous Bubba's Barbeque?"

"Okay, that's on my way home from the mall. I can meet you there in thirty minutes."

"That will be great, see you there."

I hit every red light on my way there. I guess they are all on the same timer but that's fine, I wasn't in a big rush. I was sort of just in a chilling out mood. Brandon was already at the restaurant and came up and gave me a big kiss when I walked in the door. We were seated at a table.

"Jenna, I drove straight out to your house to see you after class but was disappointed when you weren't there."

"Sorry, I didn't know you were planning on coming over tonight. I guess you shouldn't make assumptions when it comes to me."

"I'm finding that out about you."

"Famous Bubba's is a much better choice because I have nothing at home to fix for dinner. That's on my to-do list, grocery shop. I like to wait for the mid-week flyers to get all the advertised discounts before I make my shopping list, and usually hit the grocery store after tutoring on Thursday evenings. I've tried other days, but they are picked over or out of stuff that's on sale, so that's my grocery shopping thinking and planning."

"Good to know, no food in house on a Monday or Tuesday? Maybe you should just buy more when you shop so you have enough food for an entire week."

"Very funny. I do buy enough, but by the end of the

week, I'm tired of what I bought, or changed my mind. So, what's your grocery buying strategy?"

"I ask my daughter what she wants, and then I go buy it. I don't do very well with buying lots of junk food. I want her to eat healthy and I'm pretty picky about what I eat too, so I shop at a health food store and an upscale grocery store for organic, grain fed, cage free items."

"Does Kourtney like health food?"

"Yes, she's sort of grown up with it. Her mom is a fitness instructor, so she has the whole healthy food and exercise routine down pretty well. She's been healthy from kindergarten through high school, so far. I'm really proud of her, she's so beautiful, smart, and is a kind and sweet person. Even if I wasn't her dad, I'd say that about her in a non-creepy way."

"I don't doubt that your daughter is wonderful like her dad."

"Thanks."

The waitress arrived at our table and I was curious what he was going to order being Mr. healthy, but he ordered chicken breast, baked potato, and sweet tea, with no artificial sweetener. Then it was time for my order.

"I'd like a pulled pork sandwich, waffle fries, and a side of cottage cheese. Isn't pork the other white meat?" I wasn't going to worry about the food police watching what I ate. He was free to eat what he wants to eat, no judgment from me. If I were better disciplined, I'd do better in that area too, but I just ate what I was hungry for, and tried to eat some protein at each meal. That, to me, is eating well.

I knew he'd bring it up, so contrary to my normal prying self, I just let him. "Jenna, I saw you visiting with Kayla before class this evening."

"Yes, we did have a nice visit together. She is a really nice lady."

"Yes, she is. Um, I wanted to tell you that when you were gone, seeing your friend at the hospital, I took her out for dinner. It was just two friends having a meal together. There weren't any physical interactions between us. I just wanted you to know in case she mentioned it to you. I wanted you to hear about it from me."

"Well, I don't know if you wanted me to know or not, but Brandon, you are free to see and do whatever you want. I'm not going to be some needy, clingy woman. We are not exclusive and I'm glad you had dinner with Kayla. She is really great; I like her too."

"I don't get you. We make out and ever since then all I can do is think about the next time we can be together. And here you are, Ms. Whatever Ice Queen. Did I misread things between us?"

"No, that's not it at all, Brandon. I do care about you, but I'm just unsure of what we are at this point. Can you clarify that for me?"

"Well, you are in this relationship too, Jenna. How about we figure this out together?"

He couldn't have said anything that would have been more perfect than what he just said. I couldn't take his cuteness anymore. "Okay, that's a great idea, together."

I got out of my side of the booth and scooted in the seat next to Brandon. I started kissing him. He's more proper and private than I am. However, he kissed me like he was glad I was impulsive.

"Jenna, we are in public."

"Yes, we are. Don't you think others are happy that we are two adults happy to be together?"

"Your take on things is maybe not exactly how other people see things at a family restaurant."

"Okay, what are they thinking and why do you care so much what others think?"

"They are thinking why don't they get a room? Hey, that's an idea, and on a school night too?"

"I'm not that wild Brandon."

"No, you are just a little tease. Just when I think I'm

figuring you out, you surprise me."

"Is that a problem for you?"

"No, actually it's refreshing."

And with that, our dinner came, so I got up and sat in my proper place and side of the booth to eat my messy barbeque sandwich. Ever since I got back from the hospital, it's like my body thinks I had been starving, because I'm hungry all the time now. I'm getting worried that I'm going to be 200 pounds with this hungry hangover I seem to be nursing.

"Brandon, thank you for being honest with me and telling me about you and Kayla. I'm really glad we have an honest relationship. She had already told me that you two went out and I think she was hoping that you would call her again. But the next time Kayla talks to me about you, I'm telling her that I've gone out with you too. I just wanted you to know my plans before the situation occurs."

"That won't be necessary because I told her tonight that we were dating now. And she told me, she told you, and she didn't want this to change the fun dynamics in our class. I told her we are all adults, that we should be able to continue as always. She did say if things didn't work out between you and me, to give her a call."

"Well, it's nice to know you have so many great options to choose from. Anyone else on your dinner rotation I should know about?"

"Cute, and no."

"Yeah, sure."

"No really, just you. I'm ready to make this exclusive if you want that kind of relationship with me."

"Hmm, well I need to tell you about last week, and why Jacob is important to me. Then, if you still want to be exclusive, we can have that discussion."

"Okay? Why don't we go to my place and talk?"

"I do want to see your place, but not the first time when I'm telling you about another man. I know I'm weird, but let's go get Molly and Moose and we can take them for a walk. I can talk and you can help me get my dogs some exercise. How's that sound?"

"Actually, I'd rather just give you my full attention instead of managing your dogs too, if you don't mind."

"Okay that's fair, so where should we go?"

"I know a neutral place, a quiet bar, we tried to go there once before on our first date. What do you think about that?"

"Sounds perfect. Should we have this talk tonight or wait until this weekend when we aren't so tired?"

"That's a good consideration, but that might change things a bit for the location if we are changing to this weekend. If the weather is nice, we can just picnic under a tree and talk it all out. Then we have Saturday night to go out. I have a friend who is having a birthday party at a club with a live band I like. Would you go with me?"

"Sure, I'd love to meet your friends. But, Brandon, what if you decide you don't want to date me after our talk Saturday?"

"There is nothing you could say that will push me away. I'm kind of smitten with you."

"Okay, if you don't want me kissing you in public, then you can't say stuff like that and think I'm not going to immediately respond to you."

"Your honesty is refreshing." He smiled and took my hand *as we* walked out to our cars.

We kissed. He is such a good kisser, no, actually he's an amazing kisser. I cannot believe I've been missing out on this kind of romantic, passionate interactions for all my life.

Wow! He is such a good guy. How am I going to tell him I love Jacob, but have very strong feelings for him too? Honestly, that's what I have to do, tell him so at least we are starting our friendship on an honest foundation. No secrets to cause the other pain later down the line in our relationship.

Well, Saturday was finally here, and I was sort of stressed after having time to see how much money I'd spent lately and trying to figure out how I was going to pay for airplane tickets, camera, and lenses. Being off work on leave without pay for funerals and personal issues hadn't helped either.

I was in a financial mess. I just have to make payments and know that this too shall pass. It will all work out. It's just going to take a long time. I know how to keep things in perspective, it's just money.

We went to the Japanese Garden park and had a picnic. He knew me and my love for food. We sat for hours and I told him everything. Probably details he didn't need to know or want to know, but I wanted him to have the facts of Jacob and me, so he had the truth about where my heart has been. Now he had the information to decide if he wants a future with me. He sat in many different positions throughout our discussion. He asked questions and I answered. The toughest question was "If Jacob and his big money asked you to marry him, would you?"

"He already has asked that question and I answered him. But he broke my trust, and I don't know if we will ever come back from that. I don't know what he wants, but I have six months to move on with my life before he tries to rebuild a relationship, if he even wants to do that. I don't really know what he will do. But I just wanted you to know what you are getting into, and what I've been through, so you could consider your feelings in all of this."

"Jenna, you are extraordinary, and I care more about you now than I ever have. It's really interesting for me to hear you talk so logically about your emotions and feelings. I didn't know a woman could do that. Seriously, I didn't think it was possible. I'm not thrilled that you loved another man, but as long as he's your past, I want to be your future."

"Brandon, you come clean now and tell me all about

your past. I want to know everything about you. I care about you too."

"We've been sitting for a long time, so how about we pack up, take our stuff to the car, and walk and talk about my failed marriage."

"Okay, but only if I can hold your hand while we walk."

"Deal."

"My wife was full of life and fun but had an insane temper. She would lose it if I was five minutes late coming home from work or the store. She was very insecure, and everything became an issue with us. Once she threw a glass ash tray at my head in front of my family who were visiting. Nice show."

"She's also thrown my leather recliner chair out the front door and sat it in my front yard. She was mad I was spending too much time grading papers and not enough time giving her attention. She needed to be entertained and occupied every minute of every day. She found a local businessman who wanted to invest to help her have her own fitness salon, and that's when I lost her. I still care about her, she's the mother of my only child, and I'll never regret that, never.

Long story short, we interact together only when it concerns our daughter, Kourtney. She and I were young when we met and got together, and now we live in separate worlds and have totally different lives. I don't have anything to do with her personally, just stuff that revolves around our daughter. She's busy with her business and new family, so she's not really in my life anymore. So where are we now? What do you want? Where do we go from here?"

"I just wanted to be honest and didn't want to start a relationship with you unless you knew how many miles have been driven on my heart. I was married before to Tom. He was one way when we dated, and then when we got married, he became very controlling, and for me it became an empty marriage. We didn't have sex, or two-way conversations, we just existed.

Two people in one house. I was miserable. I tried to leave him once and we opted for marriage counseling. Then things got better for a while, but then back to the same old story. Then I tried to leave him again, and he said he was sick, and what kind of person leaves someone who is sick?

I stayed with him thinking that since he's admitted to being sick, maybe he'd get help. Then we moved to Missouri and Tom said he was better than he'd ever been. I knew this was only because his new Missouri doctors wouldn't give him the same number of drugs they did when we lived in Wisconsin.

His new doctors refused to give him the massive doses of oxycontin and oxycodone he was taking from his bad drug doctors in Wisconsin. So, I thought it was now or never if I was ever going to leave him. I saw a chance for me to be happy again and for Tom to get a reality check that his problem was not all me."

"I hired Two Men and A Truck, and when Tom left for work one day, my new friends in the area came to the house, and we threw my clothes in cars, took stuff that was mine before I married him, and were out of the house before noon.

I had all my stuff put into storage and stayed with a friend, so I was close to my job. I paid the moving crew to move couches from downstairs upstairs for Tom, so he didn't have to move anything heavy. I didn't take one spoon, our wedding china, nothing that I thought he'd want, etc. Just took my stuff.

My biggest regret was that I left our pug, Kisses, with Tom. That was the best dog I ever had, and I missed that dog every day, until she died in his care.

Tom lives in the area and we haven't spoken in years. He used to call me a lot, but after a while, he stopped calling. Then after a couple of years being divorced, he called me up, wanted me to know he had changed, and wanted another chance with me. He asked how I would know that he had changed unless I gave him another chance.

I told him I'd go out with him. He told me he'd call me in a couple of days and set up the time and place. Well, after seven days and not hearing back from him, and since he's the one who called me and asked me out, I was worried about him. I called him to make sure he was okay.

Tom answered the phone and apologized for not calling me, but told me he was dating someone else, and didn't feel right going out with me. So, once again, proof that Tom had not changed and I was once again so thankful I was out of his crazy, mixed up world.

I wished him the best and I was pretty sure he thought I was pure evil for leaving him. But I have finally forgiven myself for marrying the wrong man for me and for divorcing him. Now I'm very happy in my life, in my house, and with my dogs. It's been a long journey, but I'm ready to be happy again. That's a nutshell summary of my marriage. What are you thinking about me now? I don't have a good track record with men."

"I feel like I'm sort of on a retainer for six months until you are ready to let Jacob back into your life. Like a rental car that will get a few miles in before he's returned to the dealership."

"I'm sorry that's how you feel. But you are entitled to your thoughts and feelings. If you don't want our relationship to develop, it can just stop today, and I will consider you a good friend. But I'm just telling you what arrangements I've made with Jacob, and I want and deserve to be happy.

Brandon, you make me happy. I don't know what will happen six months down the road. I don't even know if he'll even call me or if I'll want to make that long distance relationship develop, but I gave him my word, and bought myself time for perspective."

"Alright, I appreciate your honesty, Jenna, I really do. You've given me a lot to think about. How about I drop you off at your house, we change into our party clothes, grab a bite to eat, and head to the birthday party for some great music and dancing."

"Sounds good to me, but I think you should kiss me before we do anything else."

"Sweet Jenna, the kissing queen."

"Well, that's better than the ice queen. And that is entirely all your fault, Brandon. If you weren't so luscious, it wouldn't be such an amazing experience! It's really too bad you can't kiss yourself; cause then you'd understand what I'm talking about."

"Stop talking and pucker up."

The kissing commenced with fervor and intensity. I really care about this man. He's a loving father, attentive boyfriend, and every day we are together, the stronger and happier I feel. Brandon is amazing.

Chapter 9

The Dance

We got to my house, took showers in separate bathrooms, and got dressed for Brandon's friend's party. While dancing around my bathroom with the radio blasting in my house, my phone rang. It was from Jacob. Unbelievable, Brandon is one room away and here is Jacob on my phone. I walked into my closet and closed the door so I could hear him with the loud music playing in the background.

"Hello."

"Hello, Jenna, how are you?"

"Jacob, I'm actually just heading out. Are you okay?"

"Yes, I just wanted to hear your voice."

"What's wrong? I can hear it in your voice."

"I've screwed things up for us, haven't I? I've blown it haven't I?"

"I'm sorry you are feeling remorseful now, but we said six months. You know you pull at my heart strings every time I hear your voice, so this is pure manipulation, and you can't do that to me, I won't let you. You need to let me go. I'm learning to live without you, and you have to give me a chance to get over you."

"But I don't want you to get over me. I want you to want me, to need me. I had everything and I blew it didn't I?"

"You are going to be okay. Give me six months and give yourself six months to live your life again. Jacob, I've got to let you go."

"Jenna, I love you!"

"Jacob, I love you too, but sometimes love isn't enough. Six months Jacob, we agreed, goodbye." Then I hung up the phone, and when I opened the closet door, there was Brandon right outside the door. He had turned off the radio and I hadn't noticed, so he basically heard the entire conversation.

"That was Jacob. Did you hear my conversation?"

"Yes, I didn't mean to eavesdrop. I just needed a razor and heard your phone ring, so I turned off the music, and I heard your side of the conversation. I thought you did a great job of standing your ground and I see this man doesn't play fair. He wants you and is not going to give you six months to get over him. He's selfish. He's not considering your wants and needs. He's self-centered."

"Maybe, but I shouldn't knock a guy for fighting for something that is important to him and making his own rules."

"You want a controlling man who doesn't consider your wants and feelings? Isn't that what you had with your ex-husband? Are you telling me that Jacob's behavior is what you admire?"

"Let's go eat and then go to your party. I'd love to dance with you tonight."

"Are we through having this conversation? I don't think I'm in the mood to go to a party now."

"Oh, don't let his call ruin our evening together."

"It's not his call, that's going to ruin our evening. It's your blindness and your attitude toward him. I don't know how to compete with that. I don't know if I want to."

"Okay, what do you want me to do?"

"I think I should just say goodnight to you and go to the party by myself."

"If that's what you really want then have fun at your party. Hey, you might give Kayla a call, she might be free tonight. I'm sure she'd love to go with you. It's hard to go to a dance when you don't have a dance partner."

He leaned down to kiss me goodbye and I just stepped back. "I'm sorry, you look beautiful tonight."

"Thank you, you clean up really nice too. I'm sorry about the Kayla comment too, it was unnecessarily childish."

"I hate it when we fight, I'm sorry. Please forgive me for listening to your private conversation and come to the party with me tonight. It won't be any fun if you aren't there with me. Please put this behind us and come with me."

"Well, I did already just put on my perfume and my new hot pink dress, so okay, but you are going to need to be on your best behavior, because as of right now you are walking on thin ice."

"Got it, thin ice, dance floor, let's go eat."

We grabbed a bite to eat and for some reason, I wasn't starving. I was just a normal kind of hungry, so I was able to eat slowly and enjoy each flavor. We put the earlier conversation behind us and decided to have a fun night together. I was looking forward to meeting his friends and dancing.

We got to the party and there were about ten couples there, so we had a really long table for all of us to sit together. Then we hit the dance floor and it wasn't a very big area, so people were crammed into a small space in front of the band. It was so much fun.

The band was really great, and his friends were fun and

welcoming. The birthday friend, Jon, had a lot to drink and started asking all the girls to dance with him because his girlfriend was home sick, and he wanted to celebrate his special day.

I told Jon I'd dance with him and then regretted it almost immediately. He was close, and in my personal space, and then his hands began to roam on my body right there on the dance floor.

Other people were dancing and doing the same thing, but I didn't feel comfortable with this stranger mauling me in public. I didn't even have time to push him away, before Brandon stepped in and escorted me off the dance floor.

"You just made some brownie points with me, no more thin ice for you."

"Glad to know I'm off the thin ice status."

His drunken friend didn't even know I wasn't still dancing with him. The next song was a slow one, so Brandon and I went back out on the floor, and it was so sweet. I loved being with him, next to him, in his arms, swaying together with the music. He was attentive, kind, and smart.

A part of me, deep down inside, knew what he'd said about Jacob earlier was true. Brandon is here now and cares about me. I care about him. Jacob is in my past and I need to leave him there. No more answering his calls or texting him. No contact six months. Swaying in Brandon's strong arms, my resolve is solid. Brandon leaned down and spoke in my ear over the loud music.

"Let's go to my place. I want you."

"Good, I want you to want me. Take me, I want you too!"

We said our goodbyes to his friends. They were all having a great time and I had no idea what time it was, but I didn't care, I wanted to be with Brandon. He said we could go to his place because his daughter was staying with her mom that weekend. Then we headed to his house. It was closer from the club than to drive to my place.

He lives in a gated community in a beautiful two-story brick home. Maybe it's a three-story. I bet he has a basement, living in this tornado area of the country, and it had an attached three car garage.

When we parked in his garage, and he was coming around to open my door, I noticed a huge boat in the third garage. I love boats. I jumped out of the car and strolled straight over to his ski boat.

"Do you take her out much?"

"Any weekend I can. Do you like being out on the water?"

"I love it, skiing, tubing, and laying out in the sun, all of it, big love."

"So nice I could impress you with my possessions."

"Well, I know where we are going next warm weekend. Date at the lake. Let's go inside and see if you can impress me as easily in there with something else. I meant a tour of your house."

"Your wish is my command, sweetheart."

We didn't stop for a tour of his house, although I considered it briefly. But with the kissing, we went up the stairs to his bedroom. I was so glad I shaved my legs today when we had gone home to change for the dance. He turned on some classical music Vivaldi's Four Seasons "Do you like Classical music?"

"Yes, but I don't think we need music to be in the mood, do you?"

"No, we don't need it. I'll turn it off if you want."

"No, actually I do like the instrumental quiet romantic tones. Now are we going to test out your bed?"

I didn't get another word out of my mouth. We were taking off clothes, he unzipped my dress slowly, and slid his hand down my back with each inch of open zipper. I felt my skin come alive to his strong, warm hands.

My dress slipped off and there it was crumpled on the

floor. I was standing in my black lacy bra, and black thong, still in my black patent pumps. I reached for his shirt. I began un-buttoning his shirt kissing each new open space his shirt revealed. A few chest hairs and then well-defined abs, man he clearly works out. I guess eating healthy really makes a difference, because wow he was impressive!

Then I loosened his belt and button on his black jeans. His firmness was growing strong and the voice in my head telling me I shouldn't be doing this was fading. Resistance was null and void. His shoes were already off and then his pants. He's a boxer's guy, and that was sexy to me. We made it to the bed and the rest of our clothes came off in a heated fury. We were absorbed in each other in a way I'd never felt before.

He put me in positions I'd never tried, and I liked it, no it was way more than like. I felt totally sexually satisfied. He was better than I ever dreamed we could be. How could I be so lucky to be with this amazing man? I felt so alive, so appreciative of his loving nature, he was breathtaking. After our intimate time together, I needed water.

"Are you thirsty?"

"I'm parched. You?"

"Yes."

I threw on his shirt that smelled like his cologne and hung down to my knees, as we walked downstairs to his kitchen. It said 3:45 a.m. on the microwave clock. No wonder we were dying of thirst. We both drank a couple of glasses of filtered water, and then he asked if I would spend the night with him, and he would take me home in the morning. Or, if I needed to get home for the dogs, he would take me home now, whatever I wanted.

I said for him, I'd make an exception, and spend the night. The dogs have a doggie door to get outside if they need to go, and I will give them a big breakfast, so they will be fine. I couldn't imagine leaving Brandon tonight, no way. We went back upstairs.

"I don't think I can dance any more tonight."

He just laughed and said, "Are you more of a cuddler?"

"Yes, at four a.m., I guess I am."

We curled up in one another's arms and quickly fell off to sleep. I love the feel of Brandon wrapped around me. I loved being surrounded with his warmth, attention, affection, power, and gentleness. How could his wife have ever let him go? Her loss my gain! Tomorrow we are definitely having an exclusive talk, because I'm not sharing him with anyone, no matter how nice she is. Sorry, Kayla, but he's all mine! Now that I know how amazing we are together I'm not letting him go.

When I woke up, Brandon was still asleep. I slipped off to his bathroom. There I looked through my purse to get my comb and fix my rumpled hair. I found my toothbrush in the container at the bottom of my purse. Now I had clean breath for my morning kisses.

I'd just taken care of those basic needs, when I looked up and he was standing quietly in the doorway, in his boxers, just watching me brush my teeth. What a weirdo.

"Do you need in here?"

"No, just checking on where you'd taken off to. Are you hungry?"

"Sure, but can I have a tour of your place first?"

"Okay, let me use the restroom and throw on my jeans and I'll be right out."

So, I sat on the bed in his shirt from last night. All I had to wear was my party dress from the night before. Brandon came out and he gave me the house tour. Very nice home, four bedrooms, three bathrooms, basement, and music room with a piano.

"Oh, do you play?"

"Yes. Kourtney and I both enjoy tickling the ivories."

When we got to Kourtney's room, he grabbed a pair of Pink brand sweat pants and zip up hoodie from his daughter's pile of laundry, he said "These are clean, she just hadn't put them away. If you'd be more comfortable than sporting my probably smelly shirt from last night, then go ahead and put these on."

I tried the sweatpants first to make sure I wouldn't be too fat for them, but they fit, so then I took off his shirt and slipped on her sweater. He just shook his head.

"No shame, you are going to kill me." Then he grabbed me and the clothes I just put on, came right back off. I was so glad I had kissing fresh breath. We were in the heat of passion when we heard the front door slam shut. He sat straight up. Then we heard her voice.

"Dad?"

Great Kourtney is here, and I'm naked on her bedroom floor. This is not good. I don't want her to hate me before she's had a chance to get to know me. Brandon jumped up to his feet.

"Get dressed!"

He threw on his jeans and headed quickly downstairs to meet Kourtney. I grabbed his shirt and her clothes, and I didn't even try to get dressed. I just ran naked with all the clothes in my hands back down the hall to Brandon's bedroom and shut the door behind me as quickly and quietly as I could.

I was so glad we hadn't gotten on her bed. We didn't make it off the floor. I quickly put on my own clothes, my rumpled, wrinkled, pink dress from the floor and just sat quietly on his bed until he came back to get me.

"Sorry about that. Kourtney wanted to work on a project and the information was on her laptop that she'd left here. She needed a flash drive to transfer the files to her computer at her mom's. Kourtney doesn't know you are here, and she will be leaving in a couple of minutes, so if you'll hold tight, I'll be back with you in a few minutes."

"I'm fine, just take care of your daughter."

Well, she got her flash drive downloaded and then she asked for her pink sweats. "Dad, have you seen my pink sweats? I thought I put them in my bag to take to mom's, but I can't find them."

He said, "I know where they are, I'll run up and get them". I had them folded and in hand when he opened his bedroom door. So glad I only had them on for a few seconds. So, she has her flash drive and clothes, and now she's leaving. I hear her mom honking the horn in the driveway.

I feel like I'm invading another woman's space and in effect, I am. If I wanted to have a good relationship with Kourtney, I couldn't meet her naked on her bedroom floor. This could not happen again. We had a close call, and I didn't want to be in that position, or put him in an awkward situation either. We agreed that we wouldn't do that again, out of respect for his daughter.

Once again, I was starving, and thankfully he was too. Brandon thought we'd be safe to have breakfast at his house. He made wheat pancakes, not my favorite, but not horrible, with fresh fruit and soft-boiled eggs, yum, yum.

Then he jumped in the shower, and I thought since I'm here I could join him, but when I offered, he said that he'd be out in a few minutes. I'm not sure why he didn't want me in the shower with him.

I felt sort of left out, but he's at his house, in his routine, I'll be fine. I was ready to get home, take care of my dogs, take my own shower, and wear some comfortable clothes of my own. I had several things to do for the weekend and Brandon and I had spent lots of time together recently.

He came out of the bathroom and said if I didn't mind, he needed to take me home, that he had previous obligations for the day.

"Not a problem. I can call a taxi if you need to be somewhere else. I can get a ride home."

"I have time to take you home."

It felt kind of weird between us, like he couldn't get rid of me quick enough. So, I just walked in front of him down to the car and this was the first time he didn't open the door for me. Hmmm, he gets what he wants from me and now no respect?

Not sure I like this behavior, what is going on? Had I done or said something? I could feel a rush of warmth flutter in the pit of my throat but didn't want to cry. Think about something else. I have no one to blame but myself for sleeping with a man before I'm married to him. Deep down I'm old school values in a modern turn, trying to meld the two, and so far, not doing such a good job.

He was kind and friendly as always, but something just felt off to me. I couldn't let it go without saying something, me and my mouth. I had his undivided attention in the car, so I couldn't hold it in any longer.

"Is there something wrong? I feel like since your daughter came home, your complete attitude and personality changed toward me. Did I do something wrong?"

"I'm sorry, it's me. I am telling my daughter to wait until marriage, and then she comes home unexpected, and almost found me on top of you in her bedroom. What was I thinking? I can't act that frivolous, I have a daughter to think about. I don't want to give her any excuses to spread her legs for a man before she's married."

"I'm sorry your daughter came home early. I'm glad we didn't get busted by her, but I guess I don't know what you mean. Do you want to stop seeing me?"

"I don't know. I do care about you, but I don't know what to do about us."

"I understand that feeling of I don't know… I was in love with another guy and had trust issues, so I trusted another guy and after one night of passion, he wants to throw me away too. Yeah, it's probably best, since you have daughter issues, and I have ex-issues, we can just be friends. Thanks for the ride home, I really appreciate it."

Thank God we were pulling down my street. The street

seemed like it had grown since I left yesterday. I spent all that time and energy telling him everything about my life for what? For him to say I was worth it before sex, but not worth it after sex. Great, that's an esteem builder! "Well, thanks so much for a fun day and night. I'll see you in class next week."

"I don't know what just happened, but I think I just completely lost you. I don't know what I want. I was just saying, we need to be careful and to take more precautions, so we don't end up hurting my daughter. I'm not throwing the baby away with the bath water."

We were in my driveway, and I was just confused and wanted out, so I said, "Well, we don't have to settle everything now. I'll talk to you soon, thanks for the ride."

"No kiss good-bye?"

I just waved goodbye and walked into the house. I locked the door behind me, slid down the door to the floor, and cried. I felt so cheap and used. Why was I sleeping with these men? This isn't how I was raised. Sex isn't just an act for me, I love these stupid men. I can't keep doing this. I can't stand the pain.

First, I have sex many times with Jacob before marriage, and now Brandon, who I was just getting to know and what do I do? Have sex with him, what is wrong with me? I've got an adult case of "SLUT!" How can you expect to be treated like a princess when you act like I have been acting?

I need an attitude adjustment. I can't keep doing this to myself. It hurts too much to lose in love. I was so happy last night and today I'm crushed. I need to start going to church and get my head and heart straightened out. I'm self-destructing from the inside out.

I finally got up off the floor and was just wiping the tears and snot off my face, when I heard a quiet knock at the door. I felt a sudden sickness in the back of my throat again. I opened it and it was Brandon standing on my porch.

"You've been crying. I couldn't pull out of your driveway leaving things the way they were between us. I really care about you, and women like you don't come along every day. I don't know how all this will work out, but I want you in my life, I'm so sorry for making you feel disposable, you are not. Please forgive me, I'm sorry. I can't go until I know we are okay."

Once again, I just cried and hugged his neck. No kissing just hugged him. "Thanks, but I've had enough pain. As good as it is between us, when I'm dismissed, it's crushing. I'm fragile and I lived through a broken heart recently, so I don't think I'm strong enough to go through that again.

Sorry, I know you are in a hurry to go to a meeting or something, so don't worry about me, I'll be fine. I'll always wish you the best. And I will still respect you in class and we will be friends."

"Can I sit down and talk with you for a minute? I really want a chance to talk to you."

"Okay, just a minute, then you need to go."

"We are new in our relationship, trying to find our way together, what works, what isn't good for us, and we are on our learning curve. I will make mistakes, but never intentionally to hurt you.

Give us a chance, Jenna. I think we deserve to be happy. I'm sorry for my behavior, I was an idiot. We are good together. I just didn't expect to care about you as much as I do, and you are more than just a sex relief for me. I really like and care about you. I want us.

Don't give up on us, please give us a chance to be happy. What can I do to make things right here? I couldn't pull out of your driveway, I kept thinking I am finally happy, I can't let her go. She likes someone who will fight for her."

I swallowed hard so I wouldn't cry in front of him and told him how I felt. "You made me feel cheap. I've never felt that way before, and I never want to feel that way again, ever. I have fresh scars from being thrown away, and then you go and do the same thing to me, reopening those deep hurtful wounds.

You knew what I'd been through, and you still treated me that way. I don't know how to move on from here or if I even can. I really cared about you and would have never guessed you would treat me that way. I shouldn't have slept with you. I don't hop from one bed to the next, so this is all new and totally wrong for me.

You were a jaw dropper for me. And I didn't think I'd find someone like you after Jacob. You are handsome, smart, funny, and most of the time, attentive and kind. You were so unexpected. You helped me find hope for my future, so thank you for that.

But I don't want, no, I won't be dismissed again or treated that way. A relationship takes two people caring. I'm not sure we have that. I'm really mad at myself for being intimate with a man and being a fool to think my feelings are the same as what he is feeling. I get it, I rushed into us because you were so amazing, but not at the cost of my heart. I won't rip it into pieces again for any man, it's too soon. I need recovery time."

"I want to start this morning all over again and tell you how I was feeling and thinking. It wouldn't be to keep you out of my shower. It would be to forget my meeting this afternoon, and keep you in my shower, and bedroom as long as humanly possible. I was caught off guard with my daughter showing up, and also with how I broke my personal rule about not having women at the house, until you.

You are a game changer for me too. I just need your patience to help me process who and what we are as a couple. I could date Kayla or whomever, but I want you. Give me a do-over. I'm not saying you have to forget, just forgive me this time. What guy do you know who ever gets it right the first time? Aren't we worth a second chance?"

"I haven't had my shower yet, and I feel exhausted. I just read in a magazine article recently that men generally speak 7000 words to a woman's 20,000 words. Now, I don't remember if that's per day or hour, but which ever it is, it clearly shows that you are going to have to work more than twice as hard as me, in order to communicate with me how you are feeling and what you are thinking.

If you think you are up for the challenge, then I will give us another chance. But just don't ever let us get into a position that could end the way our morning did. That was horrible and I don't want to feel that way ever again."

"You just tell me how you're feeling, and I'll do my best to take better care in the future. I'm sorry and thanks for giving us another chance."

"You should go for your meeting and I'll talk to you later."

"Can I have a kiss goodbye?"

"I don't want to hurt you but if you don't mind let's just say goodbye for today. I hope you have a successful meeting."

"Okay, I'll call you later, good-bye."

Chapter 10

The Proposal

Brandon and I had gotten back together, slowed it down physically, and had been dating for months. He had gone out of his way to make sure I never felt second class or neglected by him again. We decided that we wanted to tell his daughter about us. Since then, we have been dating exclusively for months and we were very happy together.

Now, it was finally time for Spring Break. Something every student and teacher looks forward to all year long. Brandon's daughter was going to an all-inclusive resort at a beach with her mom, stepbrothers, and stepsisters to Jamaica.

He wanted to take me away for the week too. I told him I had no money for a fun get away, and he said it costs the same price for one as it does for two on a cruise. We planned a full week together of heavenly bliss, on a ship in the beautiful Caribbean.

We kenneled my dogs for that week at my vet. I had left my dogs there before, when I used to go out of state on weekends to be with my dad when he fought cancer the last six years of his life. My dogs knew the people taking care of them at the kennel, and if there were ever any health issues, they were equipped to take good care of Molly and Moose.

He bought tickets for us to fly from Missouri to Miami to board a cruise ship on the Royal Caribbean Cruise line. Our trip to the Caribbean sounded wonderful to me. I had gone on a cruise once before with my sister-in-law. We had the best time ever, very relaxing. When I found out what we were planning for the spring break trip, I asked him if he minded if I invited my brother and his wife to join us. We would have a great time, and my two favorite guys could get to know each other.

"That would be fine with me. Give them a call and see if they are interested."

"Hi, Jenna, what's up?"

"Brandon and I are going on a cruise and would love for you and your beautiful wife to join us. You could get away, enjoy the sun, and get to know him all at the same time. What do you say?"

"That sounds great. Let me check and see if we can reschedule things here and make it work."

Before long, my phone rang. "Jenna, this is Jeff. We are not going to be able to join you on this cruise trip. Thanks for thinking of us, but we will get together soon. Brandon sounds like a good guy and I'm sure he's got to be better than Jacob. I will call you later and we will put something on the schedule for the four of us to get together."

Then I called my mom to let her know where I'd be for the week and that I'd be with, Brandon on the cruise. Mom and Brandon had talked several times on the phone. Brandon and mom both like to cook from scratch, so they have connected on a food level. Brandon wants to meet my mom in person and cook for her, isn't that sweet? Mom thinks he's smart and funny, and we are planning on going to mom's a couple weeks after our cruise, so they can officially meet.

Finally, it was spring break. The non-stop flight took us to Miami where we boarded the cruise line's shuttle to the ship. We had a suite reserved and it was on the top level with a walk out balcony. I didn't stay in a room this nice the last time I cruised.

This room was simply beautiful, with fresh flowers and fresh fruit in the room. There were clean, white towels formed in animal shapes, sitting on our king-sized bed. I had a strong feeling that this spring break was going to be my best week ever! And I must admit, it was my best week of all time.

I'd hit the tanning booth about a month before we were leaving for our trip, so I wouldn't burn and could enjoy the weather and excursions. I look good tan, and somehow, I feel thinner when I'm tan, don't know why, but it's a mental game I like. My new swimsuit was perfect to show off my tan.

Brandon wasn't keen on me getting into the tanning booths, he calls them cancer tubes, but he seemed to enjoy the results of my tan confidence. He's so darn cute he looks good tan or paler than me. On a scale from one to ten, he's a strong, handsome ten. And personality wise he's a fifteen, off the charts smart, funny, loving, honest, kind, sexy, patient and not necessarily in that order. Brandon turns heads wherever we go. I just smile and think, he's with me!

I loved every second of our vacation. Our plan for each port was to get off the ship as soon as we had breakfast and see the sights, take pictures every morning, and then back to the ship to put our cameras in the room safe, and then hit the local shopping and or beaches each afternoon. We could eat local food for lunch or free food on the ship, depending on how much money we spent that morning.

We were on the go from the moment we ported, until we got back on the ship each evening. A couple of nights, we were just minutes from missing the deadline to be back on the ship before it departed. We had so much fun together, it was magical.

Once back on the ship for our seven-p.m. curfew, we had to hurry to our room for showers, then dress for dinner at seven-thirty, to be on time at our table to meet with our assigned shipmates.

We got to know two other couples at our table. Both of the couples were honeymooners, one from New Orleans, the other was from Boston. I enjoyed listening to their accents at the beginning of the week. However, by the end of the week, that was a different story. The Boston couple acted like they were an old married couple, even though they were on their honeymoon. I'd guess they were in their late 30's. The men frequently argued at our dinner table in front of all of us. They were correcting one another's word choice and stories in front of us too.

I just wanted to enjoy my dinner and not be included in their couples' drama. Some people think that because it's happening to them, everyone wants to hear every detail about it. To that I'd say a loud, NOT! This is our vacation too, people, so chill out and eat already. We just tried to ignore them, eat and talk to each other in quiet voices, like we had our own table.

The captain of the ship invited us to join him at his table on the next to our last night, so of course we did. We dressed up and it was an honor to meet him. However, I was concerned that first of all, he was so young looking, and secondly, he was drinking with our table mates. Can you drink and drive on a ship in international waters? Not sure about the drinking and driving laws but I wanted him to be older, more experienced, and totally sober driving this huge ship in open waters, the ocean is so vast.

You always hear about the food being over the top

amazing on a cruise ship and about gaining weight from all the delicious food, but that wasn't the case on our ship. The food was only okay, but not on the overly impressive side. This was the only negative thing on our entire trip.

On our cruise we hit every beach at every port. We went snorkeling, rode watercraft jet skis, swam with dolphins and huge sea turtles, took tons of pictures, went sight-seeing, and had uninterrupted us time 24/7. I loved spending time with Brandon. He is so good to me I love this man. We didn't get sick of each other or run out of things to say. We were comfortable with one another and I can see myself with him for my future.

We walk together hand in hand on the beach and women are staring and giving him a double take. Yes, I'm watching all those topless women sun bathers flirt with Brandon. But he was with me. He'd glance their way and smile, but always holding my hand and talking with me. I did my share of looking around too, but not because I wanted something new, it was just looking at the beauty around me.

The next to the last night on the ship was our formal night for dinner. I tell you, this man in a tux was something to behold. I'd never seen him dressed up before and I couldn't keep my hands off him. He had a slight sunburn but suffered through it so we could be intimate. I tried to keep him covered in sunscreen, but being that close to the sun, you can burn or tan quickly here. We put our formal attire back on and went to dinner with the captain.

The ship hosted dancing clubs, casinos, bingo, shopping, rock wall climbing, swimming pools, movie theaters, a small golf course on the top deck, exercise rooms, spas, and entertainment. There was never a lack for something to do on the ship. We had such a great time I didn't want it to end.

Can we just live where we have twenty-four-hour room service and people waiting on us hand and foot? I'm sure it would get old in time, but I'd love to give it a chance. Oh, and the best feature of the ship, besides my man, was the spa. We had a couples massage on the first day we were at sea, and that was so relaxing, we actually went to our room and slept afterward.

We were on our last day of the cruise, laying out by the pool on the top deck of the ship, when Brandon said what I knew would come up at some point. "It's been seven months since we've been exclusive. I was just wondering if you've heard anything from him, you know, Jacob?"

I looked at him, his sandy blond hair blowing in the wind, on the top deck of the ship in his blue lounge chair, with his sexy sunglasses, and his slightly swollen lips from the scorching sun, or from so much kissing, I'm not sure which. I sat straight up got out of my lounging chair next to him, came over to his chair, and sat straddling him across his stomach.

"Honey, I am with you. I love you. I have not heard from my past and if I do hear from him, I will let you know. You don't have to ask me or worry about him. I will tell you when and if that ever occurs."

"You love me?"

"Yes, I do love you. I didn't want to care about anyone so soon, but you entered my life, and I couldn't let you go. I know in a traditional relationship the man is supposed to say I love you first, but it slipped out before I could stop my words. I'm not taking back my feelings for you. I just didn't want you to feel any pressure to say anything back to me. I want us to be honest with each other, always and forever."

"Jenna, I love you too, more than I've loved any other woman. You are everything to me. I love you and I'm sorry I wasn't the first one to tell you that out loud."

It was on our spring break vacation, on the top deck of the ship, where we got lost in love, started making out, and quickly had to go to our suite to express our love. I did fall in love quickly, but I didn't know I'd meet such a wonderful man, especially so soon after my heart had needed such major repair.

He's beautiful, he's balanced, communicates with me, and is kind and affectionate. I am blessed to have a man like him in love with me. I love him, he loves me. I'm so glad we found each other. I never thought I would be happy again, and I am, every part of me is happy.

"I know this is a girlish question, but how long have you known that you loved me?"

"Since I kissed you on our first date, I knew you were the one. You are the one for me. I want you to spend more time with me and Kourtney, to see if that is a place you could feel comfortable full time. I wonder if we could be your new home. I want your future to be our future. Jenna, will you marry me?"

"I know I told you I wanted to go slow, but the truth is, I couldn't go fast enough with you. I want you all the time, in every way, and yes, I could see my forever with you. I could see us as happily ever after. I smile all the time and you're my best friend. I can tell you anything.

I feel secure with you even when we have had disagreements and arguments, because we give each other time to cool down. That's about fifteen minutes, then we come back together and talk our way through the situation and our feelings. I love the way we work things out together. I feel happy that we are a good team. I love you."

"I love you. I'll ask again, will you marry me?"

"Yes, I love you too. I will marry you."

After I'd savored the moment for about half an hour, I told him we needed to have a serious talk. We were still in our king-sized bed and he sat up immediately and gave me his full attention. We really do have great communication together and I was so thankful for a man who would listen. I love him.

"Sweetheart, what are you going to tell Kourtney when

she asks you how her dad proposed? Are you going to tell her oh, we just finished having sex and I asked her right then and there on the bed? Is that going to be our proposal story? No, that can't be our proposal story. As much as I loved it, we have to think of how this will play out when you tell your family and I tell mine.

I will give you a re-do and this time you have to think about your daughter too. Baby you are going to have to step up your game with my next proposal. I will still say yes, but I don't want your daughter to be uncomfortable with our romantic story that starts our future together."

"I'm sorry. You deserved a better proposal than what I gave you. I love you and I will think of something better for you. You, thinking about my daughter, like you just did, is just one more reason why I love you. I will do this right. I wanted to be impulsive, not so planned out, but clearly a proper proposal requires more planning."

"I'll be waiting for an amazing proposal from my amazing man, lover, and friend. Oh, and by the way, I'm going to need a ring to go with that question you are going to ask me one day soon."

"Baby, there's a jewelry shop on this ship. Let's put our clothes back on and go ring shopping. Are you up for that?"

"By the looks of it, you are up for round two of something…the ring can wait." We were back together moving and loving on the love boat of the seas. Much later, we showered and went downstairs for drinks and ring shopping. We had a fun time trying on rings and found a couple that were remarkable, but they were really overpriced. Unfortunately, I had not that long ago priced wedding rings and knew this was not the place to buy the ring.

I wanted to save Brandon the overpriced emotional buy on the ship, so I just said they had great rings, but we should wait and buy locally. That way if a diamond comes loose, we can go locally and they can fix it, polish it, etc.

He was impressed with my local thinking and I saved him some money. We really are a great team.

Chapter 11

The Past Comes Knocking

While getting ready for our flight home, I was busy texting, telling Jeff and mom that I was un-officially engaged. I was so happy. They were happy for me. Jeff was just thrilled my future didn't include Jacob. He would have liked anyone that wasn't Jacob, but he was genuinely happy for me.

I hadn't heard from Jacob since the six months stay away order I gave him. He finally left me alone and I was able to move on. I had been very happy and no drama and no heartbreak with Brandon. He loves me unconditionally. Just love and acceptance for me and the crazy situations I get myself into.

I don't know if I even need to tell Jacob I'm getting married. He hasn't spoken to me in almost a year. We have both moved on. He's in Kentucky, I'm in Missouri. He has his life there, and I can keep my life and build it with Brandon and Kourtney here.

I'm very happy, heart, mind, and soul. This has been the best spring break I ever had! The best vacation and really the happiest I've ever been in my life. I've seen beautiful beaches, spent my nights dancing, and being intimate with the man I love. No distractions or interruptions from work, just me and my man, utter and total bliss.

Brandon asked me what I was thinking about. I felt bad that he just proposed to me and I critiqued his proposal and threw it back in his face. Who does that kind of thing to the man she loves?

He gives me the best gift he could ever have given me, a proposal. The gift of being with him for the rest of our lives, the verbal expression that he wants me forever, and I'm thinking of what his daughter will say, and honestly about another man, my past Jacob. Something is wrong with me. I told Brandon what I was thinking about and apologized because I love him, and his proposal was fine.

"No, you were right. Just look forward to our future and the next proposal. I'll give you something to brag about." Then he kissed me.

"I love you too, baby. I love our life together and I love that you are honest and that we have an honest relationship. We can tell each other our deepest thoughts and feelings, even though it may not be what we want to hear. We respect the truth and trust one another to guard our gift of honesty to one another. I promise I will always listen to you, respect you, and love your honest, trusting, good nature."

"I love you, Jenna, forever."

"I love you too. You couldn't say anything to me that would ever mean more to me than what you just said. Let me savor those words from the man I love for a minute. Let's go back up to our room before we have to leave our ocean of paradise. I want to give you a send-off you'll never forget, or that we'll never forget."

The next thing I know they announced all passengers

needed to place their luggage outside the cabins for customs inspections. De-boarding the ship will occur according to flight departure times. Passengers need to go to the mezzanine deck to go through customs which will begin in about an hour. We knew we still had some free time to enjoy one another before we headed for the airport, so we just floated on our bed and loved one another until our time on the ocean was up.

Heading to the airport on a ship shuttle, Brandon asked when I wanted to go ring shopping.

"Whenever you want to go, I'm ready. I'll provide the finger you provide the ring. But, with spending all this money for our week of unparalleled oceans of heavenly enjoyment, I think we might need to take our time, save some money, and wait for an official proposal."

"Babe, I've been saving for a ring since I first met you. I knew I didn't want you to get away from me, ever. We can look at rings anytime you want and I'm working on the perfect proposal so you and I will have a story to tell my daughter, our families, and friends."

"How about we enjoy the pictures and memories of our trip, our unofficial engagement trip, and then we can experience the adventure of looking for our rings. No rush, we have the rest of our lives to be together. When are we going to tell your daughter that we are unofficially engaged?"

"When I do it right, I will give you a proposal worthy of you. Then we will have a story we can proudly tell others. I don't want her to ever know about the "unofficial" proposal, so let's just erase that one. I will surprise you with a new and improved proposal that will express words to match my heart.

"Kourtney and I have talked about our future with you."

She asked "Dad when are you going to make an honest woman out of her? "Jenna is great dad. You are going to need someone to take care of you when I go off to college.

So, you don't need to worry about me, and I won't worry about you. You will have Jenna and I will have a university."

"She's growing up so quickly. But I know she loves you."

"If she didn't like me, you wouldn't have asked me to marry you?"

"No, I wouldn't have. I would have waited until you won her over, or until she moved out for college. She's my daughter and she will always come first in my life. I'm her dad first."

"That's great Brandon, but where does that put me? Second, third, where do I fit into this family picture? This is just what every woman wants to hear after a sex induced proposal, or a non-proposal. Honey, I took a vote and you passed. I love you and your daughter, but after what you just said, I would like to feel like the first person on your list of loves, but I guess I understand."

Now we were at the airport, with our luggage and we had to go through customs again. This takes forever and is so intrusive.

"I am sorry if I hurt your feelings by telling you my daughter is a priority in my life. I had no idea this would be upsetting to you. It wasn't my intention to make you feel like you're not the top of my priorities. I asked you to marry me, how is that not making you a priority? We just spent a week together of pure pleasure, for me at least, and you are going to nit-pick over one sentence of mis-speaking? You want me to communicate but criticize me for doing it. How can I win with you?"

I didn't want to blow this out of proportion. I tried to get to him to kiss him and tell him I was sorry, but the customs people are very strict until you get to a certain area. He was in one line and I was in another, so I had to keep my distance until we were finally cleared. Then we were back to hugs and holding each other.

We had first class seats on the flight home and as incredible as it is to think about, we slept most of the trip home. We just spent a week relaxing and having fun in the sun, and here we were coming home exhausted. How is that possible? We had great tans too. If I do say so myself, I looked better than I ever had, and I loved it!

We got our luggage, stopped for a late dinner, and Brandon took me home so I could be at work bright and early the next morning. I told him he could spend the night, but he said his daughter would come by his place in the morning and he wanted to be there when she got ready for school.

He wanted to hear about her spring break and see her excitement, and he missed his little girl. I said I understood, and that I was just going to take a shower and go to bed. He kissed me goodnight and left for home.

I'd just used the restroom and started to unpack my overnight bag when I heard a knock on the door. It scared me. I usually have Molly and Moose to bark when someone is at the door. I thought maybe Brandon changed his mind. I just smiled and went quickly to the door. I couldn't believe my eyes. It's Jacob at my front door. It is 11:30 pm, "Jacob what are you doing here?" I couldn't believe it was him at my door.

"I came to see you. I've stayed away for six months like you wanted, now it's your turn to give me some face time. May I come in?"

"Sure, sorry, come in and have a seat. Can I get you something to drink?"

"You look amazing, so tan and slender. I've missed you every day we've been apart. I want a chance to date you and win you back. I played by your rules, and now I'm ready to pick back up where we left off."

"It is good to see you, and you look great too. But I don't think we should see each other anymore. Brandon just asked me to marry him, well sort of asked me, and I said yes."

"Well, I asked you to marry me, and you said yes to me too. And I asked you first, so I should have some time, like you promised Jenna, to start over. Brandon has had you all to himself for six months.

If I'd had you all to myself for six months, we'd already be married. I'm here for you. Are you going against your word? Why won't you just let us spend some time together, reconnect, see if we have anything there to build on for a future? Are you afraid to spend time alone with me? Don't you trust yourself to be with me?"

"No, I just don't want to hurt Brandon. He is an amazing man, and I love him. I'm sorry Jacob, but I do love him. After you, I didn't think that was possible, but I found someone who loves me back and we are really good together."

"You and I were good together long before the Brandon show, you owe me this. Give me a week. I've taken off this week. I was coming on your spring break but heard you were on a cruise, so I changed it for this week. I can sleep on your couch, or a local hotel, but give me this week. No sparks, I leave forever. You said Jenna, you said six months and we'd try. So, give me this week. That's not asking too much. One week, I waited six months. One week is only fair."

"Okay, it's late, you've traveled far, and I'm jetlagged and tired. I have a guest bedroom you are welcome to for the week. But I'm telling Brandon you're here. I have to go to work tomorrow because I do not have any time off. But you are welcome to make yourself at home and I'll call you when I'm through tutoring on my way home at 6:30 and we can go out for a bite. I'm sorry I have no food in the house."

"I'll be fine. Thank you. I knew I could count on you to be a woman of your word. I will take any time I can to be with you. Hey, can I come with you to work, to help you in your classroom? I could read with your kids, do whatever you want. I just want to spend as much time as I can with you."

"Maybe on Tuesday, I'll think about it. Right now, here's your bedroom and your bathroom. My dogs are at the vet's kennel and I won't have time to get them until Tuesday after work. Hey if you could pick them up for me tomorrow that would save me a day's fees. I would appreciate it. I'll give you my credit card if you wouldn't mind picking them up and paying for me?"

"Sure, just leave me a list of what you need, and I'll take care of what I can for you."

"Do you have wheels, or do you need Baby?"

"I have a rental parked in the street. Should I pull up in your driveway?"

"Yes, I don't want you to get a ticket."

As soon as he got his luggage in the house, I locked the outside door, turned off the lights, and told him pleasant dreams. Then I went straight into my room and crashed onto my own bed.

I always clean my house before I go on a trip so when I come home everything is done and welcoming. I was glad I had butter soft sheets to sink into. I'm in bed when I see him standing over me.

"Jacob? What are you doing in my bedroom?"

"Can I have a kiss before I go to sleep? And are those your wonderful soft sheets?"

"No, you are not sleeping with me."

"How about we cuddle? You have to give me a chance. I kept my promise, you need to give me a chance."

"Ten minutes of cuddling and then you have to go, I have to get some sleep. I can't believe I'm letting you do this."

"Scoot over babe. Oh, you feel so good, smell so good."

"No, you have to go to your bedroom. I'm going to sleep, and I cannot deal with you tonight."

"One kiss and I'm out of here."

"Okay fine, one kiss and you are out."

Then we kissed and the memories flooded my mind like it was yesterday. One kiss turned into two and three and in moments, we were moving in motions together that felt familiar. We were rubbing up against one another and he was gently squeezing and feeling parts of me he'd known so well. I recognized his touch, I couldn't resist. We were naked and responding to the passions of the moment.

It was wrong. How could I love him after all this time, just a touch and I was totally undone? He feels so right. I am in so much trouble. How does he have this power over me? What is wrong with me? After we finished our love making, he smiled.

"You are just as amazing as I remembered. I missed you every day of our six months. I listened to what you said, I'm so sorry I took you for granted. I love you and want to spend my life showing you the many ways that I love and appreciate you."

Jacob and I couldn't say another word. He was here, we were together, and I didn't want to say no. I'm already in trouble, I might as well enjoy the journey. Before we curled up together for a restful sleep. I called in sick for work the next day. Anyone who just did what I did was clearly sick, out of her mind, and has no business dealing with kids tomorrow. I have to clean up the mess I just made at my house.

He heard me making arrangements to take off work tomorrow, and he thought that was an invitation for round three. Are you kidding me? How can he keep this up? I'm still just getting my pulse down to a safe rate. I love him, but I love Brandon too.

I climbed back into bed, and he was ready and willing to make up for six months of absence. "Jenna, I love you so much, I've missed you. I can't wait to spend this week with you. You are going to fall in love all over again with me.

You know we are meant to be together. Come here."

I had no will power; I was putty in his hands. I missed him too. I'd forgotten how much because I was so happy with Brandon, but OMG, Jacob could please me over and over and over. I didn't want him to ever stop. Ever! My mind was turned off and my body was reclaiming familiar territory.

How could he still have this power over me? How could I do this to Brandon? What was I thinking? Brandon will hate me, and never trust me again. I would be crushed if Brandon called me and told me he'd slept with Kayla. I don't know how I'd ever get over that to trust him again. How can I expect him to forgive me for this? He just spent a fortune to make me happier than I'd ever been, and I did this to him, to me.

What a dilemma. I had two wonderful men, and I loved them both. I don't know how it's possible and I know it's wrong, but I feel like I'm torn, literally ripping apart from the inside out. My brain cannot process all this intense emotion. What am I going to do? I have to talk to Brandon, when I tell him what I've done…I will die when I see the hurt in his eyes, I won't be able to bear it, but I did this to him, I will have to face him. He didn't deserve me acting this way. I have no excuse. I didn't know what to do. I have to tell Brandon the truth, so someone tell me what that is?

I love Brandon, and I love Jacob. This is wrong on so many levels, but I honestly love them both. I have two wonderful men in my life, in my bed, and tomorrow when I tell Brandon what I've done, I will lose part of my heart and break his. I need sleep, if I have to face all this, I need sleep, I'm totally physically and emotionally exhausted.

Chapter 12

Turmoil

I woke up early and slipped out of my bed. There was my handsome Jacob, sleeping peacefully in my bed and I had to talk to Brandon. I couldn't let him tell his daughter we were almost engaged and then tell her what I've done to him. I went into the kitchen and texted Brandon.

Brandon, please do NOT tell anyone we are almost engaged. Jacob was at my house after you left last night, and I promised if he'd stay away for 6 months that I would give him chance. I did tell him that, and I told you that I told him that. I have to give him that chance.

I do love you, that has not changed, but part of me still loves Jacob too. I'm torn and I need to settle this in my mind and heart once and for all. I need to be free to spend my future with the one man that wants to share his future with me. I am sorry to hurt you this way. I never dreamed. I'm sorry and I do love you.

Please forgive me and give me a week. He's going to be here this week then he's going back to his home in Kentucky. I promised him if he gave me six months, I would give him another chance. Brandon, he gave us that time, I owe him this. He kept his word I have to keep my word and give him a chance. It's just a week. I know this is a lot to ask, but this is what I'm going to do.

Five minutes after I sent the text, my phone was ringing, actually, silently vibrating to avoid conflict with Jacob. I answered the phone in a quiet voice and Brandon was in a full, loud roar (not that I blamed him), I'd never heard him so angry.

"Are you kidding me? You are telling me you love me but are having sex with another man. That's not love, that's lust. You don't need to worry about making a decision between him and me. You two deserve each other.

You have betrayed me and I'm beyond words for you right now. Talk about throwing someone away. You wait until you've gotten a vacation out of the deal, or a new car, before you love them and leave them. You are something Jenna, a real pro."

"Brandon, I am so sorry. I do love you and I never really thought I would ever see Jacob again. He deserves me honoring my promise when he honored his part of the deal to stay away and not contact me for six months."

"Don't talk to me about honor when you are engaged to me and screwing another man. I don't share. I'll make the choice easy for you. You and me, we are over! Have a good life ex-fiancé."

"Brandon, please, I'm so sorry. You are such a wonderful man."

"Jenna, stop, just stop it! You made your choice last night, so just tell me goodbye and that will be the end of us."

"I can't say that I don't want to say that."

"Well, your body already said it loud and clear.

Goodbye, Jenna. We could have been happily ever after. I can't believe you did this. I hear Kourtney coming in the front door. You are the one that took my choices away. You've tied my hands. I've got to go."

Jacob was standing in the hallway and must have heard my conversation, because he found me shortly after I hung up the phone, curled up in a fetal position, in the middle of the kitchen floor. "I can't believe I did that to Brandon. He's such a good man. I love him, and I just ripped his heart out. How could I do that to him? Who have I become? How could I put my personal happiness over his and my promise to him? I'm broken, I'm warped, I'm sick."

Jacob wrapped his arms around me. "No, don't. I just destroyed a man's heart. I'm cruel, selfish, how could I do that to someone I love? I'm poison, you have to go away and forget me."

"I'm not going anywhere. We belong together. We love each other and I'm here. I love you baby. I'm sorry your friend is hurting."

"No, Jacob, you're not sorry."

"Yes, I know the pain he's feeling of losing you, and I wouldn't wish that on my worst enemy. I really wouldn't. If you picked him, I'm sure he's a good guy. But he will survive. We did and we found our way back to each other."

"Jacob, I don't feel very well."

"You need to eat something. Let's get dressed and I'll take you out to breakfast."

"I'm hungry, but I don't think I could keep anything down."

"We need to get dressed and I'll drive you wherever you want to go."

Jacob literally had to help me get down the hall to my bedroom, I had no strength. He basically sat me on the bed and dressed me. He combed my hair, pulled it back into a ponytail, and I ended up in a pair of jeans and a tee-shirt.

After he helped me put on my sandals, Jacob got dressed, and I don't know how he did it, but he looked amazing. There he stood, in my bedroom, jeans, cowboy boots, and button down, checked blue and white shirt.

I do love him, but I love Brandon too. Brandon will never forgive me. I just destroyed my closest friend. I somehow managed to finish brushing my teeth while rushing thoughts flooded my brain. Jacob found me just staring in my mirror lost in my reflection.

Who am I? Jacob placed his hand in the center of my back, directed me to the car, and a first for him, he walked me to the passenger's side, opened the door, and put me in my seatbelt. I think if he hadn't, I'd just be standing there unable to move. So now we are in his rental and off to I-HOP for nourishment.

"Jenna, you are going to be okay. We are going to be okay, baby. But you are worrying me, I sort of think you are in shock or something. You're kind of catatonic, baby. You need to snap out of it. I don't know if I should take you to the hospital or out for food."

"Food, I'm not going to the hospital."

"I will feed you, and if you don't snap out of it, you are going to the hospital. I want you healthy and happy."

GPS brought us right to the food. Out we go. Again, I couldn't get myself out of the seatbelt. Jacob had time to walk around the car, open the door, and moved my hands gently to the side so he could release me from my seat belt.

"You are really worrying me."

"Just help me inside for food, I think I'm just really hungry." We walked in arm and arm and sat down in a booth. He scooted next to me.

"Let me have your hand."

I just flopped it in his hand. I didn't realize it, but he was taking my pulse. "We need to get you to the doctor your pulse is down to nothing."

"I'll be fine, just get me some orange juice and a piece

of ham."

Jacob summoned our waitress and then he was on his phone. Later I found out it was his friend, the doctor from Kentucky. Jacob told him what he was seeing. He said watch me, feed me, keep me warm, hydrated, and if my blood pressure didn't improve in the next fifteen minutes, take me to the hospital.

"Aren't you going to eat?"

"I will in a minute babe, I just want to make sure you are feeling better before I eat something."

"I do think the food is helping me, thank you."

"Let me have your hand."

Apparently, my pulse was stronger, so Jacob felt more comfortable to order his food.

"I want pancakes and hash browns with a side of gravy. Will you get that for me?"

"Of course,"

"Oh, and a cup of coffee, I'm dying for a cup of coffee." He ordered a skillet of food, eggs, potato chunks, sausage, cakes, and coffee. He was taking care of me. I started feeling human again. It kind of scared me, I felt I was in nothingness. I tried, but I just couldn't function normally. Only for a blip of time. That's never happened to me before. I'm so glad I had him to help me. I finally have a smile on my face.

"I'm sorry for my spacy moments. Thank you for taking care of me. I think I just needed time to process you being here."

Just then my phone buzzed. I looked at my phone, it was Jeff. He should be at work, so it must be important.

"I need to take this."

"Is it Brandon?"

"No, it's my brother. Hello Jeff."

"Jenna, what are you doing back with Jacob? You just told me you are getting married to Brandon, the man of your dreams, and hours later you are with Jacob? What are you thinking? Jenna? Jenna? Hello?"

"Hello, Jeff. It's Jacob. "Listen, your sister just fainted, thanks to your call. I'm taking her to the doctor, so get off her back. We are together and it's going to be that way forever. So be supportive of your only sister. I'm hanging up so I can get her to the doctor. I'll call you back when I know something."

We got out to the car I don't even remember the walk. I told Jacob, "I am not going to the doctor. I think I'm just tired and stressed. I just need some rest. Take me home, please, I'll be fine. I've never acted this way before and I'm sorry I'm crashing right in front of you. It's not too late for you to…"

"Jenna, lean back in your seat and rest, I'll get you home. When you're resting, I'll go get Molly and Moose. They will be glad to see their mommy. Would that make you happy?"

"Yes." Then I must have fallen asleep. My tummy was full, so it was time for a nap. We got home and I couldn't wake myself up. Jacob put me in bed and the next thing I knew, there was a strange man in my bedroom. "Jacob?"

"Baby, it's okay I called my friend who's a doctor and he called a friend who's a doctor at Mercy Hospital here in Springfield. He agreed to make a house call, just for you. He met us here at your house. You slept in the car the entire drive home. Dr. Doortea's taken some blood, and vital stuff, and we are going to make sure you are okay."

"Oh, I wouldn't go to the doctor, so you brought the doctor to me? I can't afford that. What are you thinking?"

"I'm thinking I am taking care of you now. You are not yourself I want you healthy. If I can do something to help you, I will, always. Well, doctor what's your professional opinion?"

"Jenna, you are exhausted. You might have caught something when you were out of the country on your cruise, or it could be mono. We'll know more when I get the results back from your blood work."

"Wait doctor, are you telling me that I have a teenager's kissing disease, mono?"

He just smiled. "I won't know until I get your blood work results. But you need bed rest. I suggest three days and then you should be able to function at half days for two days, then back to work at a normal schedule, if you are feeling better. Call me if you have any problems or changes, and I will call you when I receive your lab results."

"There is no way I can be off work right now. It's testing time, kids need…"

"I'm the doctor, it wasn't a request. You can stay at home and Jacob can care for you, or I can admit you to the hospital, which I think would be a good idea to make sure you are hydrated and get your pressure up from your low readings."

"Doctor Doortea, I'm afraid I will lose my job. I've missed more work this year than I've missed all my years of teaching."

"A good teacher is a true gift. I'm sure your principal will fight for you if you have my doctor's orders."

Jacob said, "Jenna, I'll have the doctor call your principal so he can let her know your condition and make the sub arrangements for the week. You don't need to worry about anything but getting better."

"Thanks." Then I just rolled over and went to sleep. When I woke up, I had Molly and Moose up on the bed licking my face and wagging their little tails. Jacob had gotten groceries and was in the kitchen fixing something that smelled really delicious. I called for him and he said he'd be right with me.

He came with a large glass of water, said I needed to drink it, and a small container of Ensure. Jacob said it was doctor's orders. I followed the directions and drank them both. I was so glad my dogs were home, and Jacob was turning out to be a pretty good caretaker. I never would have guessed that about him. But here he is in my bed, by my side, and only giving, not expecting anything in return. I do love Jacob.

We watched TV. And talked a little, but I couldn't keep awake. "Jacob, I'm so sorry this is our week together, and I'm sick. I'm so sorry."

"You can't help when you get sick. You went out of the country and wore yourself out, and I'm not going to let my mind think about that part. Then the shock of seeing me at your door, no warning, then our sex-a-thon, and I'm lucky you lived through it."

"Ha, ha, don't flatter yourself. You are amazing in bed and it turns out you have skills outside the bedroom too. I'm not only thankful and grateful, I feel like I can rest knowing you are here. Thank you."

"Are you just figuring out that I'm wonderful?"

"No, it's just nice to have you here with me, to have us as a team. Did you remember to call my brother?"

"Yes, I've talked to Jeff several times today. He knows we are back together and that you are on bed rest and doing fine."

"How did he know you and I were back together? I didn't call him, did I?"

"No, the lovely Brandon thought you needed someone to talk some sense into you, so he called your brother. And you know how much Jeff loves me, so he was only too ready to call and give you an earful for getting back with me. I do think he is coming around. You don't need to worry about your brother. He will be fine when he knows you are feeling better, and that we are fine."

"Would you take care of the dogs? I need to sleep. But I want to feel you next to me in my bed, at least until I fall asleep. Will you do that for me?" Just then the dogs started barking and ran toward the front of the house, to the front door. Then we heard the knocking on the door.

"Is the doctor coming back tonight?"

"No, are you expecting company?"

"No."

"Sit still, I'll get the door."

I sat up in bed and heard Brandon's voice. "Let me see Jenna. Get out of my way!"

"You are not taking one step in this house."

I jumped out of bed and walked as quickly as I could to the front door. "Jenna, what are you doing out of bed?"

"What's wrong with you?"

"Brandon, I'm sick." Jacob ran over to hold me up.

"OMG Jenna, what's wrong? You look terrible."

"I'm just tired, you don't need to worry about me." I felt dizzy like I was about ready to faint. I needed to put my hand against the wall to keep my balance.

"Yeah, right. Listen I'll make this quick and to the point. I'm not just giving you to Jacob. If he wants you, then he's going to have to win you back. You and I are good, better than good, together. I said things to you on the phone I regret. I was just so shocked and so angry that you would just throw us away. But I'm not letting you go. I'm fighting for you."

Then, apparently, I fainted. Something I seem to be really good at recently. And when I came to, Jacob was on one side of my bed and Brandon was on the other. I cannot wrap my mind around my dilemma.

"Guys don't fight, please I can't take it right now. I'm so sorry to put you both in this mess." Then my eyes started to tear up, so I asked them to give me a few minutes. "You've got to get out of my room."

They both just dropped their heads and started walking out of the bedroom. "Guys I love you, thank you for loving me. I'm losing it. I don't think one person is supposed to know this much love. This is literally tearing me up from the inside out. I'm doing all I can to physically keep myself from falling apart."

I saw them listening to me and then they continued to walk out of my room. I heard low, calm, male voices talking in the other room and I fell asleep. Jacob woke me up to drink Ensure and more water. All I've done is sleep, and pee, sleep and pee. "I want real food. What are you having for dinner? What sounds good to you?"

"Wait, what happened to Brandon? Is he okay, were you two good when I went to sleep?"

"He's a reasonable guy and he cares about you too. He's going to check on you when I go back to Kentucky, and we are not going to fight, so you don't have to worry. As much as I want him to disappear, I'm glad he will be checking in on you. We both want you to take the time you need to process all this, because we both want you healthy, and not having a mental break down."

"Is that what's happening to me? Am I losing my mind, have I lost it? Oh no, this just keeps getting better and better. You need to run, far away from me. Just go now before a crazy person is holding your hand."

"Baby, I didn't say you lost your mind. It's just you've been involved in a couple of very intense relationships, and we've made you fragile, and we just want you to get stronger. We are here to help you, not make things worse for you. I love you and I think Brandon loves you too."

"I love you too. Can we do something together tomorrow?"

"Nice thought, but doctor's orders, you rest tomorrow. But I'll be right next to you in this bed. I'll do work on my computer and you can rest, and get better, so you will feel like doing something with me in a couple of days."

Chapter 13

Healing

Day four of recovery and I was finally feeling strong enough to stand on my own. That was the weirdest thing that has ever happened to me. Physically, my body just said enough is enough, and wouldn't let me go on.

I had to listen and take care of it, because I didn't really have a choice. I didn't realize I'd lost so much weight, but I guess I was sicker than I'd thought. A week of not keeping anything down but some water and Ensure will do it for you.

Jacob and I were getting out of the house today. It was raining outside so we were going to the mall. He was getting me a wheelchair and we were going to buy a new pair of my wonderful sheets. Jacob had been a wonderful caretaker for me.

He said I was there for him when he needed me, when he was in the hospital, so he was honored to be by my side when I was in need. He was taking my dogs for walks, doing my laundry, vacuuming my carpets, Mr. Domestic.

I'd never been more attracted to him or wanted him more. He could see what needed to be done and do it without being asked. My ex-husband never did that for me.

After being married to someone who did not see those things and would argue with you longer than it would take to do the task, I did it all on my own, just to keep the peace. But Jacob is showing me things could be different this time if we were together. I appreciate him more than he knows. "Jacob, thank you for being here for me, you gave me strength I didn't have to give myself. I couldn't have made it without you this week."

Jacob leaned down and tenderly kissed me on the cheek, then the lips. "Baby, I'm just glad you are feeling better." Here we were at the mall, and I was exhausted just walking from the car to the front entrance of the mall.

Of course, he had made arrangements to have a wheelchair available when we came in the main entrance. A security guard stood at the entrance. Jacob told him his name and said he'd called ahead to reserve a wheelchair, and here came a wheelchair. I sat down and he pushed me through the mall.

He bought me a coffee from Starbucks, and it was just what I needed, heaven in a cup. Out of the house, fresh air, and getting a new pair of my favorite sheets ready or not, here we go. Jacob was shocked when he saw the price of those smooth as silk sheets. He reprimanded me for spending that much money on the sheet set I sent him, but he said I got the desired results I was hoping for when I made that purchase.

He didn't sleep a night without thinking of me. I knew it was the perfect gift. I love it when I get something spot on. It was worth every penny I spent, and I loved the feeling of satisfaction I got hearing him say that to me. I had a pair of butter cream-colored sheets, and Jacob had baby blue ones, so we decided on a red pair fitting for a red-hot lover bed, also Valentine's and Christmas color.

I ran into several families of my students who were concerned when they saw me in a wheelchair. I assured them I was doing much better and would be at work next week. It was great to see my little kindergarten buddies. They are so precious and loving. I miss my kids, my classroom. I hadn't thought about seeing people who knew me at the mall. But it's not like I'm out dancing on tables.

I'm being pushed in a wheelchair, not exactly like I'm faking being sick. I can't worry about what other people think about me, I just have to do what's best for me. If I can even figure out what's best for me these days.

We ate at a steak house that was new to me. It was very expensive. That must be why I hadn't visited it, but it was so delicious, I devoured my food. I was worn out by the time Jacob got me home. I took a nap and had fully intended on having sex with my boyfriend, but he said no. I thought I was in an alternate universe for a moment. He's telling me no to the offer of sex. I must look like death warmed over for him to say no to sex.

"I never thought I'd hear you say no to sex from me, how come?"

"It's not like I don't want you or desire you. I'm acting like a responsible man that loves the woman he wants to have and hold for a long time. Not just to exert myself on you with strenuous activity and have you sick for another week."

"You are leaving in a few days, and I want to be with you."

"Baby, I want you too. We'll see how you are doing tomorrow."

Jacob had been amazing during my illness. I'm so glad I'm feeling human again. I was secretly worried I was broken in a way that I wouldn't be able to pull the pieces back together. But he was my super glue. He didn't leave my side, helped me shower, actually, that was kind of fun, combed and dried my hair, dressed me.

He went beyond anything I would have ever expected him to be able and or willing to do. He loves me or he would have bolted, literally headed for the hills. But he didn't, he stayed with me, by my side working hard every day to help me get back on my feet.

Jacob said that since I'm feeling better, he wanted to talk with me, but didn't want me to feel pressured, just two friends, two lovers sharing their thoughts and dreams. I said okay. "Jenna, I want you to come back with me and live with me. I love you and don't want to lose one day of my life without you with me. I'm not happy unless you are. I mean it, Jenna.

The last six months without you in my life was a very dark time for me. I'll do anything in my power to make you happy and healthy for the rest of my life. Come home with me, Jenna. The school year is almost over, take a leave of absence and just come stay with me, get better, and see how happy we can be together. Please think about this, I love you so much."

"I will think about what you said and thank you for saying that. I love you too. But I don't think I can make a decision of that magnitude at this point of my recovery. I am weak."

"Jenna, the invitation is open, and I will have packers come pack your home and we will put your stuff in my house, we will be a blended family. I want you in my life for always. I'll be what you need me to be. I'll put your needs before mine, and I will appreciate who you are. Be with me, marry me, come away with me."

I was thinking, now this is a proposal, not an outburst after hot sex. "I can't make that decision, not yet. It's almost the end of the school year and I want to be there for the last six weeks of school. I will come out to stay with you this summer, if I can bring Molly and Moose."

"You are all welcome. When do you want to come? I'll

book your flight, it's cheaper if you buy them a month in advance."

"Okay, I can give you that." So, we got on the computer and looked at my school calendar, then booked my flight to see him three days after my last day of work. A couple days to pack up my room for end of year cleaning, and a day to pack at home and rest before I'm with Jacob.

It's his last day here, and I am feeling much better, so we spent many hours in bed. But this time for fun reasons, not recovery. We broke in my new red sheets, and they were worth the pricy investment.

Love Jacob, he's so strong and manly. He was very gentle with me, more so than usual. I kept telling him I was fine, but it was nice to be treated like I might break if he moved me too rough, or too quickly. It was a different intimacy, but wonderful all the same.

Monday came, and I went to work full time, and Jacob headed to the airport in his rental car. I was so glad he had come. I think I really was glad he came back to me, he wanted me, and I needed him. He was amazing and he didn't have to be.

He could have had work excuses, and he had money to pay someone to care for me, but he invested himself into my care. That was meaningful to me. He gave of himself and got nothing in return. He loves me, and I am still in love with him.

All this recovery time has made me realize how fragile life is, and how I need to step up my game to exercise and eat healthier. I don't ever want to get so stressed out that I go over the edge on the emotional unhealthy side and have a break down.

I felt so helpless, that was a frustrating weakness like a cloud over me. I couldn't break free from it. I wanted to climb out of the pit I was in, but it was like I couldn't get my footing and I kept sliding down this dark hole. I wanted me back, to feel like myself, to respond like a normal human would respond to normal things.

He helped me through my darkest time, he brought me back to solid ground. I'm strong because of him. He has a huge heart. He has taken up permanent residence in my heart. He has my heart in his. He's had it from our first tree swinging kiss. I look forward to spending forever with him and seeing our dreams become a reality.

My cell had messages on it that I hadn't checked in days. One message was from Doctor Doortea, who Jacob had hired. I was surprised that he called me, so I called him back. I left a message on his answering service. "I just got your message that you have test results and wanted me to call when I could talk confidentially. I was kind of worried when you left such an ominous message." I'm feeling better so maybe I'm just low iron levels or something like that. Don't get all worked up over nothing. About an hour later my phone rang.

"Jenna, this is Dr. Doortea, and I wanted to talk to you about your blood work."

"Thank you for calling me back, I hope it's not bad news."

"I'm the doctor on call today and I was checking my messages and wanted to see how you are feeling."

"Thank you so much for taking such good care of me. I never had a break down before, but I'm getting my strength back and am feeling more like myself each day. Did the tests show anything I should be concerned about?"

"Yes, that's why I'm calling. If you want to make an appointment, we can talk about this in my office, or over the phone if you prefer."

"Well since we are on the phone now, let's not prolong the suspense doc, tell me what you found."

"Jenna, you are pregnant. You need to start pre-natal vitamins and come in for pre-natal care."

"I'm sorry, what did you say?"

"You are pregnant."

"No, that's not possible. I was married for fourteen years and never used birth control, and no baby, no pregnancy, not an option for me. So how is that possible now?"

"Well, when you are sexually active with someone, that's how it happens."

"Seriously, I don't know how much you know about my situation, but I am seeing two men, Jacob and Brandon. How far along am I?"

"I don't have that information, just that your blood work came back positive. So, you need to make an appointment with an OBGYN doctor. This information is confidential, so even though Jacob paid my bill, your health information is between you and me."

"Doctor Doortea, I'm in shock. I wanted a baby when I was younger, but I'm older now, and lately I've needed naps just to take care of me. Maybe the tests are wrong, I need to call my doctor, I don't have an OBGYN doctor.

Guess I'm getting one now. What in the world do I tell Jacob and Brandon? Whose baby am I carrying? I bet it's Brandon's, but depending on how long I've been pregnant, Jacob and I had sex multiple times the night before I got sick? What a mess, what am I going to do?"

"I will have my office make an appointment for the earliest appointment to get into an OBGYN and get answers for you. Stay calm, get plenty of rest, and don't overexert yourself until you've had your OBGYN meeting and test results."

"Okay, thank you so much Doctor Doortea, for everything."

I can't believe this. How could I be pregnant? I'm thinner now than I've ever been. How can I be expecting a baby? How are Jacob and Brandon going to take this news? It's a shock. They are going to freak out. I'm going to freak out as soon as I can gather the energy to do it. After all these years wanting to be a mom, and now when I don't have a husband, I end up pregnant. I'm going to be a mom.

No wonder I've been so tired, I'm having a baby. My mom will not believe it. No, she knows me, she will totally believe this. Part of me is in shock, part of me is so excited I can't even believe this is true. I found love, now love is with me. I'm so happy.

Chapter 14

Winds of Change

I was so exhausted after teaching all day, that I had to go home and sleep. It took me a week of work and home to sleep, to gain my energy. I am just beginning to get back to normal. I keep trying to use my energy to think about what I am going to say to Brandon and to Jacob.

I didn't want to say anything to them until I knew for sure I was pregnant. I always wanted a baby, and now I've met two amazing men, and now a baby too. All my dreams are coming true. How will they take the news? I'm sure it will be shocking for them too.

I owe it to them to tell them, so they feel like I've been honest, and so they can be excited, or whatever they feel. They have the right to be a part of this too. Who should I tell first? I'll call Jacob first because he's further away and he won't rush over to my house to see me and touch my belly. Then I'll call Brandon and tell him. He already has a daughter in high school, he may not be thrilled about this. I won't know until I talk to them.

Brandon stayed away for my benefit last week, for me to get better while Jacob was here. I know he wouldn't want to add stress to my life. I hate that his last thoughts of me are of this pathetic weak woman who had problems with juggling two different men. I was going to call Jacob first, but my phone started ringing and it was Brandon. I'm excited and scared, guess I'm telling him first.

"Hi Brandon, I'm so glad you called. I was just thinking about you."

"You sound so much better, so chipper, so much better than last week. My guess is you are allergic to Jacob, and now that he's gone you are feeling better."

"Oh, Brandon, I've missed you, you are so funny. How have you been?"

"Great, just great. The woman I love sleeps with another man, and then has a break down, or something, I'm fabulous. I have to stay away from you for a week, so you don't have to deal with me versus Jacob. I'm on top of the world."

"Are you where you can talk privately?"

"Yes, or I wouldn't have called you. Why, what is it?"

"I just got off the phone with the doctor that came to my house and ran tests. He called to give me the results. I don't know how to tell you this, I've never said this out loud before in my life, but his test said I'm pregnant. Brandon? Brandon? Are you there? Did you faint? Hello?"

"I'm coming over, now. Do you need pickles or anything?"

"No, but I would love to see you, so come on over. I'll see you soon."

I hung up the phone and jumped up and down with joy. He isn't mad at me, he even sounded excited. That makes me so happy. Now I need to call Jacob.

"Jacob, this is Jenna, we need to talk as soon as possible." I just left the message when my phone started buzzing. "Jacob?"

"Yeah babe, how are you feeling?"

"That's what I'm calling you about. Are you in a place you and I can talk privately right now?"

"Yes, what's going on, what is it? Just tell me, are you okay?"

"The doctor you hired for me just called me with test results. He said I'm pregnant. I'm sort of in shock right now, how are you doing? Jacob are you there, did we get disconnected?"

"No, I'm here. So, you're pregnant?"

"Yes, and sorry to have to tell you this big news long distance, but I just found out, and wanted you to know as soon as possible."

"Umm how far along are you in your pregnancy?"

"Does that really matter?"

"Well, it could be my baby, or it could be Brandon's, so yes, I would say that it matters."

"I don't know yet. I'll keep you posted, if you want me to keep you informed. If not, that's fine too. I don't expect anything from either of you. I can do this on my own, or with one of you, or both of you. I don't know. I'm just being honest and telling you what I do know as I find out. I'll make an OBGYN doctor's appointment and when I know more, I'll send you and Brandon the latest information.

I know this is overwhelming, so I'm going to give you some time to process this. We can talk later. I am feeling better and I'm just trying to wrap my head around this news too. I just found out from the doctor's phone call a few minutes ago. I didn't think I could even have children, so this is all really shocking for me too."

"I'm glad you are feeling better. I'll call you in a couple days when all of this has had time to sink in."

"I understand."

"I've got a pressing work situation, so now that I know you are okay, I need to let you go. I'll call you soon."

After I hung up the phone, I went to the bathroom and when I came out, there was Brandon, knocking at my door. I answered the door and there he was with a huge bunch of sunflowers, my favorite. He grabbed me and gave me a big hug.

"We are going to have a baby. I'm so happy, are you happy, Jenna?"

I started crying, I was so relieved he was happy, I could see it in his eyes, his face, and hear it in his tone, he meant it. It made me so happy. He didn't ask whose baby it was, or how far along I was, nothing. He just unconditionally was here for me, loved me, and brought me flowers to show he was excited too. This man is wonderful to me.

"Why are you crying? Are you okay?"

"I'm so happy that you are happy. I was so worried that with a high school daughter, you wouldn't want to start over with a new baby. You've already gone through all this once, so I didn't know how you'd feel about being at this point of our lives and starting out together with a baby."

"I love you, and a baby is a gift from God. I will be there for you, for every doctor's appointment, anything and everything you want me to be there for, I'm all in. If you want a quick wedding, I'll do that too. We love each other and have a great foundation for a future together. I don't care about Jacob, he's your past. You and me and our baby, we are the future."

"I don't know for sure if this is your biological baby. Would that make a difference to you?"

"This is your baby. I would love your baby whether it's mine or Jacobs. I love you. I have a feeling it's mine, like 99% sure it's ours. Have you talked to Jacob yet, does he know you are expecting?"

"Yes, I called him after I talked to you, and I think he's in shock. It certainly is unexpected. I can understand that."

"This puts a whole new light on you being so sick last week, doesn't it? Can I kiss your tummy?"

"Yes, of course, thank you for being supportive, I needed your strength. Can you stay the night with me, if it's just to cuddle? I'm not ready for sex, but just having you by my side would be wonderful."

"I'm here till you kick me out."

"What about Kourtney?"

"I'll make arrangements with her mom. Let me make some calls then I'm all yours."

I felt loved and supported during this life altering event in my life. My mind raced between Jacob's and Brandon's reactions to the pregnancy news. It's shocking news, yet I got two very different responses, from two very different men. Not that one was right or wrong, just two totally different responses to me when I was scared and in need. Brandon is here for me now, and supportive, even offered to give me a quick wedding, thoughtful thinking of me.

"I don't want anyone else to know about my condition, until we get more news from the doctor. I'm not telling my mom, brother, anyone else just you, me, and Jacob."

"Are you worried about the baby?"

"Honestly, I don't know what to expect. I have never been pregnant, and this is all very new. I never dreamed this could happen to me. I think I'm sort of in shock too. I'm so glad you are here with me, to share all this with me, it makes this all real and special. You really are a wonderful man. Are you hungry, thirsty, tired? I'm thirsty and tired. If you don't mind, I would love to grab a bottle of water and just cuddle in bed until we fall asleep. I have to go to work tomorrow. Maybe we could meet tomorrow and have dinner together?"

"That would be great, but I have plans tomorrow night. You are welcome to come with me, but it's a work department meeting. Some of the instructors bring their spouses, so if you want to come, I'd love to show you off. You met some of the guys at Jon's birthday party. They would love to see you again."

"Thanks for inviting me, but I think I may just eat at home and rest. I don't want to overdo it until I've regained all my energy and strength back."

"I can cancel if you need me to be with you, you and the baby are my priority."

"No, you do your work meeting, I'll be fine. I'm not a little girl that you have to take care of. I'm your friend, your lover, your maybe baby momma. Time will tell." After getting ready for bed, he got in on his side, me on mine, and we snuggled in my fresh from the dryer, lavender scented sheets. We kissed and things got a little heated, but then he said, "No, I want you to rest."

As much as I love him and wanted to be with him, I was exhausted. I checked to make sure the alarm was set so he could get in the shower first, and then I could get in and go to work.

The next day I smiled all day long. My cheeks actually were cramping from all the smiling. I checked my phone for texts and Brandon sent me a message telling me he was thinking about me and wanted to spend the night all week. If I was okay with that, he'd bring his clothes after his meeting tonight.

Then I saw a text from Jacob. It said, "I haven't slept for thinking of your news, and how I was so shocked, that I didn't respond the way I wanted to. Please call me tonight so we can talk. I'm here if you need me. I've never been a dad before and this just shocked me, but Jenna, I would expect nothing less from you. You always have blown my mind. It's never boring with you."

I called and made my first pregnancy doctor's appointment, for the first available date which was in two weeks. I texted both Brandon and Jacob to inform them of when my appointment was scheduled. I also asked Jacob not to tell anyone until we know more from the doctor.

Brandon stayed the night every night that first week and we enjoyed the excitement together and rekindled our love.

He wanted to go with me to the doctor and I was excited for him to come with me.

I was making an effort to eat healthier, and Brandon was all over that and very helpful. He's a sweetheart. Never let me down, not once. In all the curve balls I've thrown him, he's always been there, loving me, forgiving me, and supporting me.

Jacob has been very quiet through all this. I had two days to go before my doctor's appointment and I started spotting light at first then heavier. I called Brandon in tears from work, and he told me to call my doctor then to call him back.

My doctor told me to come to the hospital immediately. I called Brandon back, and he left his job to pick me up at work, he didn't want me to drive. I told my school nurse, they got me a substitute, and Brandon picked me up. The nurse told the secretary and the principal my condition and they said they'd keep it confidential.

At the hospital they ran tests and Brandon was there with me, holding my hand when they told me, I'd lost the baby. I was just getting my mind wrapped around being a mom, and now that dream was gone again. I looked at Brandon and his eyes were full of tears.

"I'm so sorry." I pulled him on the bed with me and he just held me. Later he whispered, "Sweetheart we can try again later once we've healed from this, if you want a child. Or we can adopt, we can do whatever you want. I'm so sorry babe, what can I do?"

"I hate to ask you, but would you please call Jacob and tell him our news? I just want to go home and try to recover from this. I'm so sorry I lost our baby, Brandon. I don't understand why this happened, but I'm so sorry."

"Honey, it's not your fault. God knew our baby was so special that he wanted him or her to stay with Him. We will meet our baby one day in heaven."

I just grabbed his arm and cried on his shoulder. They

told me they needed to do a procedure to clean out the uterus, a DNC, then I'd be able to go home. Brandon didn't leave my side for any of it, he's remarkable. I got my clothes on, checked out of the hospital, and Brandon wheeled me out to his car.

He is so sweet, I'm sure he is hurting after losing a baby, but all his words and actions were about me. I was trying not to be so self-centered, to think about him too, but I just kept thinking about our baby and our loss, and couldn't think past that, as much as I tried.

I wasn't hungry but he wanted me to eat, so I wouldn't get sick and run down again. We went to I-HOP, my favorite breakfast place, for a late-night meal. I ate more than I thought I would, it tasted really good.

We had been at the hospital for almost five hours. I was so tired I just slept in the car on the way home. He took me home, stayed the night, and sometime when I was asleep, called Jacob to tell him the news. That couldn't have been easy for him.

I woke up before the alarm and was getting in the shower before work, when the tears just poured down my face. I was grieving, but I would be okay. I had a man who loved me and was there for me in my time of need. He's the one for me. Sometimes things happen for a reason, and he shined for me through this. He's my hero.

Brandon was sitting on the stool when I stepped out of the shower. "You have the day off today. I called your school nurse yesterday from the hospital when you were getting dressed and she said to follow doctors' orders and take today off. The nurse said she would tell the principal the confidential news and that no one else would know, unless you want them to know."

I'm so glad I have the day off because I'm an emotional mess. I just want to curl up in a ball and not get out of bed. Brandon said he's staying at home with me today. I told him I loved him and never felt closer to him than I do after going through this loss together. I want him, I need him, and so I said it. "Brandon, I think it's time we go looking for that ring, if you still want to marry me."

"You shouldn't make life altering decisions when you are under great stress. I do love you and want to buy you a ring and propose in a manner that's worthy of you. But you need time to heal from this loss before we can move on to celebrating our future together. Do you understand I'm not rejecting you? I'm just saying that soon, Jenna, in the very near future, you will be my wife."

"Okay, you are being logical and thinking when I'm just being emotional. Once again, we are a great team. So glad I have you, I love you."

"I love you too."

"Honey, I'm probably just going to sleep all day, so if you need to work or want be somewhere else, I totally understand. I don't need a babysitter. I'm fine. You don't have to stay and watch me sleep. But you lost a baby too, so if you want to curl up with me all day, then I want you to do what you want."

"If you really don't mind, then I will let you sleep, and I will take care of my classes. I will come back tonight if you promise you will call me if you need anything."

"I would appreciate that. I think I'm just going to sleep anyway, so go take care of your work." I sat up and he kissed me, and then I heard him shut the door. I heard his car pull out of the drive and I couldn't even cry. I just wanted to sleep, to escape, but my mind was racing. I knew what I had to do first. I had to call Jacob.

"Jacob, this is Jenna. I just wanted to call and see how you are doing after hearing we lost the baby. I'm home today, just crashing in bed. I'm so sorry." My phone rang minutes after the message.

"Jenna, you are home?"

"Yes."

"Why aren't you at the hospital?"

"They released me, Jacob. They did a DNC procedure and told me to rest the next twenty-four hours. I'm okay. How are you?"

"You told me I was going to be a dad, and my world turned upside down. I've had my builders drawing up blueprints to add on to my place so you could have a playroom on the main level. The baby didn't need stairs, so I was adding a room on the first floor at the back of the house. I have the land staked out, and they were supposed to pour cement foundations tomorrow, so I've been making phone calls to cancel things."

"I had no idea. You seemed so distant when I told you, not one word of excitement to me. I didn't think you wanted the baby. I understand shocked, I didn't know I could ever have that experience. I'm so glad to know that you were excited in your way. You just do a terrible job of telling me what you are thinking, feeling, and doing. Your heart is always in the right place, we just have a link missing in our communication."

"You didn't even call me to say we've lost our baby. You had Brandon tell me. And now you are giving me a lecture on my communication skills, you've got to be kidding me."

"I'm going to sleep now. I'm wishing you well, goodbye."

"Just a minute, just give me a chance to communicate."

"We can talk later, I'm really exhausted, and I don't have the energy to fight with you right now."

"We aren't fighting, but we can talk later if that's what you want."

"When do you want to talk?"

"Give me four hours for a nap, and call me, so I don't sleep the whole day."

"Okay, I'll talk to you in four hours." Click.

"Jenna, it's been four hours, pick up the phone. Call me back when you wake up." I didn't ever hear the phone ring and my phone was plugged in and right next to my bed.

Brandon got off work and had called to see what he could bring for dinner, and I didn't hear the phone ring with him either. Brandon was in my bedroom staring at me with a look of concern on his face when I woke up.

"If I hadn't seen and heard your phone ringing and watch you sleep through it, I would have thought you'd turned your phone off. But you were out, not responding to a sound. How are you feeling?"

"I'm sorry, Brandon. What time is it?

"Seven p.m. are you hungry?"

"I'm starving. I know you are Mr. Health Food, but can we have pizza tonight? I need cheese, yummy hot carbs."

"Sure, I'll call and get us salads and pizza. I'll go pick it up, so you don't have to wait for a cold pizza."

"Thanks, that sounds wonderful. Hey, take some money out of my purse for the pizza and salads."

"I don't think so. I'll be back in about thirty minutes. That will give you time to freshen up and wake up so you can eat."

"Thanks sweetheart."

I called Jacob as soon as Brandon left the house. "Jacob?"

"Jenna, where the hell have you been? I've called you over and over. You knew I was calling you in four hours. What happened?"

"I was sound asleep. I had the phone right next to my bed, but I honestly did not hear the phone ring at all. I just now woke up and am calling you.

Brandon came over to check on me because he tried to call me too. He's getting pizza for me, and it sounded good at the time, but now I don't think that's a good idea. I don't know. Maybe egg rolls?"

"Now that I can breathe again, knowing you are okay, do you want to talk about everything we've been going through?"

"Sure, I'm listening, what are you thinking? How are you feeling? What do you want?"

"I want to be there with you, and if you'd given me the slightest hint that you wanted me with you, I would have been there. But you had Brandon, and by the way, it's a great way to hear about you losing the baby from the lips of Brandon. That was the cruelest thing you've ever done to me, Jenna."

"Jacob, stop for just a minute. Listen to me, I'm really sorry. I just wanted you to know as soon as possible, and I couldn't talk about me losing my baby much less give you details without self-destructing. It was Brandon or the doctor to call you, and I thought at least Brandon wasn't a stranger. I'm sorry I hurt you. I thought about waiting to tell you until I was able to talk about it, but then I didn't want you to be hurt that Brandon knew about it, hours or days before you.

I tried to think of you. I thought I was doing what was my best option at the time. I'm sorry I hurt you. That was never my intention. I keep doing that to you. We keep hurting each other. We are far apart in so many ways, location, communication, family, baby. No matter how much we love each other, we keep going back to me needing you and not feeling like you are there for me.

Jacob, we need to let each other go. I love you and always will, but it rips me up inside to hurt you over and over and over. I can't keep doing this.

Brandon is a good man and he's here for me and I love him too. I will be fine, Jacob. You have to let me go. I want you to move on and be happy."

"Jenna, it sounds like you couldn't put two words together for me when it had to do with the loss of our baby, but when it comes to leaving me, you have it all figured out. So much for me having a chance to communicate. You want me gone, Jenna, goodbye."

"Jacob, please don't be mad at me. I'm sorry. I want

only the best for you."

"I had the best, Jenna. Now you are throwing me away like I'm trash. So now I am feeling like you did when I tried to protect you. Great. Well, have a good life, Jenna." I hung up the phone. I looked up and Brandon was standing in the doorway, staring at me with the pizza in one hand and a shocked look on his face. He just stood there staring at me, not speaking, then finally he broke the silence.

"Did I hear you right? Did you just tell Jacob he's your past and I'm your future?"

"Brandon, you are, but only if you want to be. I didn't know you were here yet, and I didn't know you could hear my last conversation with Jacob. I'm sorry you heard that. You told me I shouldn't make any major decisions when I'm stressed, or depressed, whatever I am, but I didn't think you'd mind me saying goodbye to a good man, and old friend, and let him move on."

With a big smile on his face he said, "There is no problem here. I'm thrilled I got to hear that conversation. You just made my year! I love you and you don't need him in your life. I promise to be here for you and to love you forever. I can't wait until you are feeling better so I can take you out and propose to you properly."

"Thanks, but right now I just feel really bad about the baby, and now saying goodbye to Jacob. I just need some carbs. Let's eat in bed. Please just be patient with me, Brandon. I'll be back to my old self in time. I need to get back on track and feel like myself again."

"Sweetheart, I'm not going to rush you, or pressure you for anything. We are a team. I want you, always have and always will. Now, do you want anything to drink with those cheesy carbs. How about some Diet Dr. Pepper?"

"We communicate so well. Yes, I need my Diet Dr., thanks."

While we ate, Brandon was telling me about his day and his classes, and he actually had me laughing out loud twice.

I love him. I really do. He is good for me and I hope that I will one day be worth all the trouble I have put him through.

Brandon was busy at work because a co-worker was in an accident. He was doing double duty covering his classes and his friends' classes too. That was okay with me because I really hadn't been alone in several weeks, and I thought I was strong enough to be alone for a while. But once again, I was wrong.

Chapter 15

Regrets

It had been weeks since I said goodbye to Jacob, since I'd said goodbye to my baby, and I did everything I could to keep busy and not think about either one of those losses, but it was overwhelming. I was running on numb and adrenaline. I hadn't really slept in weeks, and I was pretty sure it was because I missed Jacob. I loved him, and I've been miserable inside ever since I told him to move on.

Brandon told me not to make any major decisions when I was upset, but I did, and look at me now. I'm miserable. I miss Jacob. Do I just want what I can't have? Why can't I be happy?

I'm sure Brandon knows that I'm not me, I'm just a shell these days, and it's not fair to him. But I think he thinks it's because I lost the baby. But that's only part of it. Brandon has been wonderful, but he can't fill this void in me. No one can.

Well, that's not exactly true. I know only Jesus can

satisfy my soul, and I have Jesus in my heart. But my thoughts and heart keep gravitating to Jacob, and I've blown it with him forever. I can't believe I was so stupid. I tried to save him from further hurt from me, and I only hurt myself in the process. I need to learn to live like now is my forever. But I can't pretend, not to myself.

The next thing I know, I'm reaching for my phone. No, you cannot call Jacob. You sent him packing like he did to you once before. I know what I can do; I can call his brother Andrew. He would talk to me. he would tell me how Jacob is doing, without talking to Jacob, without having to hear his voice. I wouldn't have to break my heart or his again, I just want to make sure he's okay, that he's happy.

I called Andrew. Oh crap, what time is it? Good, it's only ten p.m. and it's ringing.

"Hello."

"Hello, Andrew, I'm sorry to call so late, but this is Jenna." It was silent on the other end of the phone.

"Andrew, hello?"

"Jenna, why are you calling me?"

"I kicked Jacob out of my life, and I wasn't thinking clearly. I'd just lost a baby and I was out of my head. I pushed him out of my life, and I miss him. I'm not complete without him. I've tried to be on my own, I've tried to be with Brandon, and he is nothing but wonderful to me, but he's not Jacob.

Andrew, just tell me Jacob is doing well, that he has moved on, and I'll never call or bother you or him again. He will never have to know I called you. Just tell me he's happy and moved on, so I can move on too. Andrew, did you hear what I said? Are you there?"

"Jenna?"

"Oh, dear Lord, Jacob, I'm so sorry! I thought I dialed Andrew."

"Yes, you did. I'm with Andrew and he put you on

speaker phone."

"Give the phone back to Andrew and take the phone off speaker. I have a few private words I want to say to him."

"Jenna, did you mean what you said when you thought you were just talking to Andrew?"

"Of course, I did, but I didn't expect to hear your voice, to talk to you right now. I know I hurt you, and I'm sorry for that, I really am. I had no idea you would be with Andrew this late. I shouldn't have called again, I'm so sorry. I've got to go. I'm feeling sick all of a sudden."

"Wait, what do you mean sick?" "I mean I feel like I'm going to throw up, I've got to go." I hung up the phone, then I ran to the bathroom, and threw up. I feel like I was going to pass out. The room was spinning and there I was again. How in the world did that just happen? I didn't want to hear his voice, hear his pain, his disbelief, I just wanted to know he was doing okay. Now he knows I called, knows everything I was thinking, and I've hurt him again.

The nausea and vomiting continued. I was freezing. When I had the strength to get off the stool, I took off my clothes, and sat in the hot shower and cried, and cried, and cried.

I don't know how long I was in the shower, but I used all the hot water, so I got out. I dried off and threw my clothes and my sheets in the washing machine. I wanted them clean and hot from the dryer. I sat down to dry my hair while my sheets were washing and then put on my warmest pajamas. It was late but I wasn't tired, too much on my mind.

I started to feel a little better. I had a Diet Dr. Pepper and was gaining my strength. I put my sheets in the dryer but didn't feel like I had the strength to put them back on the bed. I had just about decided to go to sleep on my couch, when there was a knock on my door. Good grief, it's almost 1:30 in the morning, and I'm in my jammies. Who in the world? No, it couldn't be him, it has to be Brandon.

"Who is it?"

"Jenna, it's me, it's Jacob, let me in." He didn't have to ask me twice.

"I can't believe you're here. How did you get here so quickly?"

"I have a private plane for business. I just made this my business. Are you okay?"

I started crying like a weak baby. "Jacob, have I ruined everything? Did you come all this way to tell me this time we are over for good? I deserve that; but please don't say it." Just then the dryer buzzer went off and we both jumped.

"Are you doing laundry at this time of night?"

"Yes, I was freezing and wanted warm sheets."

"Ever heard of a blanket?"

"I know, I'm weird, but I couldn't sleep, and I love fresh sheets. Since you're here, would you help me put them on my bed? I don't think I have the strength to do it by myself."

"Jenna, are you really this frail, this fragile?"

"Apparently, I am tonight. Why are you here? What are you doing at my door?"

"It's late, let me help you with those hot sheets." Jacob pretty much put the sheets on the bed by himself and was tucking me in bed on my side. He was getting in bed on the other side. I set the alarm so I wouldn't miss work in case we stayed up much later talking.

"I figured as quickly as you change your mind, I had better get here as soon as possible, or you would be out of my life again. I can't take this, you love me one minute, then you love me not. You need to make up your mind once and for all and stick with your decision. Know what you want, and why you want it, and keep what you want and need. Figure it out for God's sake and mine."

"I never said I didn't love you. I've always loved you, that's why I've been so miserable. I don't think I can be happy unless you are happy. That's why I called your stupid brother. But he betrayed me."

"No, when Andrew said your name, and pointed to the phone, I walked up and hit the speaker button, so actually it wasn't him betraying you. I just wanted to know why you were calling my brother at ten at night.

Then I heard what you were telling him, and it was like God heard, and answered my prayers. You said you love me and wanted me. That's all I want. I love you, and I'm not letting you go again. I'm not going to control you, but I will take care of you. I love you, and I am going to marry you. Do you want to marry me?"

"Yes, I do. I'm not complete without you with me, in my life. I've made such a mess of things over and over again but that's all over. I need and want you Jacob, you are my future. Let's get married this weekend."

"Are you feeling better?"

"I'm feeling stronger by the minute. Scoot over here and give me some sugar."

"These sheets smell so good, and you are as soft and beautiful as I remembered. Are you up for a proper reunion, or do we need to wait for morning?"

"It is morning. And I have to go to work in a few hours. But you are next to me, in my bed, and this is the best "get well" incentive I've ever had. I think I could handle some affection. I've missed you so much." I went to the bathroom to freshen up, brush my teeth, comb my hair, and hurried back to bed.

His kisses were gentle and slow, and then our love just caught fire. Our passion filled the room. It's like our bodies were just functioning, running on auto pilot before we touched.

Then when we finally found each other, our bodies were in such need of one another, and the desire was so overwhelming, it was like coming home and winning the lottery, all at once. I was so comfortable with my soul mate that I couldn't stop, I didn't want to stop. My old life is over, and my future will always be with Jacob. I was exhausted, but I didn't feel sick, I felt complete and totally satisfied.

I'm not going to keep playing this Brandon, Jacob merry-go-round with our minds and hearts. It's Jacob. I have to be with him, to have a chance at ever being truly happy. It's not a choice, Jacob is the part of me that I need, that gives me joy and peace. I love him and more shocking than that is, he's forgiven me for my craziness, and loves me too.

We will tell Brandon together tomorrow or later today. I will never be alone with Brandon again. I've made that promise to myself, and an unspoken promise to my beloved, Jacob. My past is settled, and I only want to live with and for Jacob. I want to start our future together.

The alarm went off and we were wrapped up in one another's arms. I've never wanted to play hooky more than I did this morning. Jacob was handsome, and loved his slightly rumpled, black, wavy hair. I just wanted to run my hands through his hair, but I knew where that would lead, and I had to get to work. So, I leaned over, gave him a kiss, and told him I had to jump in the shower. He offered to join me, but I told him if he got in, I'd never make it to work on time. He kindly let me escape.

He stayed in the bedroom watching me dry off, get dressed, dry my hair, put on my makeup, brush my teeth, but I didn't care. I wanted to share every part of my life with him. He just smiled and was caressing me, rubbing my leg, my arm, my back, brushing my hair. I love his touch, his smile, his smell. I love him.

"What are your plans for the day while I'm at work? Will you be here at my house when I get off work? How long can you stay? If you need to get back to Kentucky, I'll understand."

"Easy girl, what time will you be off tonight? And I will

be right here, waiting for you."

"I have to tutor two students after work, so I will be free after 6:30. Maybe you could meet me, and we could go out for dinner."

"Sure, under one condition."

"Name it."

"You don't talk to Brandon without me being with you. You are weak when it comes to him. He's a good guy but I just don't want to share you anymore, I can't and won't go down that road, ever again with you. We are from this moment, well from last night actually, exclusive. If you are in agreement, then I will meet you wherever you want for dinner."

"Of course, I won't answer my phone if he calls, until you are with me. Why don't you just keep my phone, then you will know for sure."

"I trust you. If you tell me you won't talk to him, then I believe you. You may need your phone."

"I have to go. Feel free to eat anything in the house, make yourself at home, and I can't wait to see you tonight. We will have the entire weekend together. I love you."

I was busy with my day and didn't check my phone until after school when I was heading to the public library to tutor my students. One of my students cancelled his tutoring session, so I would be finished an hour earlier. I called Jacob to tell him, and he sounded as excited as I felt.

An hour later, he was at the library doors, when I was walking out to my car. I didn't care who saw us, I kissed him to show him just how happy I was that he's in my life again. His kiss was just as expressive too.

"I am starving, do you know what you're hungry for? Something that you like but can't get easily back in the country?" He gave me the look. "I said food Jacob, you know I'm talking about food."

"How about Tex-Mex?"

I didn't care, I can always eat chips, salsa, and queso

dip, so I got in his car and off we went to the restaurant.

On our drive, Jacob asked, "Did you hear from Brandon today?"

"Yes, a couple of times, but I haven't listened to his messages because I didn't want you to think I was playing games with the two of you."

"Let's listen to them, and we need to tell him we are together, and the sooner the better." He left a message that Kourtney would be out of town this weekend, so he was inviting me over for a slumber party. I just looked at Jacob, and he gave me a disapproving glare. I wanted to laugh out loud but thought I shouldn't under the circumstances.

"Jacob, Brandon is an amazing man. I think if the situation was different, you two would really like one another."

"I'm not going to sit here and listen to you tell me how wonderful he is. You do realize that he is the "other man". If you are with me, be loyal to me."

"I'm sorry. I don't mean to be unkind or disloyal, I just wanted you to know he's really a great person, and I don't want to hurt him. Let's just tell him so we can move on, once and for all."

Then we listened to the second message from Brandon. He said he was sorry he had to cancel on our slumber party weekend, but he had a business opportunity to speak as a guest lecturer at Stanford University, due to a last-minute cancellation of one of their speakers. Brandon was excited, apologetic, and headed out of town, unless he got a call from me telling him I needed him to stay.

"Oh, we can't tell him now, not when he has to be his best in front of hundreds of people for his work. We will wait until he calls saying his conference went well, and we will tell him then. Even if it has to be on the phone, we will tell him after his work conference. Are you on board with that?"

"I'm fine with that. We are in agreement. We will tell

him as soon as he gets back from his guest lecture appearance. Let's stop talking about him and eat."

After our food, Jacob dropped me off at the library to get my car. I told him that since our recent past, I'd like to change my car's name from baby to something else. We brainstormed names and settled on "Red". It's simple enough, even I can remember it.

We got to the house and Jacob let me in the drive first so I could park in the garage. Then he got out of his car, came up to my door, opened it, and walked me into the house. There were red rose petals all over the floor, and the sweet smell was subtle and pleasant. I looked at him questioning. Then on the table I saw a vase with dozens of long stem coral, yellow, and pink roses.

"What is all this?"

"Jenna, I love you. You are the love of my life, and I want you to feel loved and treasured always. You have to tell me what you want and need, and I will always do or be what you want me to be. You don't need another man on stand-by, you can count on me. I will be here for you. I love you."

"Jacob, I love the flowers. I do feel special with you, always have, and I always will. Communication is a two-way street. You have to tell me what you want and need too, because I want you to be happy forever, with me."

"Have a seat. I want to have a serious talk with you for a few minutes."

"Okay." I thought we were being serious.

"You want a drink?"

"Yes, I'd love a Diet Dr. Pepper."

"I'll get it, babe." He brought me a soda and then bent down on one knee. He had an engagement ring in the other hand. Jacob had called the jewelry store in Branson that we'd shopped at over a year earlier and was able to get the ring I really loved and still be back in time to meet me for dinner. What a wonderful feeling to know we really are going to belong to each other finally, officially, forever.

Jacob was down on one knee, and with a sweet, yet nervous looking smile, proposed. I was so emotional I can't tell you for sure the exact words he said, but he promised to make all my dreams come true. That he would guard my heart with his love and use all his strength and power to fill our lives with joy and mutual respect. I wish I'd had a tape player going because it was a genuine first-class proposal. One I could be proud of, I think. All I could do was nod my head and say, "Yes, Jacob, forever yes!"

"Did you get your ring that I had designed for you too?"

"Yes, the ring you had inscribed for me is in a ring box. I picked it up when I got your ring. I thought I'd save us the trip back to Branson. You, my dear, have an engagement ring, and a wedding ring too. Rings are taken care of, now we need a wedding."

"I love this ring! It was my first pick of the rings we looked at. I love it, but more importantly I love you." I was so excited that's all I could think to say. "Jacob, I love you, love you, like you too!" Then I heard the music. He found my remote and started the stereo. We stood up and danced in my living room. Then he carried me to my bedroom, and we celebrated our unity with our private engagement party. Best engagement party I've ever been to, ever!

"I finally feel like sunset and sunrise all rolled up together. You make me feel healed, and at peace. Thank you for loving me. I don't deserve you, but I will always love you. When are we getting married?"

"I brought the correspondence we did a year ago with the blood work, etc., so we could get married when and where you want to."

"Let's pack my bags, get yours, take my dogs to the kennel, and go to Bora Bora for our honeymoon. I don't care where we get married. I'd like to get married in a park, someplace open and free, natural and real. And as far as my work, I'll be leaving to go with you to Kentucky.

With my year of missing so many days, I missed for funerals, murders, your car wreck, being sick, losing a baby, chances are I'm not going to get a glowing referral for this year anyway. Let's do it, let's get a preacher to marry us. I'll call Jeff and see if mom can join us tomorrow. Is that too soon?"

"I'm fine with all of that. Let me make some calls and see if we can get a preacher tomorrow on such short notice. If we can, then I'll call my family so they can fly up, and we can have an evening wedding. You will need tomorrow morning to find a dress."

"We are going to need more time than a day. What do you think if we give ourselves a week? On second thought, I don't want the big wedding, I just want us and immediate family. If you want your family here you need to call them, because I want to marry you tomorrow night. Off to our honeymoon and then it's us forever, no more delays with my soulmate, Jacob."

"I have lesson plans for the next three weeks, so that should be enough for a sub to get a feel for what I am doing in my class, routines, and procedures to keep my kindergarteners on track for their graduation ceremony in May. They will be fine without me. I will miss them, but I'm ready to live my happily ever after. Let's do it, let's get married tomorrow."

After intimate encounters, we made phone calls. My mom by this point knew it would be Jacob that would be the one for me. She knows me and sees things I don't see myself sometimes. She is just glad that I'm better, and finally decided, and settled to move on with my life. Not living on a ping pong table, as she called it, bouncing from Brandon to Jacob.

Jeff wasn't happy, but said he'd walk me down the aisle. He and his family are coming in the morning. Jacob is going to fly us to Miami, and we will catch a flight to Bora Bora from there. He's already got the e-tickets printed out and in his wallet.

"Jacob, is your family coming?"

"Yes, they are."

"I just had a thought do you have a passport? You need one to go to Bora Bora."

"Yes, I do, thanks for reminding me. Do you?"

"Yes. Give me your passport, and I will keep it with mine if you are okay with that."

"Sure, I'm fine with one less thing for me to have to keep track of. You are going to be my husband, the one taking care of me and my endeavors, so you are welcome to any and all of my stuff anytime."

We finished up our phone calls and after all the excitement, we were really tired. We went to bed, and I sat the alarm for nine because the mall opened at ten. I couldn't wait to shop for my dress.

"Jacob, do you have things you need to buy tomorrow? Or are you free to go with me to shop for a dress? Do you have a tux? We need to get you a tux for our wedding."

"I am yours to do and go wherever we can get you a dress and me a tux. Or my brother can bring me one from home, whatever you want me to wear, I'll wear it."

"This is your first wedding, but it's going to be your only wedding, so, if you want the big wedding, we can slow this down. I'm sorry for being so selfish. I just am excited to finally be your wife."

"Babe, I just want you. Guys really don't care about the wedding, just the honeymoon."

"Okay, it's just that I don't want you to ever feel cheated or slighted when it comes to your wedding day."

"I don't and I won't feel anything but relief that you finally married me. I'd love to go with you and see you undress, I mean, dress up in princess attire or wedding dresses, whatever you want to call them."

"With you by my side, I might even enjoy this wedding. I guess there is a first for everything. Can we afford this wedding and a honeymoon now?"

"We have plenty of money, that won't be a problem for us."

"Do you want me to sign a pre-nuptial agreement? I will if you want me to. I want to sign it so you won't ever think I married you for your money. You are much more than what you've accomplished. I love who you are, and who I am when I'm with you. I'll sign your pre-nuptial, just give it to me, and I'll sign it."

"You don't need to sign anything of the sort. We are going to be one in every way. What's mine is yours and what's yours is mine. Good to know we are communicating and both on the same page. I've had your name on all my stuff for a year now, so if anything happened to me, you would get everything anyway. I really love you."

"Tomorrow we are going to be married. I'm so excited. We have got to get some sleep, or we will be sleeping through our wedding and honeymoon, and we can't have that now, can we?"

"Not a chance, not going to happen. But I do agree we need sleep."

Alarm set, we jumped in the shower, brushed our teeth, dried off and crashed in each other's arms. Tomorrow I will be Mrs. Jenna Jamison, tomorrow is my wedding day. Then the song filled my thoughts before I fell off to sleep: Tomorrow, tomorrow, I love you, tomorrow, you're only a day away.

"Molly and Moose, I need to call the vet to reserve their room for a week. Put that on our to-do list."

"Got it babe, now turn off your brain and go to sleep. We have a big day tomorrow."

We were in bed for maybe five minutes, and I couldn't take being quiet any longer. I stood up in bed and started jumping up and down and squealing a high-pitched happy squeal. Jacob reached for the light and said, "What are you doing?"

"I can't sleep, I'm so excited. I'm doing my happy dance. I thought that would help me sleep. Come and join me."

Jacob didn't feel the need for jumping on the bed, he just shook his head. He had another way to relieve extra energy and excitement, and it didn't sound like anything I would say no to.

But since it's the night before my wedding, I thought we should wait until we were married. He humored me a little longer with the jumping on the bed, then I was ready to be quiet and go to sleep. Jacob turned off the lights and we spent our last night single together.

Chapter 16

The Wedding

I woke up and was so excited that Jacob and I were finally going to be united before God and family forever. I wouldn't be living in sin and making so many bad choices that hurt the people I loved. I was going to marry the man I practically grew up with, the man who wants to spend forever with me.

It must be true love because what man wants to go dress shopping with his fiancé? How sweet is that? I know it's not something he will really enjoy, but I love him because he wants to be there with me. and for me, to help me decide the important decision of the dress.

He's wonderful! I know the groom isn't supposed to see the bride before the wedding, the dress, etc., but observing all the rules of etiquette didn't make any difference for me the last time I got married.

I walked down the aisle and it was not that exciting special moment I had always dreamed it was going to be. I want to enjoy this journey with the love of my life and do things differently. This is his first and last wedding, and I don't want him to miss out on anything.

We went to a bridal shop and I didn't want the long white traditional dress like I'd had before. I asked Jacob what he wanted, and he said I could walk down the aisle naked, and he'd be happy. That isn't going to happen, so I picked a pink frilly dress that was low cut in the front, with clear, soft, baby pink mesh like lace, and buttons all the way down to my lower back. The dress was a size six and that was shocking to me, because my first wedding dress was a size 14, so I guess I've lost some weight. I feel the same, and in my mind, I look the same, so I'm not sure about their dress sizes here, but it's encouraging.

Anyway, I walked out in the pale pink dress, and Jacob asked the salesclerk to leave us for a moment. I thought he didn't like it and wanted to tell me privately. But he came up to me, felt the material, spun me around in front of the three-way mirror and whispered, "Jenna, you've never looked more beautiful than you do right now. This is the dress!"

I couldn't have been happier. I loved the dress too, it fit like a glove, and we were short on time. But I wanted him to have a frame of reference, so I said, "I love this dress too, I really do, but I want you to see me in two other dresses we picked out.

If you still feel this is the best, which at this point I am in agreement with you, then we are off to get my hair and nails done. And you, my dear, are getting a tux, with a pink vest, or tie or cummerbund, if that's alright with you?"

"I'd be glad to go back and help you get out of that dress, if you need some help."

"No, that will happen later on our honeymoon."

"Maybe you're right, we should look at other dresses, because that dress has a lot of buttons and I am not a patient man."

Okay, here came dress number two. It's a cream-colored

dress, with layers of lace and pearls, and it's a V-neck too. I liked it better on the hanger, and Jacob was in agreement, so I didn't keep that one on long. My third dress was a red, sort of a blue-red not an orange-red colored dress. It was rich looking, not hookerish. It was long and straight cut with a ruffle around the bottom. It was studded with red pearly looking beads. It was really beautiful and fit really snug in a very form fitted style.

The salesclerk said it didn't look tight, but I had to take small steps to get out of the dressing room. I needed help to step up on the platform in front of the mirrors. He walked over to me, felt the dress and said, "You look sexier than hell. I mean you look fire rocket hot!"

"Do we have a winner? Or do we need to keep looking?"

"Oh, we have a winner, that's you, baby. But my favorite is still the pink dress. That's something I never thought I'd say. But that's your dress, if you like it the best too."

"I do, I love the pink one and that dress fits the best, it's comfortable, and I love the front and back of it. It is everything I could want in a dress. I love it, how much is it?"

"$8,000.00."

"Seriously? NO WAY! Jacob, we are not paying that much. We are out of here."

"We can be out of here, but we are leaving with your dress, it's a done deal. Do you have a bag to hang it in so we can carry this to the wedding? What about shoes? Do you have shoes at home, or do we need special wedding shoes?"

"I have wedding shoes at home, and we are not spending that much on a dress!"

"Yes, we are. You are not going to feel second class, or your dress is like a cheap hotel, like your first marriage. I want only the best for you, and honey, we can afford this.

Don't you get it? I have money, we have money, Jenna.

We are not two struggling teachers living paycheck to paycheck. Your finances just got a big raise, so don't focus on the money, we are fine in that area, okay? You are going to have to get used to letting me spend money on you. I love you, and that's a way I can show you, to make you feel special. I want to do this for you, for us. You look stunning in that dress, it's you, one of a kind, delicate yet strong, it's your dress."

"Really, are you sure this isn't going to set you back?"

"Really, you look beautiful. That's your dress."

"Thank you, I love that dress I really do. Thank you for making this experience wonderful, and a happy memory. I am so lucky to have you. I can't wait till we make this officially us forever. Now we need to get your tux arranged. That should be fun."

"First let's go eat and then you can get your hair and nails done. I'll get the tux stuff taken care of and verify with the preacher and photographer the time and place. What would you like to eat as your last meal being single?"

"I'm not going to prison Jacob. I'm looking forward to my life sentence with you. But let's not kid around with those words, because I did really feel that way once, and it isn't anything to kid around about. There is no lonelier place than to be in a partnership and be all alone, that's a horrible place to be trapped."

"I'm sorry, that was insensitive. We are on a tight time schedule. Let's eat so you don't faint on me tonight. Then we can run our errands and meet for our wedding. I can't believe I am finally settling down, with the woman of my dreams.

You are the only woman who has captured my heart from the first tree swinging magical moment. It's only right that we are joined in marriage outside, in God's beautiful country. We've got a beautiful warm day for an outside wedding."

"Well, you sir, should contact Hallmark, because I think you could have a career writing cards. Women would die to hear the words you say to me when you take the time and effort to tell me what you are thinking and feeling.

I die a little every time I hear your voice, in a good way that is. And then when you talk all affectionate and loving, I am all yours in every way possible. My body just sort of melts for you Jacob, every part of me desires you, adores you, flat out loves you."

"That sounds like a good place to be, babe. We can explore those melting positions later. Now food and we're off, literally on our life adventure together." We ate a quick bite at Applebee's, and it was really good. Spending all that money and all this excitement made me hungry. He knows I like my meat and potatoes.

After our meal he took me to my hair appointment and the nail lady is at the same place, so he dropped me off and went to run his errands. I offered to help him with his tux stuff, but he didn't think we had time for that. He did that on his own, while I got my hair and nails ready for my special day. My hair stylist couldn't believe I was getting married today, but she fit me in so I could look beautiful and feel special.

She trimmed my hair and fixed it up off my back and put a few pearls here and there. I really feel like a princess. Then over to the nail table to get my nails filed and polished, clear natural to go with my soft pink wedding dress.

I can't wait to see him in his tux. I don't think I've ever seen him in anything except jeans and blazers. He's so handsome, I am so lucky, and I know it. I hope I never wake from this best dream ever, because I've never, ever been happier. I'm in love.

I've made a million mistakes along my journey, and I hate myself for that, but he's here, and wants to be mine forever, and that makes my life complete. I am finally going to live my happily ever after. Dreams do come true. I was going to say, "I do" and I mean it with every part of me.

Jacob came to pick me up and he looked like he just walked out of a GQ magazine cover. His dark wavy hair, his shirt top buttons open, his jeans, boots, I didn't think I could wait for tonight. Jacob must have been thinking the same thing, but my hair.

I couldn't mess up my hair, so we would wait. He assured me he could manage not messing up my hair, but we will never know if that would have been possible or not. It was only a few hours, and he would be mine, and I would be his exclusively forever.

We didn't have time for a wedding cake, and I didn't want a grocery store cake, so we went to a cupcake store and ordered three dozen cupcakes. We ordered cheesecake red-velvet cupcakes. Of course, we had to sample them, and oh my gosh they were so good, they almost melt in your mouth chocolate, creamy sweet, perfect for us. My girlfriend was picking up the flowers. My mom had just called, and she and Jeff were at the hotel getting dressed and wanting to know where to meet us for the wedding.

Jacob had a white limo pick us up at the house and we met everyone at the park at five p.m. We took pictures in the flower gardens and with my pink dress and Jacob's summer gray tux, we looked great in the pictures.

The photographer showed me from his screen and asked if he could use our photos in a photo contest. I am going to have the beautiful wedding pictures I always wanted, you know me and my love for photography.

This was going to be a perfect wedding. And Jacob was the most handsome man I'd ever seen. He had his light gray tux and his brothers taunting jeers about the pink paisley vest he wore. It had pink, black, and silver/gray paisley patterns and fit perfectly under the solid gray tux.

He incorporated my pink into his tux for my pleasure,

and for our pictures. I love that he did that, I didn't ask him to go all pink powder-puff for me, but he made pink look hot! I just want to run my hands in his hair and kiss him until I die.

Jeff, walked me down the aisle, finally giving me his blessing to marry Jacob. I was sad that my dad would never know Jacob and I were married, and he could never know how happy we are together. But he would have liked Jacob. First of all, he has money and that would have eased my dad's mind knowing I was financially taken care of. And he was smart, and a farm boy. My dad would have liked my man. But I am going to be only happy today, no room for sad in such a happy heart.

Jeff said as long as Jacob treated me well, and I was happy, he was happy for us. With just our immediate family and a couple of my closest friends, we made our wedding vows to each other. We both teared up when we shared our vows to one another. We had a short but beautiful ceremony at one point my hands were shaking. I was just so happy, and Jacob just reached out and held both my hands.

He whispered that if I was nervous about our wedding, that we could slow things down. I whispered back, not nervous about our future together, just so happy, my body can't hold it all in. He leaned in to kiss me and the minister said, not till we say I do. Everyone laughed and it helped my shaking.

Then when it came time for us to exchange rings, Jacob reached out to his brother Andrew, his best man for him to hand him the ring. Andrew started reaching frantically in his pants pockets, then his jacket pockets, and my heart sank. I could not believe Andrew lost our wedding rings.

Jacob just turned and looked at me then back at Andrew and said, "Andrew, where is the ring?" and then Andrew's hand stopped on something in his jacket. He pulled out a rectangular box the size of his hand. I hadn't seen one in years but, it was a box of cracker jacks. Then Andrew opened the box, and pulled out the prize inside, and there in the prize wrapper was my ring. Everyone was cracking up, I started breathing again, and Jacob hit his brother in the arm with his fist, but just a light hit, and then took the ring carefully, and our ceremony was back to intimate and sweet.

After the announcement of Mr. and Mrs. Jacob and Jenna Jamison, we took more pictures, and changed our clothes for our wedding dinner. I gave my dress to my mom to store for me while I was gone. Jacob gave his tux to my girlfriend so she could have it dry cleaned. He wanted to buy the tux to wear for our future anniversaries. How sentimental is that I thought it was cute. Now the pressure is on to be able to stay thin enough to wear that small wedding dress forever.

Jacob didn't know but I had a dress, I'd bought on my cruise, and it was short, had white sequins and it was beautiful. I hadn't had an opportunity to wear it yet, so I was thrilled to get to wear it for him. He just stared, smiled his smile, and I wanted everyone to leave so we could be alone and intimate.

I still had a good tan from the cruise, so my legs looked good when I came out in my short, shiny, all white dress. I was hungry again and ready to eat with our family and friends.

We had cupcakes and champagne and punch for the kids at the park. Then we reserved the banquet room at the Hilton Rooftop Hotel to feed our family dinner, before we flew off to Bora Bora.

We had prime rib and chicken breast for the main course, and salads, mashed potatoes, gravy, green beans, corn, homemade rolls, and *Crème Brûlée* for dessert. My favorite dessert, but red velvet cheesecake is now at the top of the list too. We ate like kings and queens. Then the music started, and we had our first dance.

We were on the roof top eating and dancing under the stars. The hotel shot off fireworks for about five minutes to celebrate us. I didn't know Jacob had arranged it. What a beautiful surprise.

We danced to a song that was from the Twilight movie. It was the theme song from their wedding, and I loved it. I didn't care if it was a cheesy choice, it was our wedding, and Jacob liked the music too.

So, until we get a different song that could be ours, we are borrowing this wedding song. I love it and may just keep that song for us forever. It was perfect, he is perfect, and I am now and forever more Mrs. Jenna Jamison. I look forward to living with that name, that family, but mostly that man, finally officially my Jacob.

Jacob whispered that we were going to need to change and get our luggage so we could keep to his flight plan he submitted to the flight towers to take his plane and fly us to Florida. We needed to catch a commercial plane to fly from Florida to Bora Bora.

Jacob was a great pilot. His plane was upscale nice for a twelve-passenger plane. Andrew was a licensed pilot too, and he rode with us in Jacobs' plane to Miami, with his cute new girlfriend, and two of his other brothers and their girlfriends. They were all going to spend the night in Florida and fly the plane back to Kentucky after their weekend. The girls were all bubbly and giddy, you'd think they just got married, but I didn't care. I was in too good of a mood to let anything or anyone dampen my mood.

Jacob was talking quietly with Andrew about watching what he drank twenty-four hours before he flies his plane home. He's a good big brother. I just talked and walked around on the plane until we got close to Florida. I felt like a kid in a candy store sitting up front in the plane with Jacob, looking out the windows, above the clouds. I enjoyed being in the air with Jacob.

We made it to our next flight on time and Jacob had first

class seating for our honeymoon celebration flight. He had his drink of choice Jack and Coke I had my Diet Dr. Pepper, and we cuddled and kissed and slept on our way to unite our eternal union. I am married and I'm happy.

I just have to keep saying it because I never dreamed my future could be this good. I never thought I could get amazing in my life. I thought I had to live with just surviving. But I'm so beyond my familiar world, and I'm letting it all go. I have all I need and all I want or could ever hope or dream for, my husband, Jacob Jamison.

We are Mr. and Mrs. Jacob and Jenna Jamison. It sounds storybook the way it rolls off the tongue, but we were real life, and united. I just hoped that our fairy tale wedding ended up in a happily ever after for our final days on this earth.

I'm in love, married, and starting the trip of a lifetime, my honeymoon, with my honey. Jenna Jamison is one lucky woman! Finally, a perfect wedding to a perfect husband, and I can't wait for the perfect honeymoon.

Chapter 17

The Future

We departed the plane and all I could smell was jet fuel. But when we got past the doors of the airplane, we were welcomed with people holding out fresh flower leis it was a heavenly tropical fragrance. They were handing out free drinks in pineapples, but Jacob didn't feel comfortable taking already poured drinks from complete strangers, especially when we were out of the country.

I love that he's balanced and thinks, because I would have just said thanks, and gulped it down. Who says no to a free drink? We are a good team.

We picked up our luggage with no problems, except my suitcase now had a large gash down the outside middle. I wasn't happy about it, but I didn't want to fight with the airline. I wanted to get to my paradise resort, with my gorgeous smoking hot husband.

We slid into our white mustang convertible, entered our GPS coordinates, and followed the resort shuttles to our honeymoon destination. The air smelled of sweet flowers, or it might have been the flower lei hanging around my neck. This was quickly becoming my favorite trip. The sand was white, and the water was so clear you could see the bottom of the ocean and all the fish that swam in it. Simply paradise. I couldn't imagine heaven being any more beautiful than this, it was beyond words. I didn't even want to sleep. I just wanted to get in that beautiful ocean, with my beautiful husband, and bask in the exquisiteness around me.

We arrived at our hotel and our room was literally like an upscale hut floating over the ocean. We have glass bottom floors in parts of our bedroom and bathroom to watch the fish swim below us.

Our deck took us out to our own private pool, hot tub, and a ladder down into the ocean. This is a movie star resort type place. I had no idea what my honey was paying for this experience, but he went way over and beyond my highest expectations to make sure this honeymoon didn't start out like my last marriage.

I love that Jacob cares about me and knows how to show it in ways I truly appreciate. I love that he listens to me and remembers the important things that matter to me. This place was really breathtakingly beautiful. It was more spectacular than I could have ever imagined.

Jacob asked what I wanted to do first. He had a glimmer in his eyes, but I halted that idea, but only temporarily. I told him wanted to take a shower and shave my legs. He smiled his sexy smile and said he was happy to give me some girl time. The twinkle was immediately back in his stunningly gorgeous blue eyes.

He said he'd make calls to our family to let them know we made it safe and sound so they wouldn't worry. I ask him to take a couple of pictures of our honeymoon palace and send them to my mom before we trash the place. She will be so happy for us. I told Jacob to use my phone, that my mom's number was stored under "mom". I'm not as techy as Jacob. He explained that I could assign people to a number and press the number and it would ring that person. I told him I'd be happy to address that later, as it wasn't a priority for me on my honeymoon.

I quickly jumped in the shower as Jacob made phone calls. I came out of the bathroom in my honeymoon nighty, a see-through, baby doll, pink short nighty, that was fitted with tiny horizontal ruffles all the way around it. Very soft, with an almost bra looking top with more rows of horizontal ruffles.

But these ruffles were covered in pink rhinestones across the bra area, very cute, and sexy at the same time. I thought since I went with a pink wedding dress, our first night as husband and wife should be pink as well.

When I walked out of the bathroom in my baby doll, nighty, tan legs, and a pair of high heeled pink pumps, I knew I'd get the desired look on his face. But his lusty smile only lasted a few seconds. I saw his smile change from excited anticipation to serious concern in a matter of seconds, as he jumped off the bed and was running to me.

I thought he must have seen a spider, lizard, or snake on the floor, so I quickly jumped into his arms. But no, it wasn't any wild tropical animal, it was just me, just a little blood, well actually it was a lot of blood. I must have nicked my ankle when I was shaving, because I got two steps out of the bathroom, feeling all appealing and there was Jacob, wrapping my ankle with a towel and calling the hotel for a doctor.

"Are you kidding me, I'm fine. It's a tiny nick, I just need a Band-Aid. Let's just get the bleeding stopped and give it a minute."

"You shouldn't have rushed through your shaving, a little anxious for honeymoon time? You needed to be more careful."

"I guess I was just in a hurry to get out to this beautiful

bedroom with my handsome husband. I wanted you to think I was beautiful, and now you just see some needy girl. Not what I was going for, at all."

"No, that's not what I thought. I saw the woman I love, whom I adore more than life itself, and your tan, long legs were something I planned on exploring in depth in just a few moments.

I love you and want to claim you in every way humanly possible, Mrs. Jamison." We took the towel off my ankle, gently washed off the dried blood, and thank goodness it was just a little scrape.

Hotel personnel was at our door with a first aid kit. Jacob thanked them and along with the Band-Aids, they brought champagne and strawberries on a silver tray. Jacob didn't just call home to let them know we made it safe and sound, he also ordered room service.

He doesn't miss a beat. I love being married to a man who can think ahead and anticipate my wants and needs without me asking or even hinting.

We put some Neosporin germ killer on my ankle, and a Band-Aid over the scratch, and I was back into Jacob's arms, this time with the look I longed to see on his face when I came out of the bathroom. The mood returned to romance.

Jacob popped the top off our champagne, I had a couple of strawberries because as usual I wanted something sweet, and then our honeymoon fun really started. I had lost track of days, nights, all time had lost its meaning and power over us. It was just me, Jacob, and this place that was heavenly.

He was tender with me, it intensified with his every caress. It was like our first time, exploring each other, but knowing what the other likes by moves or groans. When he groans, I come undone. It's the sexiest thing I've ever experienced. My body just responds involuntarily.

It's not like he's loud, it's more of a quiet, under his

breath, and just every once in a while. It seriously gives me goose bumps all over. My body just wants to please him all the more, and automatically responds to his touch and sound. I love him and I've never been this ecstatic. I can't believe I have him forever. He's better than great, he's my dream come true.

After making love and resting, we were hungry and ready to eat again. It was six a.m. here with the time change. We got dressed and walked up to the hotel lobby for a great hot breakfast. The pebbled rock path up to the hotel was smooth and to each side of the path walkway were tall palm trees and oversized ferns on the ground. It was a beautiful tropical island, and the weather was warm and humid.

Once we reached the open-air restaurant with a thatched roof to protect from the heat of the sun, I had a large cup of coffee. The fruit tasted so much fresher and sweeter than the fruit I get in Missouri. I didn't just eat healthy fruit. I had pancakes, eggs, bacon, and orange juice. We had our food eaten and we were ready to explore our stunning surroundings.

We had snorkeling gear in our room. Jacob asked about best places to snorkel, to see beautiful coral and fish. They told us we were in a protected sea life area and that we were in a prime location for viewing large exotic fish and coral.

They also noted that they book boats and sea craft equipment if we wanted to go further than our local area of the cove. The resort provided fish guidebooks in our rooms with beautiful photos so we could identify the sea life. We thanked our servers, tipped them, and walked down to the beach.

"Jacob, we are closer to the sun here, and you need some high-volume sunscreen, because you will get burnt. And I don't want my husband in pain, ever. Let's go buy some lotion, and then go back to the room so I can rub it all over your body."

That was all it took, he had my hand, and after a brief stop to buy lotion, we jogged back to the room. He was so funny. We were back in our room, feeling married again, and eventually got sunscreen rubbed in all over each other. It was time to hit the ocean, the beautiful crystal-clear ocean. The crashing waves on the shoreline of the beach were enticing.

I wanted to swim nude so I wouldn't have tan lines, but Jacob insisted that I wear my top and bottom. He said too many people have cell phones with zoom technology on their cameras and he didn't want my naked body in anyone's mind but his. As we were putting on our snorkel gear, he stopped me. "I have to tell you something."

"Sure babe, what is it? Don't tell me you can't swim."

"No, it's not that. It's something I didn't want to bring up on our honeymoon, but I just want to be honest with you, always honest, because I know you are serious on the deal breaker."

"Okay, what is it? You know you can tell me anything, so what is it?" I put the snorkel gear down, walked over and sat back down on the bed, and took his hand. He looked so serious I was afraid he was going to tell me he had a terminal disease or something that was horrifying.

"When you were taking a shower last night, and I was making calls to our family, I saw that Brandon called your phone. I know we agreed to talk to him together, but I didn't want you thinking about his broken heart when we should be focused on each other, just the two of us, so I sent him a text. I copied you so you could read it. I didn't want him to worry about where you were, or why you weren't responding to his emails, texts, and calls."

"You are my husband, I love you. Brandon is my past, and I've got this ring to prove it. Thank you for telling me and explaining what you were thinking and feeling. This is progress for us. I adore you and I'm fine with you letting him know I will no longer be in his life.

He was a good friend as well as a lover, but I would never keep that relationship, because there is too much at risk to put myself in that position ever again. I am yours, all yours, and you can trust me to be faithful to you and only you, till death do us part. Thank you for telling me and taking care of telling Brandon. I'd honestly forgotten about him. You know how you overwhelm me."

Jacob grabbed me, threw me back on the bed and our suntan lotion didn't see any sun for another hour or so. You wouldn't think that I'd be hungry again so soon, but all this activity makes me hungry.

We ordered room service and then just snorkeled around our room area until they delivered our meals. Then we enjoyed our food with our feet dangling in the water from the deck of our room.

Room service brought us a bag of frozen peas and said if we throw them in the water, the fish will come. They did. They swarmed right up to us and devoured the peas. We tried it and out of nowhere all these fish were at our feet. It was kind of scary.

These huge fish were within touching range. I was glad I was out of the water when they congregated at our feet. I grabbed my camera and tried to get some closeup pictures of the fish. Then we saw our first large shark and we both lifted our feet completely out of the water at the same time.

We laughed until we cried. Then we got up off the deck, I put my camera in the safe in our room, and with full tummies we reapplied sunscreen for a long romantic walk on the beach. It was my best day ever. When we got hot, we'd dip into the water and swim with the fish, then we'd get out and walk and talk some more.

I could live here. It was a private resort, so we didn't have lots of kids and people all around us. It was like our own private corner of the world. I was blissfully happy. Jacob seemed very happy too. I just asked him. "Jacob, how's married life treating you? Any regrets so far?"

He stopped immediately and pulled me in front of him, and said "Yeah, I have regrets." I just looked at him shocked that this would be his first response to my question. Here I was so happy, and he was regretful.

Chapter 18

Honeymoon

"Listen and hear what I'm saying. I should have never lost your trust by pushing you away from me. I take full responsibility of practically inviting Brandon into your life. But I'm a changed man, you changed me.

I will never hurt you or me that way again. I can't tell you I'll never make mistakes, or say things I shouldn't, but I'm sorry in advance for those times. I will never hurt you on purpose, because I love you more than my own life. I didn't think it was possible to love someone as much as I love you, but it's the honest truth. You are my wife, and I love every second we are together. You truly are my soul mate, Jenna Jamison!"

"Jacob, are you opposed to making love here on the beach, right now? I've warned you about when you talk so romantically to me. When you talk to me with your romantic confessions and winsome thoughts, I want to touch you and know you more."

"I love your impulsive stamina, but no public showing off of your body. You are entirely too free with being naked, Mrs. Jamison. You should only be naked at home, or inside situations. Not that you have anything to be ashamed of, I just don't want to share you with anyone, ever again. Your body is mine, and I think we should jog back to the room if you want to. Then I can let your throbbing body have its way with me."

I decided that if we were going to jog, I needed a head start, so I needed to catch him off guard. I jumped up in his arms, wrapped my legs around his waist, and grabbed handfuls of hair as I kissed him with all the passion I felt inside. I had planned on jumping out of his arms and running toward our room for a head start, but after our first kiss, I couldn't move.

I just melted in his arms, and he dropped to his knees. We fell to the sand and rolled back and forth with the tide coming in and out. But the sand and water were an added pleasure as the warm tide splashed on us with a seaside rhythm.

So much for Jacob not wanting anyone to ever see me naked in public, because he was undressing me right there on our beach. I didn't see anyone else outside, but I didn't look intently. Jacob had my top's string in his mouth, it was untied, and my top was floating in the water next to us.

His strong fingers were all over my body, my breast was in his mouth, and I was the one groaning with pleasure on the beach. I guess my moan brought him back to reality and he quickly grabbed my swimsuit top and tied it back on me and said, "We need to go to our room."

We both jogged the whole way across the beach to our private getaway. I hadn't jogged in many years, maybe high school, and only then because a big dog was chasing me. But I had never had such a great incentive to jog before. I thought by the time we reached the room we would be tired from jogging and walking the beach coastline, but I guess endorphins kicked in when you exercise, because we had a tidal wave of passion together.

I didn't think we could be any hotter than we had been, but we were off the scales rocking the room. We just lay in our bed motionless afterwards, panting, sweating, heart pulsating. I told him I was going to jump in the ocean and cool off. He said not without clothes, Jenna, my little nudist.

I pulled out my new bright orange and hot pink, very sexy bikini. I got it at the airport gift shop while he was in the restroom. He just stared at me and shook his head, "Jenna, what you do to me." I smiled and said, "Put on your suit, babe, and let's dip in the ocean before dinner." We got all salty together and then took our shower, before we went out to a four-star restaurant in search of local flavor.

I ordered blackened shark and it was like eating a white, flakey, tender flavorful steak, delicious. Jacob had lobster and steak. We had a couple of tropical drinks and then we went dancing.

I wore an above the knee length, straight black dress, with no sleeves and no shoulders. It wasn't a halter dress per se, but it was close to that. It had a silver ring that hung at necklace level and the black material tied around my neck through the silver circle I had my hair pulled up off my neck and my back was completely exposed. It was sexy on me and very flattering.

Jacob couldn't take his eyes or hands off my neck, my arms, my back, basically any exposed skin that was appropriate to touch in public.

I've never worn so many dresses. Teaching kindergarten, you are on the floor with the kids, reading and working, so I never would wear anything that wasn't sit on the floor comfortable. I love feeling beautiful and seeing Jacob smile at me. He made me feel something I've never felt before. He made me feel beautiful and desirable.

I couldn't have been happier.

Jacob was wearing jeans and a white V-neck tee-shirt with a jacket to meet the restaurant dress code. Our food was beyond delicious and the presentation was off the charts first class.

We met another couple on their honeymoon too. They were Monte and Tammy Buford, and they were from Durango, Colorado. We hit it off with them right away. Monte was very funny. He had dark curly hair and blue eyes, skinnier than Jacob, but still handsome, and Tammy was downright beautiful. She had shoulder length brown hair, blue eyes, and a perfect figure. The kind of woman other women hate because she's so beautiful, but she was great.

Her best feature was that she had a great laugh. She would toss her head back when she laughed, it was an infectious laugh. It just made you want to laugh right along with her too, and you would.

They invited us to join them at a local casino to gamble for a while. We followed them over in our convertible and had a great time.

Jacob was very lucky and won a lot of money, but after a while I whispered in his ear, "Honey, we are out of the country, and there are lots of people watching you win a lot of money. I don't want to be kidnapped or something crazy because you are showing you've got a lot of money. I'm glad you are having fun and winning but you might think about how desperate some people might be to get your money. I don't want to stop your fun just thought I'd give you another perspective."

Jacob stood up and whispered back in my ear, "They would have to kill me before I'd let anyone touch you ever. I hear your concern, and I will take care of this problem now." Jacob announced at the high rollers table, "Tammy, Monte, we are going to head out, but here is $2,000. Consider it a wedding gift and enjoy!"

They gave us hugs then Jacob said in a normal tone and voice, "I'm donating the rest of my winnings to the local animal shelter here. Do you know the name of it or the location?" The man at the cashiers' window said he'd look it up, and he said, "Never mind, I'll have my concierge take care of it for me at the hotel. Thanks anyway," and gave the cashier a $200 tip.

We walked out to our convertible, and Jacob opened the car door for me. He was looking around when he got into the car and drove off quickly. He said "I got carried away having fun and you were using your head. I am so proud to have you as my wife, thanks for having my back. We are a good team."

"Are you really giving over $5,000.00 to their local shelter?"

"I was planning on it. Do you not want me to?"

"I don't know, I'm all for taking care of animals, but there might be some other charity that would benefit from this, or you could use the money to pay for my expensive wedding dress and I wouldn't have to feel guilty at all for having the dress of my dreams."

"You don't have to feel guilty about anything. I mean it. You need to think of your dress with only happy thoughts, no guilt, no negative anything, only beautiful thoughts from my attractive bride.

Hey, do you have your seatbelt on?"

"Yes of course, I'm in the car with you, aren't I? I put it on when we were leaving the casino."

"Do you wear your seat belt when I'm not in the car with you?"

I looked away I didn't want to lie to my husband. I could feel the car slowing down, his hand moved over, and he physically grabbed my leg and squeezed tightly. "Dammit, Jenna Jamison, do you not understand how much you mean to me?

You have to be safe, you have to wear your seatbelt,

always!" He was squeezing my leg and it hurt so I knew he felt strongly about this. It's a simple thing I can do, to follow the law, and make my husband happy, but the hurting my leg had to stop.

"Jacob, let go of my leg, you are hurting me."

"Sorry, I didn't mean to hurt you. I just don't want you taking chances with your life, it's stupid and I couldn't lose you. I would never survive that tragedy. I would end my life before I would suffer that kind of loss. I can't ever lose you, Jenna. You mean everything to me."

"I love you too, you can't talk crazy like killing yourself ever, no matter what, that is unacceptable. Let's not talk like this. It's dark, depressing, and I don't want to think about you and death, killing, or murder in the same sentence, especially on my honeymoon. You kind of sounded stalkerish, and a little scary just now with your death grip on my leg."

"Sorry, that wasn't my intention. Just promise me you will always wear your seatbelt from now on, and we won't have a problem. Make it a habit, and by the way, it's the law."

"I will do that for you. I'll just pretend the seatbelt is your arm hugging me. How's that?"

"Perfect."

We were back at the hotel and Jacob put his winnings in our room safe with our other money and passports. We decided to order room service desserts, more champagne, who knew I'd like that stuff, and I slipped into my new light tan bikini.

When I got into the ocean in my wet bathing suit and my dark tan, I looked like I was naked. Jacob stared at me and just shook his head, "I should have known you'd find some way to get around the no naked in public rule I have. Cute, Jenna, cute suit."

"The water feels great tonight Jacob, why don't you jump in and join me?"

"Get out of the ocean now!" I didn't ask him why, I just swam to the steps as quick as I could, and Jacob lifted me out of the water. I turned around to look down in the water and my heart was pounding. There was a very large, eight-foot tiger shark just a few feet behind me. I started shaking where I was standing.

"Thank God you saw that shark."

"This time of night is probably their feeding time. I didn't think these large sharks came this far up to the coastline, but we can see that clearly they do." Just then, there was a knock at the door.

Room service delivered our food, fresh fruit, delicious mango margaritas, key lime cheesecake, macadamia nuts, and as requested, a bag of string cheese and bottled water. I know I'm weird, but if I eat something sweet, I need something salty to balance it out.

We thanked the guy for the food and told him about the shark. The man seemed surprised and said he needed to notify the front desk immediately. Jacob tipped him and he was gone. "If we keep eating like this, are you going to love me if I go back to my former fat self?"

"I will love you any size, anyway you are."

He is totally getting sex tonight. I was tired, but any woman dreams of a man saying that to her, it's a fantasy every woman wishes was true. It just takes the pressure off.

I don't want to get fat and lose myself under pounds of flesh. I want to stay healthy and energetic for myself and my husband, always. I told him, "I won't get fat, but I appreciate you saying that, and even more, I love you because you meant what you just said. How hungry are you? Because you thought you were lucky at the casino, well baby, you just hit the jackpot with me."

"The food will wait, what do you have in mind?" He took off my wet suit, and goose bumps were all over me. We started in the hot tub, Jacob and a Jacuzzi are a win-win experience. Sweet mango margaritas and salty crunchy nuts. I love my life, my husband, being married, Bora Bora, it couldn't get any better than this, ever.

We got out of the hot tub and my legs were like rubber. Jacob said we were in the hot water too long. He made me drink two bottles of water to rehydrate. Sometimes he's such a mother hen. I told him if I had to drink water, he needed to drink water too.

We chugged and then I jumped up on the bed and told Jacob I want to dance with my husband. We only lasted a few moves before we were on the bed and in our honeymoon motions.

"Do you think we will always be this happy and in love?"

"No."

"Why not?"

"Because every day I love you, I find new ways that make me love you even more. I am shocked that I have this much love to give, but it's yours, all of me. And every day you take more of me, and I willingly give it to you, because I love you."

"Seriously, you need to start writing because when you talk like that, I just can't get enough of you, I can't be close enough to you. I need you, my body aches for you, and you're just inches from me. I can't get enough of you."

I reached over to the serving plate, took a piece of cheesecake, and smeared it on my boobs and said, "Hungry?" Jacob smiled his ruggedly handsome smile I could tell he liked my booby trap. He was enjoying key lime cheesecake, and I was enjoying my calorie free dessert like never before. Best key lime ever!

We fell off to sleep and it was wonderful. I woke to him looking at me, moving my hair out of my face. What a wonderful life. There was a light rain outside that we could hear plopping on the ocean. It was pretty to see it bounce off the crystal-clear water. They say it could rain and, in an hour, or two, it could be cleared up and dry. Jacob asked if

I wanted to go shopping today and I was quick to say no.

"I just want to stay in our private bubble, safe, and I don't want to risk people taking you away from me because you have money."

"Is that a real fear for you? Honey we are safe, they have high security here. The way their economy makes money is from their tourists, so they don't want to have people going home with bad stories. They have a low crime rate here. Jenna, you are with me, you are safe, you don't have to worry anymore. I'm here, I'm your husband, and I'll take care of you always! You can relax."

"I know I'm just being irrational, but I've never been this happy before, and it's a little scary to me because I wouldn't survive without you. I know, because I've tried to before, and I made a mess of things."

"We had this talk last night when I was saying I couldn't live without you, and you shut me down. Just know I love you, we are fine, and we will live to be old together. We will have happily ever after, I promise."

"And I promise too. On to a more pressing subject, are you hungry?"

We walked in the rain to the hotel breakfast bar, and I had the best hot, fresh croissants ever. The chef said they were butter croissants. They were hot, flakey, and melted in your mouth. I think I ate two of them. I had hot boiled tomatoes, and I don't even really like tomatoes, but they were delicious. And fresh cooked mushrooms in butter, soft boiled eggs, and my drink of choice, coffee with cream.

They did have a green smoothie island drink that had celery, cactus juice, alfalfa, apples, and I don't know what else. But I tried it and it was different, but a new kind of delicious taste I'd never had before. I really liked it.

I had one or two made fresh every morning after that, until we left for home. I think the drink gave me extra energy and it was very delicious. I looked forward to my green sludge each morning.

Chapter 19

The Swim

After the rain stopped, we swam out about half a mile or so, the beach looked like a speck behind us. Then we turned around to go back where I felt safe. We got into comfy beach chairs, tanned, and soaked in the sun. We booked a couples massage, and they did it in the cabana huts right there on the beach.

My massage man tried to massage my naked breasts and I thought Jacob was going to physically assault him. The man said that's what's included in the couples massage, and Jacob let him know that my private parts would stay private. The man apologized.

I was really glad Jacob was next to me when it happened because I was so relaxed, I didn't realize what he was doing until he touched my boob.

Jacob was so cute. I didn't realize he was watching me. I thought he was relaxing next to me, getting his woman led massage, but clearly that wasn't working for him. Then I started thinking about it and I got tickled at the "boob incident" and couldn't stop laughing at Jacob's facial expressions. We cut our massage time short, put our clothes on, and continued to walk along the beach.

"I love that you take good care of me. Your protective nature is refreshing and something I never experienced in my first marriage."

"I was so mad that ass touched you, I can't even tell you how instantly furious I felt. I calmed myself down because I didn't want you to be robbed of a relaxing massage, but that was off limits for any man but me and your doctor. He really pushed the boundaries of professionalism."

"I'll admit, I was shocked too, but I did like the oils he used, his hands just slid all over my body. I was relaxed until I thought my husband was going to kill him. I was able to relax because you were there with me, I felt safe."

"You can't talk like that. If you want lotion, I'll buy you lotions, but I can't think of someone else touching you, it's not a good place for me to go. I'll get all possessive and angry, so don't even kid around like that. How would you feel if I was saying that about the woman who had her hands all over me?"

"I'm sorry, Jacob, I wouldn't like it at all! Actually, I would hate, hate her, and be a little mad at you too."

"Okay we agree, no more massages unless it's me giving you one, and you giving me one. Come here and let me see if you have the touch for a good massage." Later we walked along the beach and laughed about the massage experience. When we got back to our room, Jacob called room service for the massage oil and lotion. They delivered the oils and lotions, and Jacob delivered as only he could.

I had a blast giving Jacob my first naked body massage. I told Jacob to roll over on his tummy and I was going to heat up the massage oil in the microwave. While it was heating, I was stripping. The oil was warm, and I was hot.

It was fun when Jacob realized that I was naked and sitting across his lower back. He nearly flipped me off the bed when he rolled over to his back so quickly. I was going to make sure it was the best massage he had ever had. I think I succeeded and must admit we had an excellent rainy-day afternoon.

I was starving again, so we went for lobster. Yummy, so buttery and delicious, with rolls, and salad, it was all wonderful. "Jacob, when we get back home, what are we going to do? Where are we going to live? Have you thought about any of these details? I'm guessing that knowing you, you already have a plan in your mind and maybe even written down on paper."

"I've thought about it. I have some ideas and would love your take on them."

"Okay, let's hear the options. Let's discuss that when we get back to our room."

"Here's what I was thinking. We fly back, get your stuff in a moving van, and haul everything you own in a truck and drive it to my place. Then we put your house on the market and sell it. Then you can move in with me, move your stuff in my house, we can sell or give away things that don't fit. Or if you want me to build on a room for you to have a photography studio, I would be glad to do that. Whatever you want or need, I'll build it or do it, I just want you with me as soon as possible. I can cover your house payments until it sells. Or I can just pay off what you owe on it, and let it set empty, if you don't want to sell it. What are you thinking, what do you want to do?"

"I want to go home with my husband, sleep in his bed, cook in his kitchen, and make your home, our home. But be honest with yourself and me. I know you are invested in the home you built. Will you always see that house as your house that I moved into?

Do we need to build a new home that would be our home? You have lots of land, we have options. I don't want you to ever feel like I am invading your space. I want us to have our place, our space and our home. I don't want the mentality of his and hers stuff, I just want our stuff in our home. Does that make sense?"

"I hear what you are saying. I know you are a neat freak, and I am too. I hate clutter, you love antiques and collectables. I will be comfortable with you in our home. My home is your home, Jenna, from now and forever. I don't need to build another home for my benefit, but if you aren't going to feel at home in my house, then I'll build another one. We can do it together."

"I don't want you to build me a different house, I love the home you built. I just want to make sure you are going to adjust to the changes of having me in your home full time with my stuff and my dogs."

"I don't care about all the stuff, I just want you, babe. I want you to be happy and want to start our lives together in my Kentucky home. The sooner I can get you in Kentucky the happier I will be. We can get new furniture, paint, whatever you want to change to make it "ours is fine with me". I'm happy if you are."

"Okay, Jacob."

"Two-word answer? Really that's all you have to say about packing up your life and moving across the country?"

"To quote someone I know and love, "I don't care about all the stuff". I just want to be with you. There are a few things that have sentimental meaning for me that I want to take to Kentucky, but I am fine to leave things in the house to help it show and sell. I don't want to leave your side for one day, I really don't. I love you."

"Get over here. That kind of sexy talk turns me on."

"Breathing turns you on."

"Why are you still sitting that far away from me?"

"I'll meet you halfway."

"Oh no you won't." And with that, he jumped up, grabbed me and threw me on the bed. Then he began tickling me. Something he had never done before. I had worked very hard not to let anyone know I'm ticklish and apparently, I didn't hide it as well as I thought, because he tore me up.

"Stop, Jacob, stop." Two words I never thought I'd say to him, at least not in bed, not to mention on our honeymoon, but I couldn't take it. "Jacob, stop!" He sat up and looked at me like I'd just slapped him across the face. "I've had enough, just let me up."

"Are you serious?"

"Yes, I am. No always means no with me. I do not enjoy being tickled. A minute of tickling I could handle, but more than that and it's hurtful and unkind. I want to be playful and responsive to you, but I hated that. I felt controlled and trapped and I hated that feeling."

"I had no idea you felt that way. You were laughing, I thought you were having fun. I'm so sorry. I stopped. Don't be mad I didn't know. If you don't like it, I won't do it."

"Okay, I feel tense and tight, how about we get in the hot tub to relax?"

"Sure, I'll meet you there in a few minutes, you go ahead."

I got into the hot tub and relaxed. Jacob didn't join me. I should be allowed to say no, it's my body. He shouldn't be upset with me because I was honest and told him that I didn't like it. But I don't want him unhappy or upset with me. So, after I'd soaked in the hot tub as long as I could, I got out, then jumped in the shower to wash off the chlorine, dried off, and put on my baby doll pajamas.

"I'm sorry if I hurt your feelings."

"I'm fine, Jenna, we should go to sleep."

"Why didn't you join me in the hot tub?"

"Didn't want to. I guess we are both allowed to say no once in a while."

"Sure, we are, Jacob. Goodnight and pleasant dreams."

I rolled over and tried to go to sleep, but I just wanted to cry. I couldn't cry next to him, in our bed, on our honeymoon. I already took a shower so I couldn't go back to the bathroom. I just got up and threw on a pair of cut off jean shorts and left my see-through pajama top on to get out of there.

"What are you doing?"

"I can't sleep, I'm going to go for a walk on the beach. Sorry, I didn't mean to wake you."

"Jenna, get back in bed, it's late."

"I thought if I just heard the ocean tide and waves it would relax me, and I would be able to sleep. I'll be fine. I'll stay in eyesight of our room." I didn't wait for his permission or continued debate I just walked out of the bedroom. All I wanted to do was get on the beach, sink my feet in the sand, and watch the water wash up on me, and cry all by myself.

Then out of the corner of my eye I saw Jacob's silhouette standing in the doorway of our room, and my heart was sad. I don't want to hurt him. I'm not doing this to be needy or get attention. Why is he mad at me? I hate him being mad at me. We are married, he's not going to leave me, we will work this out. I had been sitting in the sand, my arms on my knees my head down and crying quietly.

I sat up so I could breathe and look at the beautiful bright moonlight reflection off the ocean. I don't know how long he'd been standing there right behind me, but now I felt bad that he wasn't in bed sleeping. I jumped up and brushed off the sand from my butt, then turned to face him. I went to hug him. He just took a step back and stood there.

"Did you get enough fresh air so you can sleep now?"

"Sorry. I didn't want you to lose sleep because of me."

"It wouldn't be the first time, and I'm sure it won't be the last."

"What is going on? I tell you no, that I don't like something and now I feel like you are mad at me for being honest with you."

"You were a little harsh, no you were flat out harsh. Just

because I'm a man doesn't mean I don't have feelings too. You were someone I've never seen before, and I didn't like the way you were acting. I was not hurtful to you, it was innocent, and you went all battered wife on me."

"Well, news flash, you are married to me, remember better or worse. You don't carry my past, you don't know everything I've been through, and I'm sorry if I came on too strong. I love you and don't want to hurt you. But I told you I was married before, and it was not a good marriage. I guess I had a flash back and I sort of freaked out, feeling controlled, and that I couldn't get you to listen to me. I know you are not Tom, and I'm sorry for overreacting. I just hate being tickled. I feel powerless, and it physically hurts me. I know that's weird but that's how it affects me."

"I'm sorry I didn't put all those pieces of your puzzle together. I'm sorry I responded cold and indifferent to you. I should have just hugged you and gotten into the hot tub with you, then we'd both be asleep right now.

But here you are on your honeymoon, crying in the moonlight, and I feel like an insensitive jerk that was over eager in the bedroom to his newly wedded wife. I'll listen when and if you say no. I want you to tell me what you like and don't like. I won't react like that again.

If I get over eager or we do something that you aren't comfortable with, it's your responsibility to tell me so I'll know. And it's my responsibility to listen and respect your wishes. You will never have to worry or be tense when you get in bed with me, Jenna. I love you. Your arms are frozen, and you are shivering. Hot tub then off to bed?"

"Sounds good. Maybe you can just hold me for a minute before we leave this beautiful beach." Jacob grabbed me and hugged me, and I saw a tear slide down his cheek. I started crying out loud. Me, who didn't shed one tear during three cancer surgeries, or my divorce, and here I am, in love, on my honeymoon, and I'm an emotional basket case.

I just jumped up into his arms, wrapped my legs around him, and he walked me back to the room. I didn't need the hot tub to warm up. We got into the shower together, washed off all the sand, and then got in bed.

I have no idea what time it ended up being, but we slept until ten a.m. that next day. Jacob woke up first and said, "Jenna, you need to wake up. We have jet skis rented with a tour group and they leave from the resort at eleven. We need to eat so you will have the energy to go all day. Do you still want to do this today?"

I jumped up, pulled my hair back into a ponytail, threw on my swimsuit and shorts and top and flip flops, and headed out our door to the main lobby area for breakfast. We had another delicious breakfast, and I had my wonderful thick, green drink, yum. Then I wanted to use the restroom before we were with a group all day on the water.

I was hurrying to get back to our room and I was on a pebble sidewalk, when I saw a lizard. Not just any lizard, a Godzilla sized lizard, right next to me on the path. I screamed and tried to move off the path to quickly get away from the huge, mean looking lizard.

Chapter 20

Not Again

Well, me being a klutz in my country and abroad and being in my flip flops, I tripped and flipped and flopped. Jacob was right behind me, in disbelief, I think.

I grabbed my ankle and was scooting on my butt as fast as I could, trying to get away from the lizard that was now eye level with me and hissing. Jacob walked around me to the lizard and with his foot, flung it through the air far away from me. The lizard was bigger than his foot, so I was really surprised he had the strength to get that thing away from me so quickly.

"Your ankle, isn't that the one you broke before?"

"Yes, I'm in pain, can you carry me?"

He quickly picked me up and hurried to the hotel lobby. The doctor on staff said the x-rays showed a new break where the old break had scar tissue. Jacob gave them permission to put on a cast up to my knee. This cast was Velcro over hard plastic, so I could get my foot wet and then put it back on and off when I walked or got into water etc. I loved this cast it was so much better than the cast I had before.

I asked Jacob to cancel my Jet Ski reservation for the day, but he could still go if he wanted. Then I asked him to come back and get me after he made those arrangements. He left the room to make the call and I just sat there and cried. Not again, I can't believe I did this to myself again. Jacob was right back in minutes and worried again.

"Are you in pain? Tell me the truth."

"Not bad. I'm just sorry I messed up our plans for the day. I'm so sorry I'm such a klutz. I really hate that I'm accident prone."

"If you wanted me to keep you in bed today, you didn't need to break your ankle to do it."

"Ha, ha. Can we go back to our room? I guess dancing is out for tonight too, so how about we just relax in the room today, or we can sit in the lounge chair by the pool or ocean?"

"I'm with you sweetheart, but if you don't mind, I'd like to go to the room and rest."

We walked to the room and we decided to take a nap. I woke up and Jacob was out on the deck talking and laughing on the phone. I got up and he said he needed to go. He apologized for waking me up and asked me if I was hungry.

"Not really."

"You are going to need to eat something to take your pain pills. You have pills for one more day. The doctor said you should take them until they are all gone."

"Walking on a sandy beach isn't something I'm going to be able to do comfortably with a cast on my foot and leg."

"If you want to go home early that's fine with me. I'm more of a homebody myself. This place is beautiful, but I get to take beautiful home with me in you. I just want you with me, as comfortable and safe as possible, and not necessarily in that order."

"Thank you, and if you don't care, then let's go home. As wonderful as all this has been, I would love to see my dogs and sleep in my own bed if you are okay with that. It's just two days earlier than our original reservations, so if it costs too much to change our plans, then I'm fine to sit on the beach in a chair for two more days and sunbathe.

It's wonderful here. I could easily stay two more days if you don't mind carrying me to and from the beach and to our room. I just think it's going to be too hard to keep sand out of my cast around here."

"I figured that you would want to head home early. I already made arrangements. We will need to leave here tonight by 6:30 to make it to the airport by 7:30, the flight leaves at 8:30 pm. We have time to eat and relax. I can get a heavy-duty trash bag and wrap your foot and cast so you could make one last walk on the beach without getting sand between your toes, if that meets with your approval, Mrs. Jamison."

"Thanks for thinking of options for me. I should have known you would literally be a couple steps ahead of me. I think I would like that final walk with you, if you want to."

"You in a cast on the sand, I'm going with you. My luck you'd trip and break the other ankle."

"Not funny."

"Okay, I could give you a piggyback ride. That might be fun, come to think about it. Hop on, Jenna, here we go. Come on, no pouty lip, and no pity party, baby."

"Giddy up, let's go."

"You are fine and not dead weight, sweetheart. Now come on, let's go out and eat, so you can keep ahead of your pain pills. Is there anything you want to eat?"

"I would love fresh fish one last time before we leave. That shark steak was seriously memorable. I'd be glad to go wherever you want to go. What sounds good to you?"

"Fresh fish sounds great to me too, babe. You ready to

go? Are you walking or am I carrying you?"

"I'm walking." Lunch was delightfully filling and flavorful. Fresh fish and fresh, juicy fruit have an entirely different flavor than what I'm used to eating back home. I could live here just for the food.

Actually, I couldn't, because I love the good old USA and would never be able to live abroad long term. But while I'm here, I'm going to appreciate the delicious food and scenery. This resort was the best place I've ever stayed, super star superior.

I took my pain pill per Jacob's persistence, drank my bottled water, and then back to the room to put my foot in a trash bag so I could walk on the beach one last time with my husband. He held my hand the whole time, not sure if it was affection or fear I'd break something else, but either way I enjoyed his physical contact.

Bora Bora was the perfect honeymoon destination. It was beautiful, private, secure, and all around a quality establishment. I'd love to come back for our ten-year anniversary.

We walked, talked, and laughed together on the beach, and just absorbed all we could of the warm sun before we had to go back to the room to clean up and pack. With the bag off of my cast, the Velcro cast unstrapped, I carefully stood in the cold shower and felt refreshed. Once out of the shower and my cast back on my clean foot, we had one more intimate encounter on our honeymoon bed and lost all track of time.

We looked at the clock, jumped up, and started throwing clothes into the suitcases. I walked quickly to our rental car and Jacob loaded our luggage in the trunk, then drove with lightning speed to make it to the airport on time.

Jacob dropped me off at the front doors with the luggage. Then he drove down a block to return the rental car and was back within twenty minutes.

There were a couple of men talking to me when Jacob

walked up, trying to sell me a time share property. I kept telling them I had no money and wasn't interested, but they wouldn't leave me alone. Jacob walked up to them with his personal charisma and the men just walked away. I couldn't believe how he made them just leave immediately.

We quickly walked inside the airport terminal and checked our luggage. We had our tickets, passports, and went through customs. We had a great trip, the best honeymoon I've ever had and that's even with a broken ankle!

What a great way to celebrate forever with the man I love. He is so good looking with his tan, sunglasses, and brilliant white smile. A three-punch knock-out, and he's mine.

We got on the plane and once in the air, I thought I'd turn on my phone. I'd forgotten to bring my power charger, but we had Jacob's phone to contact people and communicate if we needed to. So, I turned it on and had a message from Brandon. I read his text.

Jenna,

I love you (so does Kourtney) and we will always wish you the best.

You will be missed!

Yours truly,

Brandon.

I unthinkingly held my phone to my heart after I read the message, then I noticed Jacob glaring at me. I just handed him my phone, he read it, looked at me, and gave me back my phone. No words exchanged just "the look".

"Jacob, come on, he's in my past."

"If that's true, why did you just hold your phone to your heart? I'm sitting right next to you I saw you do it."

"I'm sorry, I didn't even realize I did that. I think it was more of a reflex. I thought what he said was sweet. He was a good friend I will miss him and his sweet daughter. Jacob, I married you.

You are my husband. I am moving across the country to live with you. Don't you know I'm committed to you? I'm wearing your ring. Jacob, do you honestly doubt my love and faithfulness to you and for you?"

"No, I don't. I know you love me. I'm not worried about you being unfaithful. I know I can trust you. You've always made it clear that truth is important to you and it is to me too. I'm glad we can be honest with each other."

"Good because if I don't have your trust, then I don't have your love, and we would be nothing. Trust and honesty go hand in hand. Like you and me, husband and wife, we are a team. We will have good times and bad, but as long as we can talk honestly and listen and love, we will live happily ever after. Love you, husband."

"I love you too, but can't you understand how Brandon just pushes my buttons. He's seen you naked, knows you intimately. I hate that I pushed you away and you met him. I'm sorry, but he just makes my blood boil. Thanks for letting me read your message from him. I'm calming down now, I'm okay. Are you going to respond to him? Text or a visit?"

"I'll send him a text and that will be to say goodbye. Do you want me to send it to you first?"

"No, I told you I trust you."

"Here, I'll just do it here and now and be done with the whole Brandon story, and this conversation can be over once and for all. You are my husband I don't want your blood to boil. The only time I want you hot is for me, not at me." He winked at me and I started getting my thoughts together to say goodbye to Brandon.

Brandon,

Thank you for your kind words. I will always think of our time together and smile. You are a wonderful man. You deserve the best. I will always wish you and your beautiful daughter the very best for your futures. I am happily married and moving to Kentucky. Thank you for being there when I needed a friend, I will always treasure our past.

Sincerely,

Jenna.

"Read this, does this sound okay to you? Tell me what you are thinking."

"It sounds like you are telling him goodbye in a nice and kind, Jenna way."

"I am, you big idiot. I told you I'm yours forever. I've got the ring to prove it. Now start believing in me, in us. There is no room for doubting my love or commitment to us. You should never have to doubt us ever again, got it?"

"I trust you and love you. Thank you for saying goodbye to Brandon once and for all. I hope you never talk to him or see him ever again."

"You're welcome. You'd do the same for me I'm sure if the situation was reversed." On the flight we started a movie, I got headphones to listen, and when it was over, we ate a snack, then we were landing. The trip home seemed much shorter than when we were headed to Bora Bora. We hailed a taxi and made it to my house.

I hadn't done a lot that day, but I was really tired. Maybe it was from different time zones or the pain pills. Anyway, we got home, kissed, and said goodnight. We were almost asleep and there was a knock on my front door. Jacob looked at me and I told him I had no idea who that could be.

Jacob slipped into his jeans and went to the front door. There was a large envelope sitting between the screen door and the front door. Jacob picked it up, locked the front door, and brought it back to me. "Expecting a special delivery tonight, Jenna?"

"No, what is it?"

"Here."

I sat up in bed, turned on another light next to me, and right away I recognized the handwriting on the outside of the envelope. "Oh, Jacob, I don't want to deal with this tonight, we are so tired, let's go back to sleep."

"We are both wide awake right now, and I won't sleep until I know why Brandon made a special trip over here tonight."

"Did you talk to him at the door?"

"No, but I know your looks, and when you saw your name on the outside of the envelope, I could tell it was from him."

"He was my photography instructor, so it's probably my prints. You really want to see these tonight?"

"Yes, but it's your mail, so you do what you please." I sat the envelope on the nightstand and turned off the light. Then I laid there for like five seconds and got the giggles.

"Jenna, turn on that light and open your envelope, please!" I couldn't hold it inside anymore, I cracked up out loud. Turning on the light, I saw Jacob start to smile too. Good sign, Jacob was laughing too, now I can open it.

"Wait, there aren't going to be naked pictures of you and Brandon are there?"

"We won't know for sure until we look." Then I winked at Jacob.

"You aren't going to make this easy for me, are you?"

I just smiled and opened the envelope. There were my pictures and a letter titled, "CONFIDENTIAL FOR JENNA ONLY."

Great! Jacob is going to think we took naked pictures for sure now, and we didn't ever do naked pictures or videos, ever.

I looked at the pictures and they were not only from class time, but from our weekend trip out of town, pictures of him and me, and all of the pictures from our cruise. There were lots of great, no actually wonderful pictures in that very large envelope. I hated that Jacob was next to me seeing all these pictures of Brandon and me together and the great times we shared. I had to speak because the silence was deafening. "I'm sorry you had to see these photos."

"It's not easy seeing you with him, but honestly some of these pictures are really beautiful. Did you take any of these?" I leaned over and kissed him. I couldn't believe he could look at these pictures objectively with all the history of Brandon and me.

I was so proud of him, that I put the pictures and the unopened confidential letter all on my nightstand, and just started kissing my sexy husband. "Jacob," I said, "the best man won. It's just you and me forever. Thank you for being a man I can respect and love. Are you still tired?"

"You are not going to take out your sexual frustrations from Brandon on me. I won't be used that way."

"Are you kidding me?"

"Yes, of course, scoot over."

"Oh, you are getting it. On your mark, get sex, go!" We had a great homecoming reunion. Jacob is so much fun, I love him, love him, love him. Then we really were ready to go to sleep. Back home in my soft, clean sheets and my comfortable pillows and bed. "Nightie-night, husband."

"Good-night, wife."

Chapter 21

Moving On

It was our first day back home and we had so much to do. Jacob was calling moving companies asking about their interstate transfers, age and mileage of their trucks, maintenance records, spare tires, cost of packing a house, etc. He asked about things I didn't even think of.

He got three different moving quotes. I was confident that he would have the best service for the best price. "Jenna, Two Men and a Truck, can be here in three days to pack, load, and leave. They will drive the truck, or I can drive it."

"If I had my choice, it would be a professional from the company driving all my earthly possessions, and you would be by my side to drive me and Baby, I mean Red, to Kentucky." He smiled, walked over to me, and gave me a hug.

I just squeezed him tight and absorbed his strength. We never talk about the past, about me losing a baby, but I guess that's how we are going to deal with that painful time in our lives. I have so much to get done and now, I needed to stay focused to be productive and positive.

"I was just thinking, with everything packed up, I'm going to need a day or two to clean my house and paint, to make things ready to sell. I wanted to clean the carpets leave it better than when I bought it.

I wanted someone to love my house as much as I did. It was my haven, a place I could be safe, and learn to be happy again. I'm sentimental and this will be tough for me. Jacob, I know you have adjustments with me moving into your house. We will just need to be patient with one another during this transition time."

He smiled, but seemed to be in a business mode, so no personal talk about feelings. "Jenna, the movers should have the house packed by noon, and we could have the cleaning crew here then. We could leave your home clean and beautiful so you can leave with that chapter in your life closed. If you need a day, two, ten, we will move when you are ready.

If this is too soon, then we'll go at a pace that works for you. But if you are ready to go, I found painters who would come in and give the walls a fresh coat of paint, and patch up holes from wall hangings, etc.

They can be here today to get wall colors that you want. The paint can be the same or different colors if you want them to be, it's up to you. Be thinking colors and resale value. I have a realtor friend I could call to ask what colors are trendy now, if you want."

"That would be great. I'm excited to start our life together in your Kentucky home, and the sooner the better for me too. We can leave keys with my girlfriend, and she can check on things until my house sells.

My friends are about the only things I'll miss from here. I'm okay with the time schedule and the cleaning crew. If we can get things done that quickly, then I'm on board. Do you have a place to store all my stuff until I have time to sort through what I want to keep, pitch, or give away?"

"Yeah, babe. I've got a warehouse we can store your things in. Then you could come to work with me, and you could sort and pitch, and I could be in the office working. It would be like we were going to work together."

"As long as it won't interfere with your business to have my stuff there for a while, then it sounds like that would work. See what a great team we are? Jacob, can I tell you something, sort of scary."

"Of course, what is it?"

He looked so concerned and it was so sweet, I almost didn't tell him. I felt like I was going to cry, and he just hugged me and then I really did want to cry. "Jacob, just hold me, don't look at me, and I'll be able to tell you this."

"Okay, I'm here, it's okay. Just talk to me."

"When you were upset with me on our honeymoon, I hurt deep in my heart. Not about the issue of saying "no", but because you weren't happy with me, and I was physically sick to my stomach. I couldn't stand you being mad at me and literally could not stand on my own two feet.

I've never cared for anyone as much as I love and care for you. It scares me sometimes how I've given you my whole heart. I'm usually reserved, cautious, and guard my feelings and hold back, so I wouldn't be destroyed completely if things went bad. But with you, I threw all that out the window at the point of our first tree swing encounter.

You are my everything, Jacob, and my heart is defenseless in your care. I'm in unfamiliar waters with you, and it scares me sometimes that I need and depend on you so completely. I do love you with all that I am. I love you more than I thought I could ever love anyone.

My one deep fear is that I'm afraid I'm going to lose you. That you will wake up and realize you don't really love me or want me, and I'll die, it will break my heart, I wouldn't survive."

"Jenna, you don't have to be afraid of me. I will get mad at you, because you drive me crazy in hundreds of ways every day. But I will always get over it and be there for you. You don't have to get sick every time we have a disagreement.

I'm not your dad who left you. I'm not your ex-husband who didn't appreciate you. I'm the good guy here. I am the one that tells you he loves you, shows you he loves you, and means every word. You don't need to be afraid anymore, I'm here.

I'm your husband and I will love and protect you. You can trust me." Jacob paused for a moment, still holding me in his arms like he was trying to keep his composure, or he'd cry, then he spoke again. "I love that you are honest and open to share your thoughts and fears with me.

It just makes me love you that much more, to know you love me and trust me with your most private thoughts and feelings. I want to protect you, and I will keep you and your heart safe. You are my wife, and it's my joy to spend my time, energy, money, and life with you, honey.

I thought I was happy before you, but you clicked something on the inside of me that had never been awake before. From that moment when I saw your beautiful eyes and smile in my grandma's parlor, I haven't been the same. The tree swing encounter just settled it for me.

That kiss changed my life. No way was I letting you get away. Even though we've had our ups and downs in the past year, we've managed to pull together and seal the deal."

"Thank you, Jacob, for not just listening to me, but hearing what I mean. I'm so happy to be spending my forever with you. And in case I didn't say it earlier, thank you for taking me to a honeymoon that I can tell others about with pride.

Well, I won't tell all of the details of our honeymoon,

but definitely the location." I winked. "Thank you for valuing me and making me feel special. I know it wasn't our "first time" to be intimate, but you made our honeymoon time the best, my best time ever. Jacob, you are my best time every day."

"You've mentioned me working for Hallmark in the past, but I think you could make some money there too. How's your foot, babe? You need to take a pill and eat some food?"

"My foot is fine. And yeah, I am kind of hungry. I don't have any food in the house, and we need to go get my dogs."

"We came back early the dogs are fine. Let's go get some food. What are you hungry for?"

"How about blackened shark?"

"Wrong location, babe, try a second choice."

"Oh, I know, there's a place called Chick-fil-A and it has really good chicken sandwiches and waffle fries. Or, if you want really good home cooking, then we should eat . . . I forgot the name of it right now.

Oh yeah, Cracker Barrel and they have the best green beans and potato cheese casserole side dishes, so you decide, and I'll give you directions. The chicken place is more of a fast food drive through where the other place is a sit down and eat place."

"Let's go sit and eat."

It took about forty minutes with traffic to get to the Cracker Barrel, and it was going to be a fifteen-minute wait, so we walked around the gift shop waiting for them to call our name for a table. They said, Jamison party of two, and I just looked up at Jacob and smiled. That's us. I gladly took his last name and now his hand as I proudly walked to our dinner table.

We had a wonderfully filling meal of great home style cooking. Home style biscuits and corn bread muffins along with chicken fried chicken, with white cream gravy, and potatoes. Jacob had fried chicken, green beans, and cheese potato casserole. He ate everything on his plate too. My tummy was full, and I took my pill. We both sort of waddled to the checkout to pay our bill and I saw her, Kayla, and she looked beautiful as usual.

She called my name. "Jenna? Jenna, is that you?" So, while Jacob was paying the bill, I went over to say hello. I told her I had gotten married, and she looked shocked.

"I thought you were dating Brandon."

"I was, and Kayla, he is an amazing man, but he wasn't the one for me. I hope that you give Brandon another chance because I'd love to see him happy, and you are great."

"Thanks. Are you coming back to class?"

"No, I'm actually moving to Kentucky in a week or so." Jacob walked up so I introduced Kayla to my husband. Jacob smiled and she just lit up. Not sure I liked that, but I couldn't blame her, because he is ruggedly handsome.

He just stood next to me, with his arm around my shoulder casually, and smiled. Not rushing me, just being there with me. I wished Kayla the best with her class and then we left.

We took about three steps outside the restaurant before Jacob asked, "So was she in your photography class with Brandon?"

"Yes, and she actually dated Brandon for a while too."

"No wonder you two are friends, you have so much in common."

I just looked up at him, again he's smiling, and all I want to do is tear off his clothes. I've heard that guys think about sex more than women, but I really don't think that is possible. I think about being with Jacob all the time. I may even be addicted to him, how sick is that? I've never felt this way before.

As I was thinking and processing my thoughts and feelings, I was quiet for a few seconds. Jacob asked me what I was thinking about? So, I whispered in his ear, I had to be honest, I told him everything, how embarrassing. He just laughed out loud. "So glad I could humor you my dear."

He walked me to my side of the car. That was nice. I put my seat belt on, then he leaned down and kissed me, sweet and tender. I told him the seat reclined and again he laughed. I wasn't trying to be his comic relief. He said to keep my panties on till we got home. Just for saying that I wanted to take them off then and there, but with my foot cast, it's too much work.

So, I sat in my seat like a good girl. He did a good job finding the way back home without me giving him any help. He had a good sense of direction.

We got home and he said, "Let's rest for a while and make our to do lists, so that tomorrow we can pack things for you to take in your car, and then others can pack the rest.

Do you need to do any banking or business here locally before we move? Should we turn the utilities off? Let's give the realtor three months to sell the place, then we can make the call to have things turned off. That way they can show the house with lights on and things working."

"I was just wondering, are you going to be relaxed and affectionate when we are in Kentucky?"

Jacob laughed, "Yes, I'm not going to have a personality transplant or anything like that. You know me, you know how I think, and how I act and respond to things, so I'll just be me."

"That's why I love you so completely." His hands slid into my hair, grabbing handfuls, that fell between his fingers and pulled gently. It was new for us, and I liked it. Somehow, we made it back to my bedroom.

He picked me up and threw me like a rag doll on the bed, flipping me over spanking me, all new stuff for me. Not sure I was thrilled with all those moves, but I went with it for his pleasure, but we were going to talk about this later.

When the passion subsided, I asked him if he needed a cigarette?

He looked puzzled and said, "I don't smoke, you know that."

"Well, what just happened here, because that was all new to me."

"You are just so sexy you do things to me. I just wanted you to be completely mine. And you were."

"I am completely yours, always."

"I know. I just wanted you a new way. I'm not sure why I went so frenzied. Did I hurt you, because you didn't say anything?"

"Our sex life and our bedroom will be a fun and safe place and I won't be a naysayer. I always want to be intimate with you, but I don't want to feel like I'm being roughhoused."

"Is that how you felt?"

"No, it's not, I overstated that. I want you to feel free to explore me in any way you want to, but I wouldn't want a steady diet of throwing me down and tying me up, like you were roping a steer."

Laughing uncontrollably, Jacob says "I just got the visual of that, and you don't have to worry about me tackling you to the ground and tying you up.

I know you have issues with control, or lack of control, so I would never do that unless you and I had pre-approved that kind of an encounter. Asking me if I wanted a smoke, too cute. You are smart, funny, sensitive, and really good to communicate with me, so we are in sync. I want to please you too.

You please me just by touching your lips, your hair, and sometimes when you're deep in thought, you bite your bottom lip just a bit, it's sexy, babe. Almost transcends me from where I'm standing at that moment to me being in your most private of places. You have to be careful with that, because I seriously don't know why that does it for me, but it wakes the sleeping giant in me every time. So, watch that lip!"

"Good to know, thanks for communicating, and I'll try to pay attention to the lip biting. I honestly didn't realize I did that, so now I will pay closer attention for sure. You mean like this, Jacob?" I bit my lip, and he was up and ready quicker than a blink. I laughed and laughed as he rolled me over and smacked my butt, then got out of bed. He wanted a shower and invited me to join him.

I said I'd give him a personal moment, that I had some reading to do. He looked at me and glanced over at the envelope on the nightstand from Brandon. He said okay, and my husband, with honeymoon tan lines, walked across the room, to the shower. He's so adorable.

Chapter 22

The Letter

I sat up in bed and opened Brandon's envelope labeled confidential that I'd waited to read until I had a private moment. I'm not sure what he's going to say, I hurt him, I broke his trust. I almost hate to open this letter, but I need this chapter of my life to be behind me once and for all. I took a deep breath and cautiously opened the envelope and began to read.

My Dearest Jenna,

I couldn't say goodbye without telling you that I love you and always will. If you ever need a friend, Jenna, I will be here or there for you. We have a connection that few people find in a lifetime, and even though you have chosen a road I can't travel with you, know that you will always hold a special place in my heart. Jenna, I don't care what time it is or how much time has passed, if I'm remarried, whatever, don't hesitate to call me if you ever need me. I will be there for you. Thanks for all

**the memorable times we spent together. I will cherish
our pictures and memories. You are special.**

Love you, Jenna.

Brandon

I looked up and Jacob was staring down at me, his hair
still dripping wet. "That good is it, Jenna?"

"What do you mean?"

"I just took a shower and got out, dried off, stood next to
you, and watched you breathing slow, deep breaths. It must
be a great letter."

"I don't know what to say except, a friend wrote me a
letter and I wanted to read it. You are welcome to read it,
but you will not be happy about it. He basically is telling
me if I ever need a friend, he will be there for me."

"Jenna, I want to see the letter."

"Sure, I don't have any secrets from you. I'm not doing
this to hurt you."

"I know, just let me read it, okay?"

"Here it is, take it."

I watched Jacob's hands as he held the letter, and his
knuckles were turning white, he was squeezing it so tight.
"Jacob, he's an old friend saying goodbye. It's comforting
to know that he doesn't hate me. It's such a better way to
end things as friends. I ended it I'm married."

"If he ever contacts you again, ever, I want to know.
He's playing a dangerous game and you are not a pawn to
be tossed back and forth. I want you to tell me if he ever
contacts you again okay?"

I got a sick feeling in my stomach, "Jacob, why don't
you just take my phone now. I'll give you my password to
my email and Facebook and my mail will be at your house,
so you will have total control over every word that is said
to me. It will be just like old times for me." I got up from
the bed and walked to the shower.

"Damn it, Jenna! Don't throw your Tom baggage on me.

I am not being unreasonable. I just want to know if this lovesick man is trying to overstep boundaries that you have made clear to him. I trust you and I'm not the phone, email, whatever, privacy police. But I want to know, that's not too much to ask of my wife, is it?"

I wrapped a towel around me and walked to the kitchen. I needed a Diet Dr. Pepper and noticed a Coke in the fridge. "You want a Coke? I don't have Jack, but we could run to the store."

"No, Coke's fine."

"Okay, I am going to jump in the shower now. I'll be out in a few minutes." I'm in the shower crying again. Why am I so emotional? What is going on with me? I need a physical, maybe I'm going into menopause early or something.

My cancer doctor told me that I might go into menopause early because of my chemo treatments. But that hadn't happened, so I thought he was wrong. But as I sat on the floor of my shower hugging my bent knees and crying, I looked up to get some shampoo and I saw Jacob standing at the shower door. "What is it?"

I opened the door, and he stripped, and was in the shower again, this time putting his hands and soap all over my body. He knew how to handle me to make me putty in his hands. I turned facing him and all the Brandon argument was a distant memory, like a candle flame that flickered out with each touch. I was in the arms of a man that loved me and was attentive to my needs. That's where I would gladly stay forever.

After we dried off, and got dressed, we made our to-do lists. I did call to cancel internet services and cable service to my house. But I left the power and gas service on for lights, the stove and dryer.

I told Jacob that my girlfriend needed a washer and dryer and if he was okay with it, I'd like to offer her mine, if she wants them. Her husband could come over, load them in his truck, and his son could help him install them at their house. Jacob said sure, that he had a new washer and dryer, so we didn't need two sets. So, I called and made the arrangements with my friend.

Our to-do list was getting smaller and smaller, and things were going pretty smoothly considering our timetable. I told Jacob that my Granny gave me her set of China, and I wanted to take those with us in the truck so that they didn't get broken. My dad's mom also gave me her set of Depression glass dishes.

Being the only granddaughter, it was only logical, and I treasure them, and only use them for family dinners and special occasions. Jacob thought that I should take clothes, computer, important paperwork, like our passports, marriage license, title to my car, our car, etc. So, I brought the file box with my highly important documents my camera and lenses in my car too.

Tomorrow we will clean, pack necessary items and get my dogs. Tomorrow is going to be a busy day. Maybe all these changes are why I'm so emotional. "I'm sorry I've been so emotional, I don't know why I'm acting like such a baby, all these tears, it's really a new development for me. I think when I get settled in Kentucky, I should go in for a physical and make sure everything is okay."

"Jenna, do you not feel well? Are you in pain?"

"No, I'm just so uncharacteristically emotional." Then it hit me. "Oh my gosh, Jacob, we've been having sex."

"No kidding, it's called a honeymoon."

"No, Jacob, I mean, I am not on birth control, and you haven't used any protection. I don't think I'm pregnant, but we should go get a test from the drug store, just in case. Maybe there's a reason I'm so emotional. I don't know how I missed this, but we need to check. I wasn't supposed to get pregnant or try again for six months after I lost the baby. Jacob, it's too soon, I can't be pregnant yet, but we need to make sure."

"I can't believe you aren't on the pill. I just assumed that you went on it when you had the miscarriage."

"Well, I wasn't planning on having sex for a few months, and then going back to the doctor to get the dosages set for the pill."

"Do you feel like you're pregnant?"

"I don't know. I'm just so ready for sex all the time, and I feel like I'm an emotional roller coaster. I can't remember when I had my last period. We need to get a test to make sure. I don't want to lift a box if I'm pregnant. I don't want to do anything to lose another baby, your baby. I just want to be cautious if I'm carrying your baby."

"Oh no, I was throwing you on the bed the other night. I am so sorry. If I had known I would never have done that."

"I'm fine, that was fine. But let's go to the store and get a pregnancy test just to know for sure. I'll get you more Coke and I'll buy the Jack too. I'm so sorry, I've been drinking champagne. I don't want to get all worked up, I'm probably not pregnant, but let's just go get a test and find out for sure so I can calm down, once I know for sure. My heart is racing, is yours?"

"Yes, babe, my hearts beating fast too. Let's get in the car, buckle up, and go."

Jacob didn't say a word in the car. Silent, no radio, no singing, no smiles, just serious reflections of what this could mean. How could I have been so stupid? That's what he's thinking, cause that's what I'm thinking. How could I go through this again?

He pulled up to Wal-Greens and asked if I was going inside? The car was parked, turned off, and I hadn't realized we were stopped yet. I got out, walked inside, got a cart, and headed back to the pharmacy. I bought two different pregnancy tests. Jacob bought a case of Bud Light, Coke, and a gallon of milk. Jacob didn't think I should drink so much pop with caffeine.

I just nodded and followed him as we checked out. I

threw a candy bar in the cart too. This definitely is a situation that requires chocolate.

The woman checking us out at the register was probably in her early sixties and had to talk about every item we bought. When she saw the pregnancy tests, she wished us good luck, and announced that our babies would be beautiful. I didn't think I'd make it out of there before I was going to cry again.

Jacob just looked at me and put his arm around me. We didn't say a word. He paid and I did all I could do to put one foot in front of the other to the car. Jacob drove us home but missed my street, so he was distracted too. We got home and I sat down to finish my Diet Dr. Pepper. I needed it before I faced the bathroom.

"Jacob, I'm going to go pee on a stick. I'm so sorry I didn't take care of myself." Jacob stood up, walked over to me, and took my hand in his.

"Don't apologize for loving me ever again. We will face whatever comes our way together, always."

I grabbed his neck and told him in a heart-felt whisper because that's all I could get out or I'd cry. "Jacob, I've never loved you more than I do right now." We kissed and just hugged each other tightly. He let me go, and I walked down the hall. In the next five minutes our lives could change forever. I peed on the stick, washed my hands and lay down on the bed.

Jacob came back and lay down next to me. He held my hand and told me he loved me. I didn't want to get out of the bed. I didn't want to know. I didn't want a baby. I'm too old, kids take so much energy, and I barely can take care of myself lately.

Look at me, I've broken my foot twice in a year. How am I going to manage taking care of a newborn? My mind was racing all these thoughts flooding in. I told Jacob if I was biting my lip, he could forget it. He just smiled and said, "There she is, my girl's back."

I said, "Well it's time. Let's go see if there is an addition to our family."

We looked at the pee stick and just stared at each other. Jacob said, "Jenna, how are you feeling with the results?"

"Honestly, I'm happy that we are not having a baby right now. I love you, but I'm old. I work with five-year-old children daily, and I know how much attention, energy, and money they require. They are life changers.

I have already changed my life with you, and you are more than enough for me. Do you want kids? I guess we should have had this discussion before we married, are kids in the picture for our future?"

"If you want kids, Jenna, then I will do all I can to make that dream come true. But if you don't want kids, I know that we can have a fulfilling life together without kids too.

I have a nephew now, so if I need a kid fix, I can go over to my brothers, spend an hour or two, then leave and be just fine. I never really thought about kids because I never thought I'd settle down and get married. I'm happy with our life, the two of us, very happy, Jenna.

But I'm not a girl and if you need a baby to be happy then I want you happy. A baby would be great."

"We need to be careful with sex until I get on the pill and that could take two to three months before we are safe to have sex without protection. I'm so sorry it didn't occur to me to go on the pill. I didn't need it when I was married before, so it was not a thought in my head. It was irresponsible of me and I'm sorry."

"When we get to Kentucky, you are going in for a full physical and we'll get the pill for us to be safe. You have been under a lot of stress lately. You left a job you love, got married, moving to another state, and you have an old boyfriend trying to keep you connected to him.

Plus, you are on pain pills for a re-fractured bone. You should be proud you have had all this thrown your way and you still shine."

"Just listening to you talk about it and I'm exhausted. I don't feel like I'm a light, I just feel exhausted. Are you tired?"

"A little, I didn't do a whole lot today, but why don't you take a nap and I'll get online and do some work, if you don't mind."

"Sounds good, I just need a little nap. Love you. In case I sleep longer than planned, remember we have a big day tomorrow, so don't stay up too late dear."

"You want me to lie next to you until you fall asleep?"

"Always, but you don't have to."

"I know I don't have to I get to. I'll cuddle with you, then check in on my laptop."

"Okay, let me brush my teeth and get ready for bed." Unbelievable, I went to the bathroom before I went to bed and started my period. It couldn't have started two hours ago and saved me a mini-heart attack?

I told Jacob I started my period, he just rolled his eyes and said better late than never. I said AMEN! Jacob said he was going to put my day on his calendar, so he'd know when to expect extra drama from me. I looked at him and intentionally bit my lip. He said, "No, it's not going to work this time, Jenna!"

And he ran out of the bedroom to get his phone. He really did enter "Jenna's period" on today's date. I just shook my head and laid in bed laughing. He can make me laugh after all we've been through today, I truly, completely adore this man.

We cuddled and I relaxed, and I went off to sleep almost as fast as I hit the pillow. I slept the entire night and when I woke up, Jacob wasn't next to me.

I got up. He was gone. No note, just gone. Maybe he had to do something with the packers, getting tape, or boxes, or I didn't know what. I have a phone, I'll call him. I called just as he was walking in the front door. He had coffee and fast-food breakfast.

He was all smiles and looking handsome as ever. I wanted to kiss him all over, but I hadn't brushed my teeth yet for the morning, or even looked in the mirror. He just leaned down, with his hands full and kissed me on the forehead.

"You ready for our packing day?"

"I am if you are, babe. Did you sleep?"

"Some."

"What's that mean, some?"

"A couple hours."

"Why couldn't you sleep?"

"We had a big night Jenna, I just needed to process things. I have to have time to think things through, like you have to rest to regain your strength and perspective. We are two different people who process things differently."

"I was confused when I woke and you were gone, no note, nothing."

"Sorry, babe, I didn't want to wake you. I was just trying to get back before you woke up."

"Thanks for breakfast, as always, I'm hungry. Today is the last day for pain pills so then I won't be hungry all the time. I don't know what it is with the combination of pain and hunger with me, but they must be connected in my body."

"It's not wrong to eat three meals a day, it's the normal thing to do. Here, let's eat while the food is still hot. The movers will be here in about forty-five minutes, so you have time for breakfast and a shower. I do not want you to lift anything today. Pregnant or not, I don't want you to hurt your back, or break something else."

"It's my stuff, I feel like I need to help. I want to help."

"You can direct verbally. I happen to know from personal experience that you have strong extemporaneous skills. You just tell them what you want, and we will be your arms and legs."

"Thanks for breakfast. I'll eat fast and jump in the

shower. Are you going to join me?"

"Don't tempt me."

"Jacob, is it hot in here? I am so hot."

"No actually, it's cool in here." He leaned over and touched his face to my face. Jenna, do you have a thermometer?"

"Yes."

"You do feel hot."

"Well, you look hot, I'm just trying to keep up with you, babe."

"Seriously, where's your thermometer?"

"I'll go get it. I can't be sick, I'm fine, Jacob." I walked back to the bathroom and put the thermometer in my mouth. Jacob was standing in the doorway staring at me.

"Oh, good I finally found a way for me to be able to get a word in edgewise, a thermometer." I just shook my head no and winked at him. "You look sexy even with a thermometer in your mouth. You are sick, on your period, and still turn me on in every way. What you do to me, no one has ever had that kind of power over me."

That was all I could take, I went to reach for the thermometer to take it out of my mouth, but Jacob said, "No keep it in until time is up." I just shook my head. Then the timer went off on the thermometer and the temp was 100.1

That was it, Jacob was going to call and cancel the moving and painting crew, everyone. I said, "No way. All they have to do is pack everything. I will stay in bed and drink water. You stay away because I don't want you sick too. If you have a question, call me I'll plug my phone in by my bed."

"Jenna, are you sure? We can reschedule when you feel better."

"No, I'll be fine tomorrow, I just need to get some rest, I guess. I do feel terrible. Usually, the first day of my period I feel awful, then day two I'm good as new. Aren't you hungry? You didn't finish your breakfast darling."

"Yes, let's eat and then you will have some energy." I ate an egg and cheese burrito, drank my large orange juice, and had a few sips of coffee. Then I was ready to go back to bed.

Chapter 23

The Move

Jacob took care of the movers. I didn't even hear them packing, talking, opening doors, shutting doors, nothing. I must have been really sick because Jacob came back to my bed, and I woke up and he had my pills and water and said it was two-thirty and they were finished packing and the cleaners were here cleaning.

I looked around my bedroom, and large furniture was missing from the room. I cannot believe they came in and I was sound asleep. This is very embarrassing, so glad I'm moving far away, this is humiliating.

Jacob got a cold washcloth and put it on my head, it felt wonderful. I sat up in bed and got up to go to the bathroom. I was so hot everything was sticking to me. I pulled my hair up into a ponytail, but all my hair supplies were packed, so I just used my own hair to hold it back off my face.

I brushed my teeth and felt much better. Jacob took my temperature, and it was 99.9 so it was going down. I told him I'd get better. He smiled. I asked how he was feeling, and he said he was fine. He couldn't believe one person could have so much stuff. I said, "I'm a girl, that's what we do. Girls have the homesteading gene."

He just smiled. "Jenna, I'm going to go get lunch for you, what sounds good?"

"I have soup, just pour a can in a bowl, and stick it in the microwave."

"There are no bowls, they are packed, no food, it's all packed. I called your girlfriend to come get the food from your freezer. She and her husband are really nice. They picked up the washer and dryer too. She said she has a key to your house and will keep an eye on things for us."

"What can I do to help? You've done everything for me, and I just slept."

"Yes, you did, and I'm glad you did. I'll get you some food if you are okay to be here with the cleaning crew? Maybe you should put on a bra, with men in the house and you in a weak condition, you wouldn't be able to fight them off."

"Oh, you are so modest sometimes. Okay, I'll put on a bra, but stay until I get it on."

"I'll help you, if you want."

"No way, Jacob, we have people in the house and I'm sick. You need to stay away from me. I love you and don't want to give you whatever it is I've caught. Okay, Chinese restaurant down the street for hot and sour soup for me, and you could go to Taco Bell and grab something if you don't want Chinese food. Jacob, take your time, get some fresh air, you've worked hard all day, I'm fine. Love you!"

Jacob left and I got out of bed and walked through my house. It seemed so big with everything packed and loaded into the moving truck. Wow my carpets were dirty, so glad they are cleaning them. It smells clean. The paint is the same colors, light gray's, whites, and green colors.

The cleaners told me they start at the ceiling and dust light fixtures and the walls, then they paint, then clean carpets and while carpets dry, they scrub the tile floors in the bathrooms, clean mirrors in the bathrooms and then they should be through. They said they would do windows if they had time. Jacob checked every box on their work order, so we are clear on what he wants and expects.

"Well, he'll be back with lunch, so I'll let you all get back to the great work you're doing. It's happening so fast I can't believe how quickly you've worked and how quietly." They all just smiled and got back to work. Then I counted six people in the house working.

Good grief, no wonder they are almost done, they had almost one person per room. They asked me to give them twenty minutes and they would vacuum and clean my back bedroom floors. They said, "Mr. Jamison said not to paint back there because he didn't want you breathing the fumes. We will come back when your friend can come let us in and we will repaint this back bedroom."

"That's fine thanks."

I moved out to the kitchen and sat on the counter, so I wasn't in the way. Jacob showed up about fifty minutes later. He wasn't happy that I wasn't back in bed, but he just smiled at me and gave me my soup. I sat on the countertop, and Jacob leaned against the bar, and we ate together.

"Jacob, the house is clean and empty. You did a great job orchestrating all the move details. Thank you so much for taking on all the stress of packing, painting, and cleaning details today. I know you did all this for me, sweetheart, and I just want you to know your efforts are recognized and really appreciated."

"You're welcome. Actually, it went really smooth today. Both companies were very professional and worked quietly and quickly. I am going to pick up your dogs at five and there will be room to put them in the back of the SUV with us. I've got a bag of their dog food, and both their crates in the back seat.

The rest of the moving truck is piled pretty full, but

anything is adjustable if you want it to be. There is one change of plans. I need to drive the moving van, and you will have to drive our car, if you are up to it."

"I'm sure it's all fine Jacob. Do you know where my purse is located?"

"Yes, it's locked in the car with your phone and phone charger. Your laptop is in there too."

"Thanks."

"You still feel warm. You probably have been up the whole time I've been gone."

"Yep, I was holding down the fort. I didn't want any slackers on my shift. I do feel better after eating. I'll lay back down and sleep until I hear two barking dogs." I got up as soon as he returned with my dogs, knowing Jacob would have his hands full.

They were glad to see me. I didn't want them on my almost dry carpets or touching my freshly painted walls, so we took them into the fenced back yard to run until we were ready to get in the truck and head out to Kentucky. I made sure they still had a water dish outside and it was full of fresh water.

The cleaning crew wanted Jacob to check their work so they could get paid and leave. I was impressed, but Jacob made them go back a couple of places and spot clean some high traffic areas on the carpet. I love that he's a perfectionist. I love having him fight for what I want, even when I can't. He is my man.

They left and Jacob said he needed a nap before we left for our long drive. I told him I'd nap too if he was going to sleep. But only if we are back-to-back, I don't want to breathe on you and make you sick. I said, "Let me have a nap, you take one too, and I'll follow you anywhere, even across the country sweetheart."

"I was really tired. I needed to shower first. I'd be really quick, then jump in bed."

"Okay." I curled up in bed and when I woke, Jacob was

curled up around me. I hope he doesn't get sick. I would feel horrible if he did. I felt better, but I should have, because I'd done nothing but sleep and eat. I love the feel of my hairy man wrapped around me. I'm hot and need to use the restroom but don't want to wake him up. I looked for my alarm clock, but it's been packed so I have no idea what time it is.

I tried to stay in bed, but I had to pee really bad, so I got up, and went to the bathroom. I walked down the hall, out to the garage, into the car, and found my purse and phone. It said seven o'clock. There was no way we were leaving for the road trip at night. We need to go in the morning.

After I used the guest bathroom down the hall, I just slipped back into bed. The next time I woke up, Jacob was still asleep next to me in bed. I went to the bathroom, slurped down some cold water, and threw some on my face. Jacob heard the stool flush and came to the doorway. "How are you feeling, sweetheart?"

"Much better. Thanks for asking. How are you feeling?"

"Bad. I overslept, and now it's morning. Are you up to jumping in the shower and then driving through to get food, so we can get started on our trip?"

"Yes, I am if you are."

We jumped into the shower, but could only find one towel, so I just pulled my wet hair up and threw on my sweats. We fed the dogs and made sure everything was turned off. We drove through Burger King for breakfast, ate together in my car, then I drove Jacob back to our fully loaded moving van. We loaded the dogs into the crates in my backseat, and we headed to my husband's home in Kentucky.

I don't know how Jacob could drive that huge truck. It was windy, and we ran into some rain on the road, and some areas with crazy traffic, but we just plowed through it all to get me home. I have to pee way more often than he does.

But he was patient to stop when I needed to go. He'd get out and stretch his legs, fill the trucks with gas, and walk the dogs. We had a long trip. Jacob wanted to drive until we got to his house.

I told him I could do it if he didn't mind if I smoked. He thought I was kidding, but I said no, if I had pop and cigarettes, I could drive across the country with no sleep. He said just this once, and said he'd never figure me out. But we drove on, and we made it from my door to his door in twenty-seven and one-half hours with food, gas, and bathroom breaks. The trip wasn't bad, but when we got to Jacob's, I was so excited I felt wide awake.

Jacob parked the moving van at his business, and said he'd have his workers unload the truck tomorrow, and his guys would return the truck. He'd pay them for their work. I'm so glad Jacob has money. It totally takes the pressure off for the basic things.

Then he got into our car and drove the rest of the way to our house. We got to the house and Jacob wanted to carry me up the stairs over the thresh-hold, like a newly married couple. He's so sweet, as tired as he was, and he wanted to do this for me. "I love you, Jacob." Then he put me down and walked me through the kitchen to the back door. Then he turned on the porch light.

He had his brothers, and his workers build a wooden fence so we could let my dogs outside and not worry about them running off. Jacob is so thoughtful. We went out to the car and got the dogs and let them run in their new back yard while I walked through the house, used the restroom, and tried to enjoy the feeling of motionless flooring under my feet. Jacob had the car in the garage and was unloading stuff. Where did he find the energy to do all this?

"Jacob, can we go to bed? Aren't you tired?"

"Sure, babe, just wanted you to have the car empty if you wanted to run to town, or whatever."

"I want you healthy, you've been going one hundred

percent for days now, and I need you healthy and strong. Please don't overdo it, because I couldn't take it if anything happened to you."

"I'm fine, let's go to bed." We jumped into the shower, and I felt human again for the first time in days. We went to bed and slept almost thirteen hours straight. I was really glad we left the dogs in the backyard to run and move, because we were both dead to the world.

We got up and we went to town to check on my stuff being unloaded in his warehouse. Everything was unloaded, stacked neatly in the corner, and it hardly took any room in his huge warehouse. The moving van was gone, so we assumed the men he asked to take care of it had done so. We were hungry so we went to eat and then to the grocery store so I could cook for my husband.

"Jacob, I love this house."

"It's our house now, you, me, Molly and Moose. I want you to feel comfortable in our home. It's not my house anymore it's our house. I may mis-speak from time to time, but I will always feel that this is our home from now on, Jenna. Honestly that's how I feel, what's mine is yours."

"Jacob, are we really going to wait weeks before I can get into a doctor before we have sex again? Because I feel better, and I miss you and want you. Do I need to bite my bottom lip?"

"Do not do that to me. I should have never told you my weakness, you will use that against me."

"There's a whole lot I'd like to hold against you, just naked. You have those soft beautiful blue sheets they are calling my name. I did buy them with this very thing in mind. I'm giving you to the count of ten, then I'm biting my lip."

"I'm not going to be Mr. No, but I saw your face when you thought you were pregnant, and that was pure panic. Baby, I love you and want to be intimate with you more than anything, but I don't want that look on your face ever again. It scared the hell out of me."

"I love you, and once again, you are right. Do you know a doctor that could get me in before three to six months?"

"We will call around tomorrow. We will get you in somewhere tomorrow. I do know a few people in the area. I think we can get this resolved quickly. You are tired and run down, so you should conserve your energy for a few days anyway."

We kissed and cuddled, and it was enough just being next to him. I love the smell of him, the feel of his thick head of hair in my fingers. I even love stroking the hair on his arm back and forth as I'm falling asleep with his arm wrapped around my middle, right below my ribs. He comforts me and relaxes me.

Chapter 24

Home Sweet Home

Jacob had been with me non-stop for two and a half weeks. I knew he had tons of things to do for his job, but he never complained, or made me feel like I was taking up too much of his time. He was very attentive to my needs and all the adjustments we were making together.

He offered to drive me to my doctor's appointment, but I told him I had GPS on my car, and I could find my way. That way he could get some work done today. "I appreciate the offer, but it's really not necessary. You are welcome to go with me if you really want to go, but I know you've missed a lot of work."

"Babe, I'm sure you can manage your doctor appointment without me. But call if you need me."

"Okay, but, Jacob, you do know I always need you right? I need you to be happy and healthy and sexually satisfied, so I'm off to the doctor."

"You and your honesty, it's, it's, it's…"

"What, Jacob? What is it?"

"I'll let you know when I figure it out."

"Fair enough, I'm off to see the doctor."

I liked my new female doctor, and she started me on contraception medicine "the pill". It was the same brand I had taken years earlier when I was first married. Then when we were told we couldn't have kids, I stopped taking the pill, and we pretty much just stopped having sex too. Maybe that's why I'm so sex hungry now. Maybe I'm making up for lost time, lost years, I'm not sure. It was a good doctor visit and I set up my next appointment for six months down the road. I had the rest of the afternoon to go explore my new surroundings.

I stopped and purchased some fresh flowers and a pretty deep blue glass vase. I located an authentic Italian grocery store, so I bought the ingredients to make spaghetti, garlic bread, and meat to make homemade meatballs for my husband and our first homemade meal in our happy home. And, of course, I purchased all the fixings for a healthy, colorful salad too.

Jacob said he'd be home about five. At five-thirty I called him and he said he'd be leaving in a few minutes. By seven p.m. I was so hungry, I just ate by myself, left the food on the table, and went to bed.

I don't know what time Jacob got home, but I was asleep. He didn't wake me, talk to me, nothing. When I got up the next morning he was gone already. I went down to the kitchen to make some coffee and there was a note from Jacob.

My second letter from Jacob, he apologized for being late last night, and thanked me for a delicious meal. The flowers were a sweet touch, and he was sorry he wasn't there to hear about my day. He was really behind at work and was just overwhelmed, but he'd get caught up and make it up to me soon.

Now is as good a time as any, to go to Jacob's work, start going through my stuff, and sorting and pitching. But I wanted to talk to Jacob before I began this process. Maybe he won't mind if I stop by the warehouse and just begin. I remembered how to get to his office. I pulled up and there were lots of cars in the parking lot.

I walked into the front doors, in my jeans and nice, fitted, button-down white blouse, with a black belt on the outside of my shirt, and black boots to my knees, one cast, one boot. I thought I looked good to be meeting people he works with, and then to get work done in the warehouse too.

I introduced myself to the receptionist and she was polite. She asked if I had an appointment. I said no, I'm Mrs. Jamison. She just smiled and said one minute please. She called a number and then smiled again. She told me to follow her. She walked me to the back of the building, past lots of offices with windows and people working. We got to the back and there was Jacob's name on the door. She knocked and opened the door.

He had about eight men sitting around a large mahogany conference table. They all had laptops and were vocal about the topic at hand.

Jacob stood up and said, "Gentlemen, this is the reason I've been playing hooky from work, this is my wife, Jenna." They all stood up and said hello. I smiled and felt like a huge intrusion.

I said, "May I borrow Mr. Jamison for a moment please?"

Jacob walked to the door and shut it, allowing us to have a private word in the hallway. "What do you need, honey?"

"Sorry to bother you. I just wanted the key to get into the warehouse so I could have something to do. I would like to go through my stuff, if it's okay with you."

"It's your stuff, help yourself. I need to get back to work. If you need anything, just ask my secretary and she will also get you a key." Then no kiss, no love you, all business, he was on the other side of the door and gone.

"Love you too, Jacob."

I walked back down the long hallway to his secretary who was younger than me and very pretty, and I asked her for a key to the warehouse. She looked at me like that was going to be a problem, but just then she got a phone call from Jacob, I presume, because she said yes sir, and hung up the phone. Then I had the key in my hand, and she was walking me out to the warehouse.

"Mrs. Jamison, if you need anything to drink or have any questions, just dial my extension 33, and I'll do what I can to assist you."

"Thank you. Are there trash bins available for things I need to get rid of?"

"Yes, use the gray trash bins, they are on rollers, so they will be easy to move around."

"Is there a local shelter that could use clothes, housewares, etc.?"

"Yes, and they would come by and pick up clothes, furniture, you name it. Just let me know when you want them to pick stuff up, and they will come by and get them."

"Thank you, Ms. Extension 33."

"Oh, I'm sorry I don't think I introduced myself, I'm Twyla Snow."

"Thank you, Ms. Snow." Twyla had shoulder length hair and it was a beautiful strawberry blond color. She had a smile that made you want to smile too.

I'm glad Jacob has a good Administrative Assistant to run things for him when he's so busy and his business so large and successful. I could tell from our short conversation that she was really smart, had an extensive vocabulary, and was a nice lady. I think could be friends.

Twyla headed back down the hall and I got to work. I started pitching lots of things I just didn't care about anymore. I called my mom to see if I had anything she would want. She said when I get everything sorted, send her a picture from my phone and then she could make an informed decision. My mom is techier than I, that's just sad to admit out loud.

I still don't have a picture of Jacob in my phone for when he calls me so his picture could show up on my phone. I need to take a computer class or something down the road. I wish I knew how to play music on my phone too, and then this sorting process would be much more fun. I should call my uncle Thomas, I'm sure he could tell me how to do that. I'll do that tonight. It will be fun to visit with him and catch up on what's going on.

I worked until I was so hungry, I couldn't stand it any longer. So, I locked things up and since Jacob's truck was still parked in the parking lot, I didn't want to go home and eat alone, so I went to a local restaurant. I wondered if Alice the waitress will remember me. I went and ordered a greasy cheeseburger, with onion rings, and of course my Diet Dr. Pepper.

Alice did remember me and sat down in the booth with me to have a smoke while I ate. I liked Alice, but the smoke I could live without. She was honest and spoke her mind. She said she couldn't believe the news that Jacob finally got married. Alice was funny and knew everyone in town.

She gave me the scoop on everyone in the building. I asked if there was a movie theater or bowling alley nearby and she laughed in my face. No, the closest town with those options was forty-five minutes away.

I told Alice nothing that I didn't want the entire community to know. I told her things like how much I loved the beauty of Kentucky and I was looking forward to meeting the women in the community. I wanted to get to know them and become involved in the community. Then Alice said, "With Jacob's money, you will be welcomed with open arms."

"Thanks, Alice, I wouldn't want anyone to like me for

who I am, only for my husband's money. Those are the kinds of people I want to surround myself with. Can I have my check please?"

"No, Jenna, I'm sorry I didn't mean to be so blunt. I just say what I'm thinking sometimes too quickly. Can I ask you a personal question?"

"You can ask, no promise I'll answer."

"Everyone is wondering, I'm just the one who's brave enough to ask. Are you pregnant? Is that why Jacob married you?"

"Alice, thanks for the great food. Hope you have a great day." I gave her a five-dollar bill for a tip, and I thought I was being kind. Alice said under her breath, but loud enough for me to hear, Jacob usually gives me ten.

I just smiled no way was I going to let her know she got to me. And I said, under my breath, hmm maybe I need to get a job here. I heard her co-worker laugh at my comment. I smiled and left the premises. Apparently, I didn't like Alice as much as I thought I might.

Well, I'm in a state where I basically don't know anyone, with no job, no friends, and a husband who works all the time because of his heavy workload. Alice mentioned the biggest town was forty-five minutes away, and I was sure Jacob would be working late again tonight, and then he'd come home and crash. So, I had time to do more exploring. I filled up the car and headed over to the nearest town, compliments of my GPS.

I found a new favorite coffee house called "Above the Grind". It's so exciting to have something familiar a delicious cup of perfectly brewed coffee. I parked and went inside. The scent of freshly brewed coffee was heavenly. Just what I needed, it tasted like home, warm and comforting.

A younger college man in front of me in line bought my drink for me. I thanked him and he asked if he could sit and visit for a moment. I didn't care and he just bought me a drink. He sat and told me he was a student at the University and was studying foreign affairs.

I told him I was married and didn't believe in affairs. He laughed at my sense of humor. This kid in his baseball cap, jeans, and a tee shirt, was really cute. He had dimples and piercing green eyes, totally a looker. I liked him right away, not just because he's adorable, but he's funny and nice.

He has a girlfriend who is studying dance. He was telling me about all the courses he was taking and said I should think about going back to school. I told him I already have two master's degrees, but I love learning new things. I told him I'd check out the course catalog to see what was being offered next semester.

He smiled and seemed pleased. He told me when I come back to town give him a call, and he and his girlfriend would take me and my husband to some fun night clubs in town. How cute is this college man?

I thanked him for the coffee and conversation and Larry asked for my phone to put in his number. I gave him my phone and he entered Larry the coffee man into my phone contacts. I thanked him again, told him I'd love to meet his girlfriend, and that I needed to head home, it was getting late.

It was about ten p.m. when I got home, and Jacob's truck was in the driveway. Good he's home early. I came in the house, glad to see my husband. He smiled, but not a big, happy to see you smile, just a smile you give when you feel like it's expected of you. I went up and said, "Honey, I'm so glad you are home. How was your day?"

"Fine, how was yours?"

"Fine, thanks for asking."

"I heard you talked to Alice today and was rude to her. Jenna, you need to be nice, she's a great girl."

"Really, Jacob, is that what your old girlfriend told you? Well, I was told that my five-dollar tip wasn't as nice as your ten-dollar tips. I was also told that the town thinks I'm pregnant because why else would you marry me? I was kind to your old girlfriend Alice, because I was representing you, as your wife, and I was not rude to anyone. She was rude to me.

Why do you care so much about what she says or thinks anyway? And I find it interesting that you are too busy to talk to your own wife today, but Alice, the ten-dollar whore, gets your ear. Nice, Jacob, thanks for supporting your wife who's out there on her own, trying to make her way in a new environment. Thanks, husband, I'm feeling the love."

"Jenna, Alice is Twyla's good friend, and she called Twyla as soon as you left this afternoon around four. I asked Twyla if you were still in the warehouse, and she told me she just got off the phone with Alice, and then relayed to me the conversation that took place."

"It's late, Jacob, you hungry?"

"No, I just had leftover spaghetti. You hungry?"

"No."

"Did you eat dinner?"

"I had a late lunch remember, your Alice."

"She's not my Alice."

"Whatever, I'm sure you are tired and so am I, so if you don't mind, I'm going to jump in the shower and go to bed. You don't need to stay up for me, Jacob. I know you are working hard, so go ahead and crash if you want to."

I didn't kiss him, hug him, anything, I just turned and went to the shower. I got out of the shower and Jacob was standing in the doorway with his shirt off and his hand running through his hair. He looked so hot.

"Jenna."

"Babe, what's up?"

"I have a question for you."

"Okay, what is it?"

"You want to tell me who the hell Larry the coffee boy is?"

I dropped my towel and turned around. "You checked my phone while I was in the shower? You went through my phone?" I felt sick, I wanted to run, but my legs wouldn't move. "You don't trust me, are you checking up on me?"

Jacob saw the horror in my eyes from my past and quickly said "No, that's not how it happened. You went to the shower and your phone buzzed. I saw it sitting there and that's what came up on the phone identification name and number."

I picked up my towel from the floor and asked to have a few minutes and I'd be out. I sat on the stool and buried my face in my towel. For a minute there I thought I was trapped in another marriage with a man who was controlling and didn't trust me.

Just the brief thought made me sick to my stomach. I got myself together and was throwing cold water on my face, when I heard Jacob at the door.

"Are you okay?"

"Yes, I'll be out in a minute". I came out and he had the lights on in the bedroom. I walked over and turned them off and crawled into bed.

"Why did you turn the lights out? Aren't we going to talk about this?"

"Not tonight, goodnight."

"Jenna, you haven't answered my question. Who's Larry?"

"Fine, we'll talk, that's what you want, so we'll do what you want right this very minute. He's a guy I met at the coffee shop today. He is a young man who bought me a coffee. He had time for me and made me laugh. He's really funny and wanted me to meet his girlfriend.

He wants you and me to meet him and his girlfriend and go to some dance clubs soon. That's who Larry is, and I don't even know his last name to tell you any more than that. It's totally innocent, Jacob."

"I know you must have thought you were back in your

Tom days, but I told you I won't treat you that way."

"No, you don't have to, because you've got eyes all over the countryside, reporting my every conversation and move. And putting their own twist on what really happens. How about getting both sides of a story before you make a judgment and find me guilty?

How about give your wife the benefit of the doubt. You should know me better than to believe what she said about me. That was hurtful. Not what she made up, but that you believed it. You are supposed to know me best, and you didn't have my back."

"That's not fair, I wasn't checking up on you. I just asked if you were still at the office and I got the voluntary account of the lunch conversation."

"Yes, an account from another woman's perspective, from another woman and not from the source. If you want to know something, ask me. You have a phone, I have a phone, you want to know something ask me. I'm sorry, Jacob.

You asked about Larry, and my past and present had a brief crash. It's late and I'm sure you have a busy day tomorrow. I'm sorry I bothered you at work today, but I did get rid of a lot of my things. How was your day dear?"

"I work with a bunch of men who are all about the fast buck and have no vision for the future. They just want profit now, not a vision for investments and future benefits. It's frustrating."

"I'm sure if they are good businessmen, they will think about what you've told them, and with time to reflect, they will begin to catch your enthusiasm and vision. You are a strong competent leader. I'd follow you anywhere, oh wait a minute, I've already done that."

"Thanks."

"You're welcome, sweetheart. Good night and pleasant dreams."

"Are you tired, Jenna?"

"I'm Exhausted."

When I woke, Jacob was gone to work. He left a note next to my pillow that said, I will be home early tonight for a date night with my wife. That was sweet of him to make an effort in this busy schedule for me. He's trying to be a better communicator. I do love him, and miss him, and appreciate his effort.

I need to go to the city, find a nail salon, get my nails done, then come back and fix a nice dinner for my hubby. The last time I fixed him a romantic dinner and bought him flowers, he worked late, so I ate alone and so did he. Maybe this time I'll fix a wonderful dinner and should buy some new sexy sleepwear too. That's the ticket that sounds like a fun day.

I showered, shaved, and headed to the city for a nail salon and then found a Victoria's Secret store and stocked up on sexy bras, underwear, and thigh hose. I stopped at the store and bought a case of Coke and a jug of Jack Daniels. Tonight, should be a great night. I think I've covered all the basic stuff for dinner and after dinner.

I was back at home around five. I took my cast off for the night. I put a little black dress over my naughty night wear and eagerly awaited my husband and our date night. After six o'clock, I got hungry, so I decided to try Jacobs's drink of choice. I poured a Coke and Jack. It was pretty good, but a little strong for me.

At seven o'clock, with no call saying he was going to be late, I closed down the computer and decided to watch television, but I couldn't find anything on I wanted to watch. I looked for a book to read.

At eight o'clock, I took off my dress, and stretched out on the bed. I wanted Jacob to come home and see what he had missed.

I woke up and Jacob was crawling on the bed and kissing me and trying to wake me up.

"Jenna, baby, I'm sorry it got so late. I had such plans

for us tonight and by the looks of it you had a few ideas too." I looked up and smiled and he said, "You tired?"

"I was asleep. Aren't you tired?"

"Yes, I'm tired, tired of waiting to be intimate with my wife. I want you, Jenna, I need you."

"Good, because I need a husband who can make all my dreams come true." I sat up, "Are you hungry? I could fix you something to eat."

"Not right now. I don't remember seeing that outfit before, is it new?"

"Yes, I picked up a few things. You like it?"

He just smiled his sly sexy smile and started slowly gliding his hands over what little material I was wearing and that's all it took. We hadn't been intimate, in days, and we were both yearning for the sexual pleasures we could only find in each other.

My nighty shopping spree was worth the time and effort I spent picking it out. Jacob was excited, enthusiastic, and he felt wonderful all over me. I truly was happily married, personally happy, and my husband was happy.

Those three things together make me happier than I've ever been. I went through dark and lonely years before Jacob, but now I'd go through all that pain again if it meant I got Jacob in the end. I would live through that all over again if that was the price, I had to pay to be happy with Jacob.

I feel at home in Kentucky, comfortably intimate with my soul mate, safe financially, emotionally, and loved. I'm finally appreciated and desired for simply being me. He's seen me at my worst and loves me. For some strange reason, I don't know why, he loves me.

But I love and adore him more than I could ever dream was possible. I love him more each day and can't believe I could experience so much love, but he brings it out in me.

He's my love generator. This really is my happily ever after. He said, "I do", and married me of his own free will.

I'm so happy when we are together, it scares me that I could be this happy. I have everything I could ever want, a healthy family, Jacob happily married to me, and me happy to be with him.

Jacob is my favorite place to be in the entire world. I still woke up some days amazed that we were married, but I thanked God every day for the gift he was to me. He made me smile on the inside. Would things always be this wonderful? It was pure joy being Mrs. Jenna Jamison, I'd never had wonderful before.

About the Author

Sonny D. Stone was born and raised in the Midwest. She's lived in rural settings in Kansas and Missouri as well as large cities in Louisiana and Minnesota. She enjoys writing, photography, travel, family, friends and pets. She has a great sense of humor and enjoys many styles of music, and a variety of card games, board and video games and sports. Sonny wanted to share a story of romance and mystery. She had a blast writing this trilogy taking readers on travels with twists and unexpected turns.

Author's Note: Please don't miss book three, coming soon, **The Back and Forth of a Woman's Love**. *Find out how the Jenna Lee series concludes.*

Read book one of the series to find out how the story began, **The Ups and Downs of a Woman's Heart**.